Other

Philip Machanick

Minor corrections: 7 October 2025

Set in Cantarell 11 point.

Author:	Machanick, Philip, 1957–
Title:	Other / Philip Machanick.
Publisher:	RAMpage Research, 2025.
ISBN:	978-1-0370-5708-3 (pbk.)
Subjects:	FICTION / Political / Cullinary

Other titles by this author:

- *Vent*, 2025, ISBN 978-1-0370-4124-2
- *The Superpower*, 2020, ISBN 978-1-326-59791-7 (lulu.com e-book) and 978-0-620-90347-9 (paperback)
- *MIPS2C: programming from the machine up*, 2015, ISBN 978-0-620-90347-9 978-0-8681048-7-4
- *The Day it Rained Forever*, 2013, ISBN 978-1-4825609-9-2
- *No Tomorrow* (2nd edition), 2008, ISBN 978-0-9804510-1-6
- *An Object-Oriented Library For Shared-Memory Parallel Simulations*, 2008, ISBN 978-0-980451-02-3

Contents

Chapter 1

In the News

The usual crowd has shown up, shuffling in with the usual degree of enthusiasm, but with obvious pleasure at my special day and the guests it brings with it. I smile, recognizing the regulars. I get cheery waves, the shuffling as always is a physical disability not a lack of pleasure at entering the dining hall. The food is steaming; the plates are lined up; the tables are laid.

Then something strange happens.

Strangers are flooding in. Cameras, audio recorders and TV cameras break into the space.

Martha abandons her serving station with startling celerity for someone that large and blocks their progress with her formidable bulk – a ladle wielded, instantly transformed into a weapon.

Before the regulars, my special guests and I can make sense of it all, Henrique barges through the throng, who resolve themselves into reporters, food critics and TV crews.

"Haven't you heard?" Henrique yells breathlessly. "You

have been awarded a ... "

I slowly lower my serving spoon and delicately shake my head, cutting him off before he can finish. "What matters now is that we have dinner to serve. As always, the residents go first. The rest of you can have what is left and of course if you can afford to pay, whatever you put in is most welcome. With a slight difference this time, of a very private party. Here with the consent of the residents.

"Whatever the story is, it can wait. This is not about me. This is about completing service, as it would be at your restaurant."

The cameras flash and the media go crazy. But Henrique sees what must be done. He grabs Martha by the hand, and the two of them form a formidable barricade, ushering the media throng back to the entrance, from which they glower at him.

Henrique displays the authority that has mastered his own kitchen: "You will just have to wait. This is not our space. Be respectful and you will get your story."

As a reporter thrusts a microphone in his face, Henrique pushes it away. "*Non!* This is most definitely *not* about *me*. Now be civil. Martha, my dear, get back to your station." Eleni pops through the crowd and her glare completes the rout. Clearly, the media crowd is cowed.

But I get ahead of myself. You need to know where and how it all started.

Chapter 2

Farm Boy

It's a warm day. We are running around in the hills, far from the house. Sipho and I are best buddies. We run around barefoot with the gang. My gran, who runs the farm with a will of iron, insists that we all speak Zulu as her schoolteacher experience says that learning a language from those fluent in it is always best.

I spot a snake and yell: "*Inyoka!*" We all flee in terror. When we get to the farm, I try to describe it. The detail is a bit hazy, but I remember it as very shiny. No one else has seen it.

"Aha," says Sizwe, one of the older farm workers. "That is the most dangerous kind of snake, *avuzayo amanzi.*" It is only many years later that I wonder if he is having me on – I never again hear of such a snake with a name that means "leaking water".

This is life on the farm. My gran runs everything. I barely knew gramps before he died. My parents are in a distant place, not able to cope with me. I have no idea why. I seem pretty decent to myself and to the farm kids.

I have fond memories of the farm – cows, strawberries, cream, butter, a carefree outdoor life with kids blacker than me and a common language. Occasionally we have the intrusion of outsiders speaking English. Fortunately, thanks to gran, I am fluent in that too.

Compared with the farm kids, we live a luxurious life. We drink water from a rain tank and very occasionally have electric lights, when the generator is working. There is a hand pump outside to get water out of the ground, but gran says we can't drink that: it's only for washing.

We even have a telephone, a mysterious thing called a party line. Everyone in the district is on the same phone line and you used different rings to signal to different people. Ours is two shorts and two longs. You can pick up the phone when other people are talking and listen in but gran says that's rude and we never do that. That does not stop her repeating gossip others share with her when we have guests for tea. I am too little to get involved, and have my own tea on the stoep, catching only snatches of conversation and laughter. I decide my gran is funny, and being funny is the thing for me too.

Mostly, I spend my days on the farm but occasionally go shopping with gran. One time, she takes me with her when she has to go to the dentist, an experience of significant curiosity to me. I am granted permission to watch. The most scary part is when the dentist injects her in the gum. He talks about "deadening", which sounds terrible, but I trust gran to know what she is doing. Then I find there is actually something even more scary, when he operates a drill. The sound and a smell like burning hair put me on edge. On the way back to the farm, I quiz gran on the procedure.

She concentrates on driving while answering. Her car is very bouncy on the rough farm road. "I had a filling. There was a hole in my tooth and the dentist had to use a drill to make the hole clean." She grins, then turns back to the road. There is a shiny new patch on a tooth.

"What was that needle? I didn't like the word 'deadening'."

"That stops me feeling the pain when he is drilling. I have to be careful what I bite until it wears off, because I still can't feel anything in my mouth."

I file this all away for the future; my teeth don't have holes in them. But I do know that they will all fall out and new ones will grow. So I ask: "Gran, why do teeth get holes in them?"

"Luke, some people are lucky and have strong teeth. But I stopped putting sugar in my tea because sugar can be bad for your teeth." I pull a face. I like lots of sugar in my tea. She sees this out of the corner of her eye. "I used to like a lot of sugar too, but I slowly cut it down. Is that something you could try?"

I contemplate this gravely, then decide: "Gran, can I try that after I lose all my baby teeth?"

She laughs happily. "You are such a funny boy. Of course you can."

Some time later, out of nowhere, my parents appear, rattling over the rutted farm road in a Ford, spewing clouds of dust. I remember it as a smallish Ford, but bigger than gran's Morris Minor station wagon. The brother Jamie that I barely know is not with them. They have a long discussion with gran about things I can't follow. Then they go. I barely get noticed, though it is obvious from gestures and looks in my direction that I am talked about.

I spend a lot of time looking at them. I don't often see older people besides gran and the farm workers. They both look fit and healthy. My dad is tanned, has short hair that is a sandy colour. My mother has light skin and fairer hair. I don't see their eyes. I like gran's eyes. They are grey and she laughs with her eyes. I don't know how to explain this, but it is how I remember her.

Once the dust cloud from their car has subsided, gran beckons to me to sit with her. She is looking serious. She is not generally a serious person, even though she has taken on the tough job of running a farm.

"Luke, you are going to school."

I nod; school is something I have heard of. I have even made a head start, thanks to gran encouraging me to enjoy reading.

"There isn't a school near here and you would have to go to boarding school." This is a concept I have vaguely heard of. I nod appreciatively. I am being brought into the world of grown-up decision making.

"Your mother wants you to go to a school near to her, instead. You are to live with your parents."

Now I am puzzled. "Why? This is my home."

"Your mother has had a lot of trouble in her life. Your dad too. But I am getting old, and someone has to look after you when I am gone."

I nod very solemnly. "I don't want you ever to go away." She gifts me with a lingering hug.

This is a very big moment in my life. I have no idea how to process it. All I know is that much that comforts me is soon to be in the past. Sipho, Sizwe, the other farm kids and workers, the sunny hills where we all run free. And the only older person I really know well, gran.

That night, I curl up in bed with Noddy and Bigears and the impossibly friendly Mr Plod who, I will later learn, is not like any real policeman. Well, almost.

Chapter 3

School Starts

Johannesburg. The big smoke. The gold-mining capital of the world. South Africa's centre of both wealth and poverty, at its peak in the 1970s. The gold price is on the way up and the Carlton Hotel in the city centre epitomises opulence.

My parent's home is in Yeoville, which has a trendy air, but plots are small. It is nothing like being on the farm. I have no Zulu-speaking friends. In fact, I have no friends. I arrive in July, experiencing an icy winter for the first time, without the pleasure of snow. Johannesburg is dead dry in winter and for the first time, I feel discomfort being barefoot – my soles crack up from the dryness. I am forced to wear shoes for the first time, aged five.

My parents have a social life that I can't relate to, even if I was allowed to. When they have friends over, they are loud and get drunk. I retire to the garden if the weather is good and read. If not, I try to read in my room. They go out partying with such friends late into the night and for the first time, I spend time with my older brother, who is commanded to "baby sit".

When this is mentioned, I round on my mother. "I am not a baby!"

She is unimpressed. "It is just a turn of phrase. The older child is responsible."

"Why? I can look after myself. I ran free on a big farm and I was not scared of snakes. Big ones that can kill." I am lying about the fear, but I do not respect my mother, so it does not count. She has shown no signs of affection. It is as if I am a toy she can't discard.

Jamie sniggers. "There are no snakes here. You know nothing about life. You lived in the sticks. I know my way around a big city and I am going to a top boarding school next year. There is a lot I can teach you." I don't like the sound of this and, sure enough, as soon as the parents are out of the door, the bullying begins.

Six months of this is more than enough; Jamie is shipped off to his fancy boarding school in a remote part of Natal that I haven't heard of and whose name escapes me, except that it doesn't sound Zulu. So things get a little more peaceful. Apparently, without an older brother around to bully me, I am no longer a baby or don't need to be sat. I don't bother to ask. I treasure the solitude. School at first is not too bad. It is an easy walk from home, so I am free of my non-parents as soon as I step outside the gate. I am ahead of the class as I have been reading since I was four so school work is dead easy and dead boring. I take a lot of books out of the library and soon exhaust its limited selection.

Between reading, I remember a lesson from gran. I go outside, and focus on the far distance. This is her secret for enjoying reading without losing your eyesight. Yeoville lacks the far distance worth staring at that I enjoyed so much on the farm, but my eyes are my most important muscle, so I don't neglect them.

Unlike gran, my "mother" never reads to me, and seems to be faintly amused that I am so bookish. Her favoured son is off at an expensive private school and here am I slumming at a public school and learning all by myself. Yet even this does not turn to affection – it is as if I am living the wrong life.

I still do not understand why she has so little affection for me. I could understand if my dad thought he wasn't my real dad but, even at age five and three quarters, I know enough to know that there isn't much uncertainty about who the mother is.

The early years are uneventful – only spoilt by Jamie's return home for holidays. As we head for the first July break, I demand to be sent to the farm. I can't bear another winter of cracked feet and bullying Jamie. But I use the winter weather as my excuse.

My entreaties hold no water, so I find gran's phone number and talk to her. She sounds well enough – to my relief – but insists it is up to my parents.

"You are my parents! These people don't care about me!"

There is a silence. Then: "Very well. Even if I have to pay for it myself, I will get you on a plane to Durban. But I will have to talk to them. Are they in now?"

Well, obviously not, otherwise I would not have sneaked a trunk call at whatever bloated cost that implied. I say: "No, but they should both be home by five."

Later, after a phone conversation, with sullen looks between my "parents", it is arranged. I don't know the details and don't care. I am going home, even if it is only for 3 weeks.

The day that school closes, I am at the airport with my "mother". She hands me over to a friendly person in South African Airways livery and doesn't wait to see me board. That unaccountably makes me happy. I am with someone who is being paid to look after me. Somehow this trumps being with someone who is not paid and doesn't care.

The plane is an enormous beast. A Viscount, with four massive engines, with propellers driven by turbines – halfway to being a jet plane. The nice SAA person explains all this to me while I wait but gets stuck when I ask technical questions, beyond suggesting that it is quieter than a piston engine. Apparently at age six, I am not supposed to be so difficult. But she is nice, so I don't make a thing of it.

Once on the plane and over the excitement of doing something new, I observe that it is not super quiet. But I am on my way home, so nothing is worthy of complaint.

Chapter 4

The Chain

Life settles into a pattern. I am miserable at "home" and visit the farm that I regard as my real home every winter. The mild Natal climate, playing with my Zulu friends and my gran just being there is a wonderful respite from feeling unwanted.

School at this stage of my life is still going well – I am ahead of the work, if a bit of a loner. Being good at school work apparently is not the path to popularity. But I have my farm friends and my gran, so for three weeks of the year, my batteries are recharged.

The longest stretch of the year is summer, when I have to do time with Jamie. His bullying is relentless if subtle – he is not stupid enough to get into trouble as the favourite son, sent to the expensive private school.

Luckily my report cards arrive when he is away. He would not enjoy seeing me do well – though he does every now and then hint that school work is so much easier at a government school.

The "parents" do not do the traditional Joburg summer

thing of charging off to the coast. That means that we get uncrowded use of the local public pool. I walk there often without the others but even when I meet them there, it is big enough to get away from them. I am not a brilliant swimmer, but it is a way of doing my own thing away from a hostile house.

In my eleventh year, everything changes. Gran gets too unwell to look after the farm, and lets us know she is selling it and moving to an old age home in Durban. I go into mourning. I stop reading. My next report card is the worst ever. For once, I am in trouble over school results. My "dad", who never cared when I did well, gives me a strong talking to. My response: "I miss my gran. She cares about me. You don't. I want to see her."

Luckily I overhear the name of the old age home she is moving to so I do my phone subversion trick again. I manage to talk to her. Her voice sounds weak but she is still the person I remember – there is still a spark there. I ask if there is a way to visit her.

She says: "I can still afford to buy you a plane ticket, as I did every other time. But there is no space for a visitor here. But, you know what? I am sure you can sleep on the floor. Let me sort it out."

And she did.

That July, as before, I head to Durban on a plane. SAA has upgraded to an all-jet fleet and the Boeing 727, despite a sleek modern look with a third engine going through the tail, is pretty noisy. Still, it gets me there.

Gran's floor is one of the best beds ever. She is just a room away.

I find she is a bit slow and finds it hard to move, so I offer to help with the cooking. Under her expert eye, I learn a lot. How to cook vegetables so they don't taste like mush, how to make a lemon meringue pie with a crispy top, and so on.

The next year, I expect the same, but the news is bad. She has been moved to frail care, and there is no way she can have a visitor on the floor. Jamie gives me hell the entire winter and it gets so bad that the "parents" can't help notice. But what do they do? Nothing.

By the time Jamie leaves for school, I can almost feel the chains closing in. The next school term is worse than ever. Teachers who appreciated me are starting to complain, and the bullies have decided it's time to put the knife in. No longer teachers' pet, I am a soft target.

By the time we get to the September break, I have had enough. Getting out is so easy. I wait until no one is paying attention, and play outside in the yard, barefoot, wearing only shorts, as the weather is warming. What they don't know is that I have saved up all my meagre pocket money over the last year, and have it in my pocket.

I walk out of the gate, and orientate myself roughly southeast, the direction of Durban, 500 km away. And start walking.

By the time it is getting dark, I am on the N3, in the middle of nowhere. A truck goes past, then stops. The driver beckons to me. I run up to the truck, not sure if I should trust a stranger.

He is Indian and looks at me in wonder. "Boy, what are you doing here in your shorts?"

"My gran is in frail care and my parents won't let me see her. She is the only person who cares about me."

"Oh, and where is she?"

"Durban. I know where, I have been there before."

The driver looks solemn. "Maybe I will get into trouble for this, but I know how it is. My granny was also the one who looked after everyone. Hop in. I have to be in Durban by morning."

Not sure if this is luck or if I am putting my life in a stranger's hands, I decide there is only one choice. If my gran dies before I see her, it's more than my life is worth. I jump in, and the truck gradually eases up through the gears, into the teeth of the darkness, the sunset at our backs.

I have dozed off and wake with a start when we draw into a fuel stop. After refueling, we move to a parking bay. The driver says: " Watch the truck while I go to the shop," as if I can do anything if a crook shows up. He gets back with a pie in his hand. I feel the weight of my life savings in my pocket and decide I had better not spend rashly as I am not close to starving. I try not to look at his pie but suddenly he has thrust half of it in front of me. I take it silently; as he pulls out of the fuel stop, we both eat contemplatively.

The kindness of strangers does not require thanks. We both understand this instinctively. I have broken my chains and he is my accomplice.

Chapter 5

Farewell

The driver tells me he is going right past the old age home. He has lied as I see when he maneuvers into a totally different direction after dropping me. It does not matter because we shared in each other's humanity.

I shiver slightly in the uncharacteristic cool of the Durban spring air. Then I turn to the entrance of the complex, and open the door to the main office. It has clearly just opened, as the staff are settling in, and not yet doing actual work. I get a rather surprised reception: "What are you doing here?"

"I am here to see my gran, in frail care, Mrs Timson."

The administrator takes a closer look at me. "You are the lad who slept on her floor, totally against the rules."

That is a big surprise. I never thought of gran as a rebel.

She goes on: "Do your parents know where you are?"

"My gran is my only real parent. The ones who made me wish they didn't." The tears are threatening to flow, but I am determined to be strong so they will let me see my gran. "Please, I must see her."

"Only after you give us your parents' phone number."

"I have no bargaining power. So here is the number."

The administrator is amused by the piece of wit. She picks up the phone.

"Now wait a minute: you said you'd let me see my gran after I gave you the number, not after you phoned them."

She shakes her head. "I am not phoning them, I am checking with frail care. I will phone them once I have established that your gran will see you."

She talks rapidly and nods grimly.

"OK, you can see her. I will send someone to fetch you. But first, a question. Why are you only wearing shorts?"

"My parents would never have let me go, so I sneaked out when they thought I was playing in the garden."

"And how did you think you could travel all the way to Durban like that?"

"I didn't think. My gran mustn't die without seeing me again. That is all that I care about."

A nurse appears. The administrator talks to her. Her eyes go wide. Only when the nurse ushers me out does the administrator reach for the phone again. We do not go straight to frail care. The nurse leads me to a room full of lockers. She looks me straight in the eye. "Do you really want your gran to see you like that?"

Rather than wait for the answer, she opens the locker and produces a T-shirt. "I brought this for going to the gym this afternoon. Put it on." It is very big for me, but I understand the thought behind it. She leads me up a flight of stairs to a corridor of small rooms with a stench of illness about them. My gran is in one, lying very still in a bed with high sides. I walk up to her and touch her arm. She is obviously very weak but smiles.

"You came. I knew you would. Make me a promise."

I nod silently.

"Don't let nastiness of other people destroy you. You are a wonderful child. There is something badly wrong with your mother. You just have to get through school and you will be fine. Trust me."

"I have no one else to trust." Then I think of the truck driver, the administrator and the nurse. "Besides you, only strangers are good to me."

"When your grandfather died, everyone told me to sell the farm. They never believed I would cope. I made a life for you and did my best to make a life for the farm families. Believe in yourself and the kindness of others will follow. If you don't believe in yourself, nothing matters."

She squeezes my hand with surprising strength.

"I know I don't have much time. I am so glad you were naughty enough to sneak out to see me."

"How did you ..."

"No one takes a plane trip without shoes and wearing a T-shirt four sizes too big. You don't have a naughty nature so if you have been naughty, it's for a good reason."

We sit together in silence as long as we are allowed to – there is nothing more to say.

Chapter 6

Legacy

Two weeks after my naughty trip to Durban, there is a knock on the door. I am the only one home and check through the spy hole. It is a stranger in a suit. Strangers have been good to me – a trucker, a nurse. But a suit?

"Who are you?" I call through the locked door.

"Your uncle, Geoff, your dad's brother. From Pretoria."

I have vaguely heard of him, but he is not part of the social circle. I await detail. After a silence, I add: "If you want to see my parents, they aren't here."

He smiles reassuringly. "It is you that I want to see. Are you going to let me in? I have good and bad news and I have to deliver it in person."

I hesitatingly unlock, and remove the door chain. He walks in and shakes my hand, something no adult has done before. I decide he may be OK, and lead him in to the living room. "Would you like tea? My gran taught me to cook."

"I would like that very much."

As I go into the kitchen, I see he has brought a briefcase

and is starting to open it. I bring out a teapot, strainer and two cups. "My apologies, I forgot to ask if you take sugar and milk."

"No thanks, I like it straight." Same way as me, I think. Odd when he isn't gran's son. I wonder how his teeth are.

I pour tea through the strainer, while he looks on, observing that the ritual is proper. He takes his, then looks at me solemnly. "I am sure you know that your gran has been poorly for a long time."

"I know. I saw her last month. I wasn't supposed to but I did it anyway."

He grins. Then looks grim. "I am sad to tell you that she has had a severe stroke. We don't know how long she will live, but she is unable to talk and shows no sign of understanding anything. It could be days; at most months."

I put my tea down carefully and he follows the motion closely, first with his eyes, then by putting his own cup down. "I see I am the one who broke the news. I can't say I am surprised. Your mother wasn't exactly close to her mother."

I am feeling numb – not surprised, as I knew that the time when I sneaked out to see her was goodbye. But here I was as alone in the world as if I had no family. Then I remember something. "You said good news?"

"Yes. I am a lawyer and the only member of the family that your gran really got on with. When she sold the farm, she said she wanted you to have whatever was left of the proceeds after she died. It isn't a huge amount of money, but she left instructions to keep it in trust until you turn 21, and only to release funds for your higher education."

I consider this slowly. It is a lot to take in for a pre-teen.

"You mean my parents get nothing? Or their brat?"

"Correct. And I made sure the paperwork is tight. Do well in school and you will be free to go to university without needing for anything. There could be a bit left after that. But this is your gran's legacy. She was a great teacher and she wants you to be educated. What do you say?"

"I would rather have her than an amount of money."

I get up slowly, aware of the need to keep control, and tea that could spill. I walk over to him and give him the first hug I have given anyone other than my gran.

Chapter 7

High School

Though there is a perfectly good high school nearby, my "parents" decide to send me away to a boarding school. Not a fancy one in an obscure part of Natal, but a government school in Durban. Perhaps this is some idea of a joke as it makes it possible to visit my gran, but each time, this is a very sad occasion as the bright, encouraging personality is nowhere to be seen – just dull staring eyes.

By early March, I am learning that there are levels of bullying beyond anything I knew before. Jamie was awful but I could avoid him by playing outside, and he was not around most of the year. In hostel, there is no escape. In high school, even more than before, being bookish is not a social asset. Finding time to read whenever I can makes me a figure of ridicule. The school's unofficial motto is, "Have a school your rugby team could be proud of". That I had no interest in rugby or inclination to learn about it doesn't help.

The only plus about the school is that it has some good teachers – expats who have come to South Africa via former

British colonies, including some with degrees from exalted places like Cambridge. But even there, my luck doesn't hold – the teachers mistake my bookishness and lack of interest in socialising for rebelliousness and I am forever getting into trouble for things I didn't do. There are also Afrikaners, who are determined to instil apartheid culture in English speakers, and I often rate their ire; rebels divide Afrikaners. They are either admired or reviled, sometimes with no logic.

Around mid-March, the inevitable happens. I am called into the principal's office to take a phone call from Uncle Geoff. I know what it is before he starts speaking. My gran is no more. The principal is good enough to let me off school for the rest of the day but the bullies do not get the memo. I am sitting on my bunk when the first of them walks into the room. His name is Simpson and he is a merciless bully. Seeing me looking down, he immediately moves in on me, followed by his retinue. I look up, fortunately not tearful, as that would have led to being savaged even worse. I stand up, determined to hold my own.

"Haha, mummy's boy is sad. Oh, wait. Mummy doesn't care. It's granny's boy."

Something snaps and before I know it, Simpson's face is a bloody mess. Before anything else can happen, a teacher appears. De Villiers, the biggest rugby fanatic and hence my natural enemy. He takes a look at Simpson and a look at me. "Simpson, you idiot, wash your face. The rest of you, get out. I must discipline Fredericks."

The other kids clear out. De Villiers confronts me. I expect the worst. At least 6 cuts with his cane, at which he is notably adept. Six is the legal limit, but this is the law of the jungle. I assaulted another kid and can't complain if he breaks the rules.

"Right, Fredericks. I know about your gran. What those kids did is unacceptable and Simpson was long overdue for correction. I will never punish anyone for standing up to a bully but you pushed me close. Next time, do it without drawing blood." This leaves me stunned as I never read De Villiers as anything but a bully himself.

De Villiers puts a friendly hand on my shoulder. "I know you don't like rugby but you have to do some kind of sport. We don't do karate in school but there is a club down the road. Why not take that up, and I will excuse you from school sports? Get that anger under control before it gets you into trouble where I can't help you."

I join the karate club. I am no good at it. But it doesn't matter. Word gets out that I am not to be messed with. Bookish me is back without interference. I drift through the rest of high school, not making friends. I cope with time back at the "family" home, particularly after Jamie's mediocre finish of high school, after which he starts working on dropping out of university, amortizing the cost of his expensive private school education.

I have my eye on university and gran's legacy. It is not just about the money, it is about her caring nature and her final advice to me. I try to visit Uncle Geoff when I am out of boarding school whenever I can, taking the slow train trip to Pretoria. I sense that Geoff is a little lonely. His divorce is long past and his only son, Ian, is away studying in Cape Town. He shows real interest in my progress. He cannot replace gran, but it is good to know there is someone who cares.

Chapter 8

University

Finishing school is something of an anticlimax. I can't say I much care for Durban. The sticky humidity gets to me. I have bad memories of waking up with sheets sodden with humidity and sweat. But it was gran's last home, and that is not something I can forget.

So the question is: where to go to university?

Not in Johannesburg, because that is too close to a place I can't call home. Cape Town has some appeal because it is about as far from Johannesburg as you can get and still go to a good university.

But Durban...? The University of Natal has two campuses: Durban and Pietermaritzburg. On a visit to Pretoria, I mull over options with Uncle Geoff. After all, he is the only one who cares – and he controls the purse strings.

After going through the options, he says, "You know, your gran studied in Pietermaritzburg. What are you thinking of studying? That is actually a better starting point."

"Two subjects I liked in school: English literature and

history. But school history is boring, all memorising dates."

"I am sure university history is more interesting than that. But what do you really want to do?"

"I like reading a lot and sometimes I wonder if I could write as well. I like history but it doesn't grab me the same way."

"Then that definitely leans you towards a BA in English Lit."

There's a pause, and I ask the tricky question. "Aren't I supposed to work out what career this results in?"

Geoff laughs. "Look at me, a highly paid lawyer. Guess what I studied in my first degree."

I sit silently.

"I had a passion for the ancient world. I did a BA in classics, including Latin and Greek. Then I got interested in some of the political trials and discovered quite by accident I had done some subjects required for law. Latin, for example was a requirement. I had to pick up a few courses, yet here I am. A classics scholar with a strong law practice."

"I'm not sure if I want to be a lawyer."

"That's not my point. Get a good starting point and you can go anywhere. Look at top people in business – very few of them have a degree in a relevant discipline. It's the ability to think logically and to solve hard problems that counts. And being able to communicate. Communication is the number one skill and studying English Lit gives you that in spades."

So here I am in Pietermaritzburg, doing a BA in English lit, with no career prospects but, if Geoff is right, that won't really matter. And I am spending gran's money, so I aim to do her proud.

Because I like reading, study is not that hard – in the first year, I have read a lot of what is needed already and easily get ahead of assignments. The next two years aren't much worse: I develop a rapport with my lecturers who confide in me that a student who takes an interest is a rarity. Why, I wonder. What are you doing studying English Lit if it doesn't interest you? It's not as if there is a lucrative career like plumbing at the end of the pipe.

Getting so far ahead in reading frees up time for a new pastime: movies. I go at least once a week and take to popcorn. It is stupidly overpriced, especially when you consider that each kernel blows up to mostly air as it cooks. Early in my third year, one of my teeth starts to trouble me. I keep putting it off but eventually find a dentist. He looks into my mouth with a lot of tut-tutting and pronounces the need to do a filling. "Do you want deadening or are you one of those people who don't like needles?"

"Can I try it without a needle?"

He gives me a funny look but goes with my wishes. As he starts, I tense up, then it suddenly occurs to me: I can do nothing. I put my head in a different place and stop worrying. I almost fall asleep.

At the end of the procedure, the dentist says: "You should sell whatever you're taking."

"Oh. I just found a way of going somewhere else. I don't know if that can sell for actual money. But what I would really like to know is why I had a cavity at all. I don't have sugar in tea or coffee and don't eat dessert a lot."

"Any starchy foods?"

I think for a while. "Popcorn at the movies?"

"Ah. When it combines with saliva, it can get very sticky and converts to sugars in your mouth. You need to clean your teeth soon after, or drink a lot of water to flush it out." He gives me a lecture about the proper way of flossing, something of which gran obviously was not informed.

That puts me off popcorn – but whether this advice is right or not, I also don't have a need to visit that dentist again for cavities. On his insistence, I go back after six months for a check up and am just as relaxed as he prods at me and cleans my teeth. At the end of that he says: "Good, no further damage. But you still have that remarkable relaxation trick. I thought you were falling asleep."

I still go to movies. It fascinates me how they are so different from the literary art forms. A novel or play is very hard to convert to a movie – you can't do it too literally, but you can capture the essence. And should in my view. For this reason, My Fair Lady is my least favourite movie – it completely loses Bernard Shaw's attack on class in Pygmalion.

Towards the end of my third year, I visit Geoff again, anticipating positive results and graduating. I decide that I would value his views on what to do next. After a 3-year degree, there is the option to do an additional Honours year. I am pretty sure by now that law is not for me.

Discussion takes a serious turn. "Luke, if you do not go on to study further, the army will grab you. It's just gone up to two years."

"I was thinking of doing Honours anyway – won't they allow deferment for that?"

"Yes. But what are your views on going to the military? I must tell you, since I started following political trials, I have no inclination to support the system and I would not like to see you pushed into that."

I look at him levelly. "I've thought long and hard about that and I value your advice. I didn't get much into protest but there is a growing move that way on campus. I've been reading the student press and, if they are right, there is a lot going on that the major media aren't reporting.

"Could you tell me more about the political trials?"

Then begins my political education, building on my long-standing discomfort about the injustice of leaving my farm friends behind.

By the end of the visit, I am convinced that I am not going into the military, but I would like the extra year to decide on options. So I apply for BA Honours in English Lit, hoping that my results will be good enough to get accepted. If not, I will need to accelerate my plans. I need not have worried. Even before I receive my official results, the phone rings. As usual, my "parents" are nowhere to be found but the call is for me.

"I would like to speak to Luke Fredericks."

"That's me."

"Professor Glassman here." The head of the English Department. I belatedly wish I had been gramatically correct and said *That is I*. But I need not be concerned as he goes on. "We have a small number of student assistantships on offer. If you wish to do Honours, we will cover all costs, and require that you do six hours of tutoring per week. Do you want to..."

"Yes!"

"All your lecturers said you were an enthusiast. They weren't wrong."

"My late gran was a teacher and encouraged me to take up her legacy."

"Mr Fredericks, the paperwork will reach you soon. We look forward to working with you."

As I put the phone down, I realise that I have graduated in several ways. Somewhere along the line, Uncle Geoff has become Geoff, and a professor has promoted me to "Mr".

Chapter 9

Doing the Honours

Covering all costs turns out to include a reasonable but not generous amount towards living costs. I chat with Geoff about money. He agrees that there is enough left in the bequest to upgrade to slightly better accommodation, leaving a nice amount for future plans – like travel. There is a block of flats just off campus that houses better-off students, who can afford to upgrade from digs or res.

"Besides," he adds, "once you reached 21, the money was all yours. You could actually do what you like without consulting me. We could dissolve the trust any time, if you want complete control of the funds."

"I like having a trusted person to talk to. When the need arises, we can think about dissolving the trust. Meantime, living on my own gives me the opportunity to hone skills like cooking and doing my own laundry."

Geoff smiles. "Speaking of independence, I have a surprise for you. Ian graduated last year and is off on his own, and doesn't want his hand-me-down car any more. Would you be too proud to take it over? It's a rather basic VW Golf, well looked after."

So here I am back in Pietermaritzburg, a stone's throw from the campus, with my own one-bedroom home and – for the first time – my own car. The flat has a 1950s look about it, with an over-decorated built-in electric heater in the living room, in the style of a fireplace.

I drive my car out to the shops and buy a few essentials – tea, a few staples, ready-made curtains, basic cooking utensils, crockery, and a thin mattress. The last item is homage to the last time I spent with my gran before her stroke. I will sleep on the floor for now, until I can afford better.

I am installing myself, when the skies open up. Most of the academic year falls outside Pietermaritzburg's rainiest months but I am early, before start of term and it seems someone else is too. There is a knock on my door, just as I have ensconced myself. A bedraggled sodden figure greets me.

"Hi, I was caught in the rain and haven't had time to unpack. Can you lend me a towel?"

"Of course – would tea be good as well?"

She favours me with an appreciative grin. "Thank you, that is so kind."

I direct her to the bathroom and put the kettle on. By the time she is a bit drier, tea is ready. "Apologies, but I don't do milk in tea and forgot to buy some. I also don't have any sugar."

"That's fine – anything hot will do it for me." She gives me a pointed stare that makes me wonder what my temperature is. "I'm sorry, forgive my manners. My name is Harriet."

I take her hand delicately. "Luke." As I touch her, it is as if an electric impulse has shot through my body. She reacts as if she feels it too and grabs my hand tighter.

I don't know what is happening. I have been a loner so long that I have not had a direct physical experience like this. She clearly has, and makes light work of me. It adds new meaning to the expression "doing the honours".

I can't describe everything that happens from that moment on – it is an intense experience yet somehow most of the detail eludes me. For two weeks, leading up to the start of term, we are constantly in each other's company.

Then, suddenly, for no apparent reason, she dumps me.

I arrive in my Honours class in a daze. Apparently I do OK as I am not fired as a teaching assistant and there are numbers on my transcript that indicate good results. But I have no recollection of any detail. I have a reading list from a course and have since reread some of the books – and it is as if they are totally new to me.

Every now and then Harriet drifts past. She has a boyfriend or more than one. I really don't know or care, or recall much of that either. All I know is that what was truly intense for me was nothing to her. I do my dental drill thing when I see her; I am not sure how often I do that at other times. All I recall of that year with any detail is cooking and running. The cooking is a kind of comfort, a reminder of my gran. The running is an escape but it takes me nowhere. This is my first and only experience of physical fitness. I suppose I would like it if it had a purpose.

At the end of the year, I am back with Geoff. It's my first stop after clearing out my student flat. How exactly that happened – whether I sold my stuff or gave it away – totally escapes me. It's as if getting into my car and heading for Pretoria erases everything Harriet set in motion – even things that preceded her. It's crunch time. Either I find a way to study further to dodge the military, or I have to deal with that issue, one way or another.

"So, Luke, you're looking fit and well. Do you want to study further?"

I mention the running and how I developed a taste for vegetarian, a reaction to all those years of horrible hostel food. But the Harriet story is what pours out. And that is what creates a desire to move on – anywhere but more university.

"Aha, a first love that didn't work out. I hope you are not planning on joining the French Foreign Legion."

"No. But I am too wrecked to study further and, after what you told me, the army is not for me."

"The good news is that you don't have to burn your bridges. If you take an overseas trip and give the military a foreign address, they will send you letters reminding you that they exist, but there is nothing they can do while you are out of the country."

"I have never travelled further than Durban. I'm an emotional wreck. How is this going to work out?"

"I have a good friend in San Francisco who is sympathetic to South African draft dodgers. We studied together for a while. I was on an exchange programme and met him at Stanford. We can send you there, and you can take some time to work out your options. Luckily your call up is for July, so we have plenty of time.

"Stan has some writing connections, so he may be able to find you work, but he made no promises when I asked."

"One-way ticket?"

"No, that is surprisingly expensive. What we can do is get you a ticket with an open return date, good for up to a year."

"We? I still have money ... "

"You will need that to cover costs once you are there. Trust me, it won't go far. Besides ... When you accepted a car from me, you became my kid." Geoff looks extremely serious as he says this, so much so that I can only burst out laughing.

Having lightened up, I go on: "OK, you are the nearest I have to family. I appreciate your support. How do I get a passport?"

"Easy. We are in Pretoria and all that is best done here. I would very much like you to stay here until you have to leave." That answers a question – where is my actual home, now that my off-campus lease is terminated?

"Offer accepted. I never felt at home once I left the farm and you are more of a parent to me now than they ever were."

It also raises another question: do I need to go back, ever, to the Yeoville house, with its bad memories? I decide no. Do I even need to let them know? If they care about me, they will ask after me. Geoff is after all family and they know who he is and what he has done for me. But he forces the issue: "You should phone your parents, to let them know, and make a plan to go over there to fetch your things."

While I am mulling this over, Geoff is also contemplating something. "One more thing. Stan is gay."

"Gay?" I ask, puzzled.

"Homosexual."

"I know what it means. I just don't understand why it matters."

"Good lad. I am sure you and Stan will get on."

I make the phone call, and my "dad" answers. What follows clearly surprises Geoff. "Hi? Luke here... Listen, I am going to live with Uncle Geoff while I sort out where I go next with life. You can dump my stuff however you like... That's right, everything, clothes, books – whatever is mine in your house. I'm not going back." I put down the phone without waiting for an answer. All that is left of my past life is the clothes I am wearing, a small amount of money in my pocket, a car and a trust fund. But I have a person I can relate to in lieu of a parent and prospects of a new life.

Geoff is agog but eventually gives me a tight grin that turns into a nod. "Wow. A clean break. I didn't think my brother would talk to me any time soon anyway. Sadly, that break happened a long time ago for me. After I got into a big fight over the way you were dumped on your gran..."

"Is that why I hardly knew anything about you? I remember once or twice, my gran mentioned your name, then she changed the subject. Favourably, as I remember – I often wondered why she did that."

"Yes. Your gran agreed that one split in the family was enough, but she also felt she could rely on me to look after you, if things went bad with your parents. I could never understand why she was so much better able to relate to you than to her own daughter. Come on, let's go shopping."

I am soon kitted out with new clothes, new bathroom gear, a suitcase and a backpack for carry-on luggage.

Over the next week, I visit various travel agents and study my options. The cheapest option goes via Paris. The second-least expensive ticket goes via London; I decide that a break in the trip there would be good and worth the small amount extra, over a stop in Paris. I discuss the layover options with Geoff before committing.

"I agree," he says. "London is a fascinating place, as is Paris, but if you don't speak French, Paris can be intimidating. I am sure we can find an inexpensive place for you in London – a youth hostel, perhaps. Or you could just visit the city in the break between flights without an overnight stopover. The tube system is good and you can see a lot in a few hours."

"I am keen to get to San Francisco – maybe a few hours in London will be enough. If I do head back, I could take a longer break in London then." Such prophetic words.

Chapter 10

London the First

The BA flight to London is a whole new experience. I have never travelled overseas before, let alone in an intimidatingly large plane like a 747. Fortunately I am seated well ahead of the smoking zone. Even so, as people at the back of the plane light up, I have to wonder why no one has thought of having peeing and non-peeing zones of a swimming pool.

As I am settling in and pull my book out of the seat pocket, a member of the cabin crew leans over and asks with an excess of civility: "One of your neighbours is separated from their companion. Would it be a terrible inconvenience if you move?"

"Not at all – as long as it's far from the smoking zone."

"Of course. We have a bulkhead seat. It has a little more legroom."

I move without fuss, wondering why it has to be done in such an apologetic fashion. No sooner do I have my book out when the same person approaches me.

"I really am terribly sorry, but we have a baby who needs

their bassinet to be attached to the bulkhead. Could we trouble you to move again?"

"It is absolutely no trouble, as long as I am well clear of the smokers."

She ushers me to my new seat and meal service starts. Before the drinks trolley arrives, a member of the cabin crew in fancier livery approaches. *Uh, oh, not another move.* But no. He says: "Because you have been so decent about moving, can I offer you some champagne from first class?" I nod enthusiastically. Why is it that I always do so well with strangers?

The rest of the flight is uneventful, though I find sleeping sitting up impossible and am pretty tired when we land at Heathrow. On my way out of the plane, the cabin crew give me a friendly send off and hand me a whole bottle of champagne to thank me for not making a fuss about moving.

It's really early in the morning and I am grateful that my suitcase is checked through to San Francisco and I only have a small backpack to lug around London, though weighted by an unexpected bottle of champagne. In a bit of a daze, I check out travel options, and decide to take the tube, despite the appeal of a fast train to London. It gives me time to doze and, as I do not have a destination in mind, I don't much care if I sleep through a stop. All I need to worry about is getting back to the airport by 11am to check in to the flight to New York.

I am on the Piccadilly line from Heathrow; that is all I need to remember to get back.

I wake up with a jolt as the train stops at Hyde Park Corner. This is something I have heard of. I get out of the train and take out my map. I find the station easily, so I feel happy that I will not get lost and emerge to the slowly dawning day. I have this image of Hyde Park Corner of a big line of people wanting to vent crazy rants in this bastion of free speech. But clearly it is not like that as I can't even find the correct spot.

Anyway I do not have a rant lined up and instead start wandering through parks, until I find a coffee stall. I buy a cappuccino and start to feel a bit more awake. Just as it is starting to get sunny, the clouds start to shift in. Even so, some people have taken their shirts off to catch what little sun there is. As it starts to drizzle lightly, they are still there, lying shirtless on the grass. Though I was never a beach kid, this strikes me as totally nuts.

While the drizzle isn't too bad, I decide that getting wet is not for me – particularly as mid-May London is not super warm – and I find a restaurant near the tube station to get undercover and have another coffee. The way I am feeling after my sleepless flight, there can't be enough coffee. When the drizzle slows, I take another walk and find some fancy destinations: The Dorchester and Park Lane. But time is marching on and with nearly an hour back to Heathrow, I pack it in and find my way back to the tube.

With a bit of time to kill, I wander around the duty free and conclude that it should actually be called "duty expensive". I find a novelty massive Toblerone, a variety of chocolate unfamiliar to me, that is on special and hence is not hideously over-priced, and decide to get one as a gift for my host in San Francisco. To add to the champagne. Then I make progress on my book, such as I can with drooping eyelids, at my departure gate.

Chapter 11

California

My arrival at JFK is a bit of a blur. A bit? More like total. If I was tired in London, I have no description for how I feel arriving in New York. Somehow, I navigate processes of passport control, claiming my modest suitcase, taking it through Customs and checking it back in for the rest of the trip to San Francisco, on American Airlines. We go via Chicago but fortunately there is no plane change as, by that time, I am too tired to process anything.

Finally, in the early hours of the next morning, I land in San Francisco, after actually managing to sleep fitfully on the last leg of the flight. I find my suitcase and emerge from baggage claim in a daze. There, right in front of me is a friendly face. "You must be Luke. Stan. This is my partner, Simon."

"How did you know..."

"Geoff sent a photo. Come on. You must be really tired and you need a while to get over jet lag. What time is it back in South Africa?"

I look at my watch. I haven't reset it all this time. "6pm – or is it 6am?"

Stan and Simon laugh. "6pm most likely. Set your watch to 8am. Come on, let's find the car and get you home. You desperately need a shower."

"And sleep."

"Not quite yet," says Simon. "Staying awake with sun exposure is the best way to get into the time zone. Coffee first." I look around as we head for the car. The sky is blue and it is appreciably warmer than early-morning London.

I am not quite sure what kind of car it is other than the electric blue kind. My eyes can't focus on anything. The trip from the airport would probably be more exciting if I was fully awake. I doze off again, despite my aversion to sleeping sitting up and wake up as we pull into a yard with a low fence. As I get out of the car, I spot an impressive structure over in the distance. "Is that Golden Gate?"

Stan grins. "We get a small view of it here. You have to be pretty rich to live somewhere with a clear view. Ironically when it was first built, it was decried as an eyesore. But more later, let's get you settled."

After a shower and yet another coffee, I feel more human, if still pretty tired. The house is compact but clearly cared for, with artsy furniture and a well-appointed kitchen. I present my hosts with my champagne bottle and Toblerone.

Simon takes them deferentially. "A giant Toblerone is a pretty traditional duty-free gift. But a good bottle of champagne... Geoff said you were living on a shoestring. We didn't expect this."

I explain about how I scored the champagne from BA. Simon is suitably impressed. "I only wish an airline treated me half as well."

"It's my lack of travel experience. I thought if they were polite, it was only reasonable for me to be helpful. I'll know better next time and be rude." This scores a good laugh. I am already starting to feel that I will fit right in.

Stan insists on taking me out for a walk before I've explored the house. "Sunlight is the thing. Resets the body clock. Come on, we have a park just down the road and from a high point you have a better view of the bridge."

I follow, trying to stay interested. The rest of the day is much like that – we stop at coffee shops periodically, there is a lunch I totally forget and eventually, back home and I collapse in bed and wake up with the sun streaming through the window.

I get up slowly and find my way to the bathroom. I don't remember unpacking anything but my kit is all there. I shave and debate taking a shower, but decide instead to dress and explore the house. Stan and Simon are out but there is a note on the kitchen table: *Make yourself at home.* So I prowl around the compact but well-stocked kitchen. There is an impressive array of knives, a fancier coffee machine than I've seen outside a restaurant and a fridge with an inviting array of ingredients in it, some I have never seen before. Clearly, this is a foodie household.

I pour myself an orange juice and make some toast. The bread has a surprisingly sour tang to it but I am too hungry to worry if it is off. It tastes good enough with a generous slather of butter and raspberry jam, though I don't quite finish it before the need to explore further kicks in.

Simon gets back as I am contemplating the impressive cheese drawer. "Aha! You are sufficiently awake to explore culinary delights. What do you think of San Francisco's finest?" He points at what's left of the toast.

I try to put it politely. "The bread has gone a tad sour."

Simon has a good laugh. "Don't you get sourdough back home?"

I cover my embarrassment by shifting the conversation. "It seems you guys appreciate good food."

"You bet. We met at grad school and a group of us decided that if we couldn't afford top class restaurants, we should just learn to cook for ourselves. We challenged each other to beat the last best meal. Now, we challenge ourselves to find a restaurant that cooks better than we can."

"I like cooking but I'm not at your level."

"Don't worry. Plenty of time to learn. We are throwing a party in your honour tonight, in the possibly optimistic expectation that you will be awake at dinner time. Do you know how to fillet a salmon?"

"No, but I am willing to learn."

"Excellent."

My first attempt at filleting the salmon is a bit of a mess but Simon is a good teacher. By the time Stan gets home, we are well on track to completing what the two of them call "prep". Part of this involves removing pin bones, a task I happily take over in the cause of keeping awake.

As Simon predicts, by dinner time, I am struggling to keep awake. I have a vague recollection of forgetting introductions and animated conversation. I also recall thinking that I am not used to happy parties and am glad I've been introduced to the concept while too tired to stumble over social skills. Being introduced to Chablis is one of the few things that sticks. Chablis is a great friend; my introduction is something like this: "Luke, meet Chablis."

"Chablis who?"

"Chablis the classic Chardonnay from Burgundy."

This conversation is a complete fabrication – I know what Chablis is from future encounters. Anyway, wine doesn't talk unless you are very drunk or in a magical realism novel.

Memories of any kind of detail of that night? Not so much. But I can say that I now know how to fillet a salmon and how to make a good cream sauce – starting from that first experience.

Recovering from jet lag is no fun. Simon tells me it is worse heading east and that is not a great help. But after a week in San Francisco, I am ready to start making my own plans. Stan has several options for part-time work: editing for a small publisher, proof-reading for a magazine. I find this work easy if boring and dispose of it faster than it comes in, so I have time to explore, while summer moves in and the chance of rain recedes further. Toto, this isn't London, I find myself thinking. And definitely not Kansas, from what I've heard of *that* state.

I ask Stan for options and he starts to gives a list. "Golden Gate Park. Alcatraz. The Cable Cars..."

"What? Where are the mountains?"

"Mountains?"

"Isn't a cable car a thing you use to get up a mountain? We have one in Cape Town."

"Ah. I should explain. A San Franisco Cable Car is like a streetcar that picks up motive power from an underground cable."

"This I must see."

"You can actually pick one up not that far from here. You

may want to take it to Golden Gate Park. I have a map."

So I explore the Cable Car system that day; somewhere I pick up a pamphlet advertising Green Tortoise tours to Yosemite. That looks interesting – actual real mountains. I bring this home and show Simon who, as usual, is the first one home.

"Green Tortoise? Looks a bit dodge. I guess you get what you pay for."

But I am not so easily put off and, when Stan gets home, he sells me on Yosemite. He pulls out a book of stark black and white photos by Ansel Adams. This I have to see in person, though mulling over it takes me almost to the end of May. So, having booked with Green Tortoise, I pack my backpack for a few days away from home. And the start of the biggest adventure yet.

Chapter 12

Green Tortoise to Wherever

The Green Tortoise depot is in a shabby part of town. Stan and Simon drop me off. I can tell from Simon's body language that he doesn't approve. The bus is an old GM model, possibly from the 1950s. A bunch of mostly hippy-looking people are milling about, waiting to board. One or two of them look surprisingly normal, even conservative, in their dress.

Then the driver arrives and introduces herself. "I am Millie and I drive this bus. We will all have a great time but we must all remember, when we are in nature, it is not our space. We have some strict rules and I will remind you of them. Otherwise, be cool and we will all have a great time."

Her companion, Charlie, introduces himself but is obviously a person of fewer words. He hands backpacks into the luggage compartment, while Millie warns everyone to keep out whatever they will need for tonight, as we will be driving through the night.

We get into the bus. The front half is seats and the back is a bunch of mattresses. Millie directs us to make ourselves comfortable at the back if want to sleep. I don't want to – not at first anyway – and take a conventional seat. The bus starts with a reassuringly smooth purr and off we go.

As we head out of San Francisco, I catch as many of the sights as I can until it gets properly dark. I have my book with me but there is no reading light so I give up on that. One of the more conservative-looking people is sitting next to me and strikes up a conversation. I don't recall about what, but this is his fourth trip on the Tortoise. So clearly he is not as conservative as he looks. Or possibly he has to escape "conservative". I don't quiz him and conversation tails off as we watch the growing gloom through the windows. Eventually, I try lying down at the back of the bus and it is only marginally more conducive to sleep than a plane seat. Even so, I do eventually fall asleep and am awakened by the lurch as the bus stops.

Millie stands up and surveys her charges. "Right, now this is where we all follow instructions. I want as many of you as possible to lie down in the back. This is how we get to enter the park cheap and keep our prices down." It's still a little dark, so I don't know why the subterfuge is necessary, but Millie is soon back on the bus and we are on our way.

Soon after dawn, we stop again at an impromptu camp site. Millie and Charlie invite us all out of the bus to watch them make breakfast, which is quite a performance in itself. Nonetheless it tastes great and leaves me feeling ready for what else the day will bring. Millie gives us a list of destinations: Yosemite valley, where we will stop for much of the day to allow time to do mountain trails, Tuolomne Meadows, Mona Lake. Not necessarily in that order.

Yosemite valley is pretty spectacular. As we stop, Millie intones: "70% of tourists never get off the valley floor. They drive around in their cars or tour bus and take photos and go home believing they're Ansel Adams. We aren't those tourists. Be back at the bus at noon if you want lunch, otherwise grab a snack bag and be back before sundown."

This seems pretty informal. I ask formal-dress who sat next to me on the way out: "How many people do they lose on the average trip?"

He grins. "Surprisingly, none. But I wouldn't like to be their public liability insurer." This is not actually reassuring, so I decide to stick with a group who look inclined to survive.

I look around. There is a young woman about my age, looking a bit lost, but not quite the hippy type. She is medium-height, petite but with some muscle – obviously someone who walks a lot. Her light brown hair looks slightly red as it catches the light. I go up to her and ask: "Are you planning on doing a mountain trail?" As I catch her eye, I see she has brown eyes with flecks of green. She holds my gaze.

"And getting back to the bus safely? Yes."

I decide this is what I am looking for. "Hi, I'm Luke. You sound British."

"And you sound... let me think... South African?"

"Very good. The locals don't get that at all. I've even been accused of being German."

"Really? But excuse my manners. I'm Hazel. What brings you here?" She looks slightly suspicious.

"Draft dodger."

"Ah." She looks interested. "Politically motivated, or just

averse to being in the military?"

"The first." I tell her about my farm friends, what my uncle Geoff has taught me about political trials and how a relationship fail put me off the option of further study.

"Well," she says, "I am rather boring compared with all that. I'm about to start a job at the BBC, a new international service that will go out on satellite. Doing background research on news, though I hope eventually to get into a bigger role. A rare talent, a journalist who can count – though I hope I don't get stuck with that because I like to write."

"That isn't at all boring. I wish I had an exciting career ahead of me. All I have is elementary proofreading and editing. Breaking into real writing jobs is tough."

Others are starting on the trail and I point them out. We hurry to catch up. Yosemite is every bit as spectacular as promised. The clear June air and the near-summer light give everything a stark, fresh look. Ansel Adams was a true genius to have even come close to capturing its essence – but you really have to see it firsthand to appreciate it. I'm not big on remembering names but I remember spectacular waterfalls and a huge lump of rock called Half Dome named thus for obvious reasons. Perhaps also it's the company that distracts me from remembering much besides a sense of awe at the scenery. Somehow I open up to Hazel – we talk the whole way about nothing in particular, almost as if we are old friends.

We're back at the bus, and once everyone is ushered on board – and I note no one is counting – we head out to a quiet spot to camp overnight. As we stop, we all get out and Millie is last out of the bus brandishing a spade. "If you need to take a dump, dig a hole and bury it. Not burying it is truly disgusting!"

Fortunately for me I had used the facilities in the valley; this does not seem an enticing option at all, though one of our fellow-travellers enthusiastically marches off with the spade, to reappear after an interval with every appearance of satisfaction.

Hazel has hooked up with someone else and I sit alone, munching on bread and veggie burger, with a generous mound of leaves. I don't mind. I am a loner and, after my Harriet experience, I am not ready to hook up with anyone. And anyway, he clearly knows the moves and I don't. The burger is messy to eat but not dreadful so I focus on that.

The next day, we visit Mona Lake, a good distance from the valley floor. There are weird rock formations in the lake called tufa, resulting from some natural chemical process in the lake that Millie does not explain super clearly. What she does explain clearly is her contempt for Los Angeles, which is draining the lake as a source of water supply at an unsustainable rate.

From there, we take a drive to a place with a hot spring, about two bodies wide, where we are meant to take a short break. Some of the more adventurous types alternate lying in the hot spring with jumping into a neighbouring icy stream. This, I decide, is not for me, and wait at the bus. The hot spring is reasonably enticing as we are past the midday peak and the air is starting to cool; it is the icy part I do not relate to.

Then we are all loaded into the bus, and it won't start. Millie excoriates herself. "If I knew my stuff, which I don't, I could fix this." Yet again, something that is not super-reassuring.

We all exit the bus, which has acquired a sheen of dust, something not so noteworthy until we have extra time to contemplate it. Someone writes in the dust: "Visualise world peace." I add: "Or running bus." This scores a little mirth.

Charlie flags down a passing car, and is whisked off. Millie promises that he is organizing a backup bus and suggests we meantime enjoy the site, brandishing the spade for whoever wants to use the facilities.

I decide that the hot spring is enticing enough after all, noting that my conservative neighbour from the first stage has stripped off and is lying in the hot stream. I decide to do likewise, as he gets out. I almost doze off; the water is just hot enough to be restful, if with a rather rocky bed. Then I notice Hazel is there next to me.

"Hi stranger," I say shyly. I wonder where the other guy is. But I am here now and he isn't.

She looks my way, not peering too closely in a way that would violate privacy, a delicate touch when we are both lying naked in a hot spring. I reciprocate by not looking her way, after my initial glance to recognize her. It's a nice feeling to have someone who's not a total stranger close and I don't want to ruin the moment.

She breaks the silence. "Did you feel that I abandoned you?"

"Oh, no. I enjoyed talking to you and it's nice to talk to you again."

"Good. I am in San Francisco a couple of days after we get back..."

"If..."

"Quite. But let's be optimistic. Perhaps you can show me some of the sights?"

"I'd like that. I haven't been there long enough to see much myself."

A car stops and Charlie gets out. There is an animated conversation between him and Millie. Millie calls us over.

Hazel and I emerge dripping. We both forgot to bring a towel. But no one seems to notice, as we coyly wipe water off ourselves, while at the fringe of the crowd.

Millie announces: "I am not sure if we can get this bus going soon. The company is sending another bus. When it gets here, you can collectively decide if you want to finish the itinerary."

So it seems we are stuck here for a while. I borrow a towel from now fully-clad conservative guy and hand it to Hazel who is shivering. I wait my turn. Once we have our clothes on and Hazel and I are contemplating a more organized soak in the hot spring, the bus suddenly roars to life.

"All aboard!" We scramble to obey Millie's command. Once going, Millie announces: "There is no other bus. We are going back now."

So much for collectivism.

When we get to San Francisco, it is not far off the time when we were supposed to return and Stan is waiting for me. I clutch a piece of paper with Hazel's local phone number. Stan and Simon are in for quite a story when I get back to the house.

The next morning, I connect with Hazel. As planned, we see the sights. Embarrassingly, since I am not much of a tourist, Hazel makes most of the suggestions once I exhaust Golden Gate and the Cable Cars. But that is not my big recollection – it's what happens when we finally part. I lightly touch her shoulder. "This has been such fun – I wish I had someone with me when I was in London on my way here."

"You should visit. I can show you the sights – and I already know my way around."

"Really? I have a ticket back home that I can use any time until May next year that has a stop in London."

"Do you want to go back?"

"Not until I can go back without the dubious choice of the military or jail but, once I am in London, I can make plans. I am doing boring work here. Maybe there are better opportunities in London."

"Well, I would love to have you as a visitor. I have a small flat but there is space on the floor for a visitor. Which," she hastily adds, seeing a sharp reaction from me, "could be filled with a camp bed or mattress."

"Sleeping on the floor brings back a memory. A good one." I tell her about my gran but stop short of telling her the whole family story, and my crazy barefoot shirtless trip.

"That's so sweet. Let me know when you are ready to visit." We swap addresses and phone numbers.

Chapter 13

Back to London

My work does not get less boring. That's why there is a lot of it; no one else wants to do it. Sadly, being able to read doesn't mean you are good at writing. At least, that is what everyone believes when I try to get a writing job. It's still more editing, proofreading and vague hints that I may even make subeditor in a minor paper. One positive of all this boring work is that I accumulate savings quickly.

The only really good part of being in San Francisco is Stan and Simon. They have a great social circle, absolving me of the need to network, not exactly my strong point. I increasingly take over the cooking for their parties, which they are happy to take in lieu of rent. And I am happy to mostly be in the kitchen as my social awkwardness doesn't apply there. Fortunately their parties are generally the dinner kind and not so big, so I can usually find a quiet spot to chat with one of the guests, rather than trying to play party animal and failing.

Stan and Simon like my cooking philosophy – start from

the classics, cook from fresh, keep it simple. Between us, we thrash through ideas of what is good or not to eat. We decide land animals are out – seafood, if not overfished, is better for your health and the environment. Vegetarian is good but you can have too much of a good thing. In one of our discussions, I decide that this should be called vegaquarian. Stan responds: "I like it but if you look up the official name, I think you will find it's 'pescatarian'."

To this I reply: "Not me, I'm not religious." This gets a good laugh.

One of my big discoveries is how many varieties of salmon there are in the Pacific, so salmon features often. Different flavours, handled different ways – on its own, or in combination. One of my experiments is adapting a classic Marseilles bouillabaisse recipe to the Pacific Northwest, to much acclaim.

They have a pasta maker, and I explore options – various shapes and sizes, filled pasta and so on. Ice cream, we decide, is a major food group, so we get an ice cream maker – and the leftover egg whites lead me to discovering macarons. If I can't be paid to write creatively, I can exercise creativity in the kitchen.

This house mostly drinks French wine – California and Australia, Stan says, are pretentiously overpriced. Chile is a police state and no one talks about South Africa.

As I thought, when the subject first came up with Geoff, gay is simply not an issue and I don't know why it is for anyone. If it was a house full of highly social heterosexuals, I would have enjoyed cooking for them just as much – and been even more socially inept because these guys appreciate different. I am not even sure what fraction of the guests are gay.

The one kind of writing where I can be myself is letters to Hazel. Mostly banal stuff, but she seems to appreciate the way I express myself and writes back. In six weeks or so, I have learnt a lot about her end of London and she has learnt a lot about my end of San Francisco. Then she asks when I can visit. I reply: as soon as you invite me.

Her next letter says: "Remember that patch of floor with your name on? Any time. Here's my phone number in case you lost it. Let me know when you are on the way. My home is right near the Edgware Road tube stop – dead easy to get there from Heathrow. Just a few train changes. Heathrow Express is faster, but tube works too. If you can get here late on a Friday or early Saturday, we can work together on the jet lag."

So I am on a plane again, heading out of San Francisco, pretty much the reverse of my previous trip. But this time, London is my destination, not a stopover. As I head east, I remember how Simon said this would be worse than jet lag heading west.

As a more practiced flier, I manage to catch a bit more sleep on the flights. My San Francisco flight leaves really early on Friday morning and I get into Heathrow at approximately the same time on Saturday – after adjusting my watch. My sense of time is badly thrown out.

Once I find luggage and find my way through customs and immigration, it's still early. But I decide: why wait? I find my way to the tube and switch to the Bakerloo line and I am out of the Edgware Road station in less than an hour. It's still before 9am, but Hazel is expecting me, so I study my map and set out for her flat. It is below street level and I have to go down a flight of stairs to knock on the door. But I have barely touched the door when it opens.

"Look at you! You need a shower and a good dose of coffee."

I grin. "You are so like my gay friends in San Francisco. That's exactly what they prescribed."

"I hope I am gay enough for you then." She winks conspiratorially. "Or is that not compulsory?"

"Not at all. I like them for what they are. Same with you."

She leads me in past a compact kitchen. Jet lag prevents me from taking in much. There is a bare patch on the living room floor, next to a small table with four chairs, with a rolled up camp mattress next to it. "My bed. Marvellous."

"But no gran," Hazel adds.

Perhaps my pronouncement on the "bed" came across as sarcasm, so I instantly move to remedy that. I put my suitcase down and hold both her hands. "I have everything I need. Thank you so much for inviting me." I am not too tired to remember her eyes and the way the sun catches her hair.

Chapter 14

Making London Home

Simon is right. Jet lag this way around is much harder. But with a difference. I am with someone I know. After struggling to stay awake to a reasonable bed time, I wake up when it is still dark. I see the bedroom door is shut, so I hope that a light won't disturb Hazel. There is a small study at the end of the corridor, so I go down there with my book. There are no curtains, but it appears to look out on a wall that's barely discernible with the afterglow of my reading lamp – a consequence of living below ground, I guess.

After a while, I feel tired again, and go back to my mattress. I doze off for a while, but never fully get to sleep.

It is starting to get light outside when I hear her door open. I see her head to the bathroom and after the flush, she sits on the floor next to me. " Do you mind?"

"It's your floor."

"Actually, my parents'. They downsized after I moved out. But mum missed her garden, so they moved out to Greenwhich where they got a bargain on a house too small for a family, and rented this out. When the last tenant moved on, they offered it to me."

I am lying on my back and when I look round, I find she is in the same position. She smiles coyly. "Takes me back to that hot spring. That's when I decided you could turn out to be a good friend."

"Oh?"

"Stripping off and getting into hot water with a strange guy was an impulsive thing – it was in the moment. Then I thought, 'Uh oh, is he going to make a move?' You didn't. In fact, you barely looked at me."

"Was that a test? Did I pass?"

"It wasn't meant to be but you did. Do you mind if I ask a personal question?"

"Go ahead." I am staring at the ceiling, visualising the hot spring and feeling content with the way the world is.

"Are you gay?"

"You mean why no interest...? No. But maybe you need to know something." The whole Harriet story spills out. I haven't even told Geoff as much – I was suppressing and surprisingly now remember much that had previously happened between us – the whole roller coaster of falling wildly in love and being pushed off a cliff.

"Oh, wow. An 'H' name. I am almost ashamed. Don't let one person's horrible attitude wreck your life. I also have had more than my share of dud relationships. Just being friends works for me. How about you?"

"That and more time in this spectacularly dry and not particularly warm hot spring. And I like that you echoed my gran's advice about life."

I must have dozed off again as I wake to brighter light and

a kettle whistling. I stand and Hazel calls out: "Tea? How do you like it?"

"Straight, no sugar or milk." I take the few paces to the kitchen. There is a fancy cappuccino machine and I take a closer look.

"Oh, that. Mum thinks I need to learn to cook and she keeps showering me with equipment that I never use." As she pours boiling water into cups with tea bags, I take a look around. There is a row of books including an impressively large and unsullied *Larousse Gastronomique* and several by Julia Child that I recognize from Stan and Simon's collection – all looking pristine and unused. "Those? Part of mum's plot. Sadly, cooking isn't my thing. I do toast and I can whip off the lid of a peanut butter jar like a pro. But that's it – otherwise ready meals for me."

"I like cooking. Got it from my gran and learned a lot from Stan and Simon. While I am here, you don't even have to cook tea again."

"Deal! You can have a patch of my floor, and I can escape the chore of cooking. What are we going to have for breakfast?" She hands me my tea and picks up hers, looking expectant.

I think long and hard, with copious pondering gestures, then exclaim: "Toast!" We almost spill our tea.

The rest of the weekend is jet lag recovery time; feeling tired at the wrong time, waking up at the wrong time, going out for what little sun London offers (thankfully, in July, appreciably more than in May), shopping. Saturday morning is our main shopping trip to remedy the shortfall in fresh food. I pick out a selection of cheese, a nice-looking loaf of bread, decent-looking coffee beans, vegetables including shallots, cream, olive oil, butter and a piece of salmon. I also find a bottle of Chablis – the only item Hazel lets me buy. She insists that she must entertain her guest even if he is doing the cooking and I insist that I have to get something, and Chablis is my thing, thanks to my stay in California. At this, Hazel looks puzzled. "I thought California has its own wine."

"Yes. But Simon told me it is vastly over-priced. They mainly buy French. To get decently-priced wine, it seems you must get it from a police state like Chile."

"Or South Africa?"

"I never saw that in any places where we shopped – but I am a draft dodger, remember. I can't be too nostalgic."

"Do you miss South Africa?"

"In some ways. I miss hearing African languages. I miss our birds and wild scenery. I don't miss racism and personal abuse."

"Harriet?"

"Not only. Some time I must tell you about my parents. And boarding school. But not now, let's not spoil a good day. Particularly when I am about to fall asleep."

Saturday lunch is a high point. The Chablis is in the fridge. I am pin-boning the salmon as best I can without tweezers, making more of a mess than I would with the right tool. I cook the salmon with a cream sauce, using the shallots as a base and deglazing the pan with a shot of the Chablis. With this goes some bright green beans and boiled potatoes, crisped in the pan along with the fish.

I bring out two plates while Hazel puts out cutlery. She stares at what I made in amazement. "I hope that tastes as good as it looks."

She starts to sit down and I say: "We are missing something. The bottle of Chablis is still in the fridge. I didn't get it just to make the sauce." I fetch the bottle and she produces two rather fancy wine glasses. I do not need to ask: her mother again.

Just for long enough, I am wide awake. As we finish the meal, I look her straight in the eye. "Is the deal still on?"

Apparently so, as the next three weeks develop into a pattern. I go out looking for work opportunities while she is at work, and I do all the cooking – at least 2 meals per day, sometimes a dinner party on a work day, and just once, a nice lunch for guests on a Sunday. And at regular intervals, I call "home" – meaning now, Geoff in South Africa, and Stan and Simon in California. Socially, it is bliss. I don't need to work at it. I can always escape to the kitchen when I run out of conversation and Hazel's friends are just as undemanding as Stan and Simon's. If I miss a social cue, they switch to someone else.

The big plus is Hazel is my exclusive company when a party's over and I never find her challenging to talk to. On the downside, the work I get is minimal – at least as uninspiring as in California and less of it. This is depressing, so – just once – I quiz her about work.

"Oh, that? Dead boring. Remember what I told you before? I'm that rare creature, a journalist who gets numbers. So they give me the background work on all the science stories. Not what I wanted to sign up for, but it got my foot in the door." I decide it is not the moment to express envy. She has an actual job, after all. I am just the domestic help, I think with a hard dose of irony, given the way the domestic help is treated in South Africa. No, that is not what this is. I should unthink that. I am not a victim.

I put my hands on her shoulders and give her a deep look. "I believe in you. Give it time. You will get what you want. Whatever that is."

Chapter 15

Meet the Parents

On Monday of the fourth week, Hazel gets home looking just a little excited – but also a bit subdued. "I have been chatting to my boss about the kind of work you are looking for and the kind of work you are actually getting. We do news, but he talked to someone over at BBC Two and they have a new series and the script writer has taken ill. They are willing to give you a chance."

"Great. What happens next?"

"The thing is, I told my boss that you are a South African draft dodger and he says you should apply for refugee status so you can legally be employed. The bad news is that asylum application is long and tedious – but he also told me about some organizations that can help. It can take as much as two years."

"So where does that leave me?"

"Why don't you chat with those organizations to find out how to go about it? And meantime, just get on with our lives. I have a short list – maybe start at the top?"

"OK, good, I will look them up. How good do you think the job prospect is?"

"I can't be sure since there's a big difference between my work in background research for our international satellite channel news and domestic drama. But: foot in the door..."

I note that she has not said that two years is too long to occupy her floor, implicitly answering a question I sometimes raise with myself but am too scared to ask her.

The next day, I find the offices of the Committee on South African War Resistance, which is affiliated to the broader anti-apartheid movement. The process is indeed tediously long but with no other options, I make a start. Learning to pronounce the acronym COSAWR takes up a good part of my time. I leave, after providing a few details of my situation, with a promise that someone will be assigned to my case by early next week.

When I get home, Hazel is back and has an announcement. "My parents will be over for dinner on Saturday. Can you do something nice for them?"

"Has anything I did so far not been at least 'nice'?"

"That did come out wrong. Nothing has been short of spectacular. That first meal you made for me would be great. They both like salmon. Mum likes a good New Zealand Sauvignon Blanc. They aren't big on dessert but if you have some macarons left..."

I share the news from COSAWR. "They are going to assign someone to my case. I need to go back soon. I did some initial paperwork to get into the system, but there is a lot more to do, to keep it moving on. And yes, it could take as much as two years. But they will push for getting me permission to work a lot sooner than that."

At Hazel's insistence, I phone Geoff, who enthusiastically endorses the approach. "I miss having you here, but it's your best option. Go for it. The trust fund is not going to last much longer. You need a paying job."

On Friday, in the build up to Saturday, we do a little extra equipment shopping. I finally acquire pin-bone tweezers. I also buy a pasta machine with a cutting attachment, a stone mortar and wooden pestle. When Hazel enquires as to what it is all for, I say: "Have you ever had linguine al pesto?" She nods. "I'm not sure you *really* have. I will show you tonight. Made from scratch. Anyway this is my little present for you. As long as you have someone in your home to make pasta, you're set." I reject her protests. "Your mum buys you cooking stuff. I do that too but I don't expect you to use it."

I take her to buy ingredients we don't have already. Basil, pine nuts, Italian double zero flour, good Parmesan. I only made pasta a few times with Stan and Simon, but it isn't hard if you have the basics, and pesto is one of the things we made several times.

Once home, I set to mixing the dough and getting it to the right texture, before starting on the pesto, to let the dough rest. After rolling out the dough and cutting it to size, I drop it in boiling water and the pasta is done in a minute. I spoon a bit of the cooking water into the pesto, mix and serve.

"Wow! From a mess in my kitchen to a meal in forty-five minutes."

"Shut up and eat. I want your review."

She digs in and says nothing until the plate is empty. "I see what you mean. I never had pesto this good. What do we do with all that leftover pasta?"

"Hang it on coathangers to dry. Then we can pack it in

ziplocks or Tupperware, if you have any, and it will keep as well as factory pasta, but still taste better. Where can we put them so they are out of the way of our dinner party?" Hazel leads the way to her bedroom, the first time I have been in there. It does not feel like a transition as hanging pasta to dry has no romantic connotations.

We clean up together. This place has never before felt more like home. I dismiss thoughts of whether two years is too long, or whether I will have to find better work that will pay for my own place. I have enough money to buy a pasta machine for my friend's home. That is the moment I am in, and it takes me through the rest of the day.

Saturday opens quietly. Hazel asks about the drying pasta over lunch. I contemplate. "Should be ready to pack away, but let's focus on the dinner tonight; we can put it away afterwards." I have a slightly uneasy feeling about invading her space again; when we put the pasta there, it happened naturally. Am I overthinking?

I have everything I need for the party and we just chill until half an hour before, when I do some of the prep. The parents – I'm not sure which – knock forcefully. But the dad is first inside. Hazel introduces me. "Dad, this is Luke."

"Ah, our chef for the evening. Robert. Pleased to meet you." He extends a hand and nearly crushes mine. I nod politely.

"And mum..."

"Yes, dear, I heard who he was the first time."

She doesn't extend a hand but I feel the need to break the ice and add: "Pleased to me you. Hazel tells me a lot about you." Actually she only tells me about her mum's obsession with making her like cooking but Hazel only responds by throwing a dark look my way.

The mum casts her eyes around the kitchen. "Hmm. At least you have more equipment than when I last bought you something. Are we getting pasta?"

"No mum. Luke bought that for me yesterday and exercised it by making pasta with pesto last night. We're doing salmon today."

I explain my vegaquarian approach, which is received without comment. The mother shifts her gaze to me as I look her way. Favourably? I'm not sure. I am no good at body language. We proceed to the living room. I blurt out: "There's Chablis in the fridge " – then remember that we bought something else for the occasion – "and a New Zealand Sauvignon Blanc."

Robert grins. "My, quite the wine list. If Carol sticks to her preference, it will be the Sauvignon." Robert neatly fills the void where the mother had neglected to introduce herself. I am rapidly reaching the point where whatever I call her, it won't be mother.

I pour three glasses, each properly half full, as I won't have any until I am done with the cooking. I take them to the table and excuse myself from company to cook. I haven't asked, but don't test my assumption that the mother supplied the fancy glasses; she takes hers without comment. As the prep is all done, it doesn't take long and in fifteen minutes, I bring the plates then go back for my wine glass.

Even with my weak social skills, I know when something in the air is not right. Robert breaks the silence. "Hazel wasn't lying. In fact she undersold you. If she doesn't want you here any more, we can always find a space on our floor."

"Dad!"

I am about to say no offence taken when Carol breaks in. "You know, it is rather odd to have a chap living with you like this, without being in a relationship. I mean, we aren't in Victorian times, but what if you do find yourself a boyfriend?"

"Mum please. It is my life and Luke, I am sure, would be perfectly fine if I did find someone who wasn't a complete jerk and brought him home. You didn't find it at all weird when I was in all of those broken relationships. This is different and I happen to like different."

I don't know how to handle this. We have never discussed her acquiring a boyfriend but she is absolutely right. I have no role in such choices. I say nothing and clear away the plates, returning with macarons. Macarons have never been a social disaster.

Even the macarons don't fix the situation. I can't say anything. I feel like the kid whose parents talk about his problems as if he isn't there. The only plus is that Robert and Hazel are both in my corner.

Eventually Robert breaks the uncomfortable silence. "Rain is in the offing. Best we get home before it really comes down."

There are polite goodbyes.

We wash dishes in silence, then sit down in armchairs adjacent to my sleeping space. I don't know what to say. I don't want to be the centre of a family conflict. Everything has been so good up to now. Surely Hazel and her dad being on my side will paper over the cracks but I am scared of saying anything in case it comes out wrong.

Hazel breaks the silence. "You know, my mum is not wrong. It is weird for us to live together like this." There is another silence. I say nothing. She goes on: "You should go..." and I blank out totally. My world has gone inside out.

What's smooth is sharp. What's friendly is a threat. I no longer know who or what I am or where I am.

I have my suitcase. I am packing at breakneck speed. She is saying things that I can't hear, it is as if the sound is from the other end of a sewer. I am out of the door. I toss my keys into the doorway as the door closes. It is me and my suitcase and the now drenching rain as the skies open in a London September night.

I find my way to the tube station on autopilot. I board the first train without noting where it is headed.

Chapter 16

Mr Plod

I keep changing trains. I lose count of the number of times I change trains and track of where I am going. Eventually, it seems to be enough as I emerge onto an empty platform. There is no one there and there is just one bench. I find my way there and sit down, my head between my hands, my sodden suitcase between my sodden knees.

Everything is draining. The rainwater, my past, the place that seemed like home.

Then there is a tap on my shoulder. I look up to see a friendly, smiling face that takes me back to my childhood reading. It's Mr Plod the impossibly friendly cop. "Son, you can't stay here. They're closing this station tonight for repairs. You need to go home."

Then the tears flow like a waterfall down my face. I finally manage: "I have no home. I was staying with a friend and she threw me out."

"Oh dear, dear. Look, I can't put you out in the street. There is a place for the homeless just a few blocks away. Let me take you there. They won't turn you away, even at this late hour. Not if I have anything to do with it."

I don't have anything else to do so I get up and follow him. The rain has stopped so I drip out some of the water on the way, though it is starting to get unpleasantly cold. I am a shivering wreck when we get there. Mr Plod hits a buzzer and a weary voice answers. Soon Mr Plod ushers me in and a rather dazed person lets me in. There is a conversation between them and Mr Plod wins the day.

"They can't give you a bed this late in the day, but you can have a shower and sleep on the floor in the dining hall. It's the best I can do."

I don't have the voice to tell him it's the best anyone has done for me all day.

I am grudgingly issued with a tatty towel and get shown to the showers. The dining hall is grumpily pointed out. It is a big empty space with piled up chairs and tables in a corner, a mop and bucket in the other corner. The serving space is shuttered off. I am too tired to take in much more. After a warming shower and changing into clean shorts and T-shirt, I hit the floor and sleep. There is no gran, no camping mattress and no Hazel. I have never been more alone. But still, I sleep. Mr Plod to the rescue.

As it is getting light, I wake up, a little stiff for sleeping on a bare floor. The floor. My thing. At Hazel's. When I visited Gran. When I met Harriet. I try to picture my Honours year flat. I bought furniture. I try to picture that event. I can't. I try to picture the building. I can't. There is an image of a tree-lined street. Pietermaritzburg has tree-lined streets. But my building? Gone. As if I had never been there. I have no idea what it looked like – the facade, the number of stories.

Erased. I switch focus to the interior. I can't picture the layout. Cooking. That was my thing. I can't remember preparing or eating a single meal. Not even making a cup of tea. Harriet ... did she like the way I make tea? Nothing. I do not remember a single thing. I try to review my courses, my tutoring. It is not even a blur. I remember nothing. Just the highs and the lows – how wonderful it all seemed then the crash when she dumped me. The ordinary: gone. Just gone. It's as if Harriet sucked me out of a vacuum then blew me back into it.

I briefly think back to Hazel. I certainly have not forgotten that. But it's too raw. I have to focus on the now. I stand up and take stock.

My pants are still not quite dry though I did have enough presence of mind to stretch them out on the floor, so I find another pair in my suitcase. My shirt is also a bit damp but it's warmed up enough for my T-shirt to do for now. I am now ready to explore my new terrain. I say a quiet thank you to Mr Plod if only for being a friendly face when that was the last thing I expected.

Chapter 17

Officially Homeless

When I was staying with Hazel I suppose I was already homeless. But wasn't that the case in San Francisco? Was I at home with Geoff? My Honours year home is effectively erased, the only time I ever had my own place. Even my birth family's home was never really mine. I have effectively been homeless since gran sold the farm. Up to that point, I always had the option to go back. Even in her old-age home, I was a visitor – and a contraband one at that.

Here I am at a homeless shelter. So I am now officially homeless.

I pick up my damp clothes and suitcase and look for signs of life. There is an office at the entrance and a different person there than the one who delivered that grumpy greeting. The new guy stands as I approach. "Aha, you will be the late arrival. Slept it off I hope."

A sharp wake up. This is where I am now. "It isn't like that. I was staying with a friend and she threw me out. I got disorientated and landed up here, thanks to a friendly cop."

"My apologies. Late arrivals are usually stoned or drunk if not worse. I gather Fred did not exactly give you a friendly reception. He more or less expected me to throw you out at first light."

"I have nowhere to go. Is there some way I can stay until I work out my options? I can work. I can cook. I can do anything..."

"Now wait a minute. We are getting ahead of ourselves. I would not have put you out into the street no matter what Fred said and he knows it. I will have to hand you over to the manager when he gets in. Now, can I offer you a cuppa?"

So I get to know Bill, who takes the early morning shift, over a steaming mug of tea. I sense that he is happy for once to talk to someone on his shift who is compos mentis. I start telling him about my South African draft dodger story and how I have barely started the asylum process. I start to hint that this will be my opening and he stops me sharply. "No, no, no. You don't want to tell management stuff like that. Next thing law enforcement is onto you and you're on the first plane home. You were staying with a friend who threw you out. You don't know where to go. Stop at that."

"Are you sure? The asylum process is supposed to allow you to stay in the country until you get to the end."

"Are you a lawyer? I'm not. I just know the law of the street. Don't play your weakest card. Only say what you have to. Besides, if you don't want to fight in the apartheid army, you're a good kid in my book. They should just let you stay without all that bullshit."

We have a good chat about places I've been and what's good and bad about them, until eventually management shows up and I make my case. Bill is pretty much on the money. All I need say, really, is I have nowhere to go. Being able to cook? "Present yourself to the kitchen ahead of the next meal and it's up to them. I know nothing about cooking. We don't expect residents to pay their way. This is not a workhouse."

"As in Dickens?"

"As in this country in his time, yes. Do you read much?"

"English lit major." I decide to skip mentioning Honours – outside South Africa, it's a complication.

"Aha. Let's hope you are not as difficult as some of our educated residents."

"You speak as if this is a long-term home."

"It shouldn't be. But we have very limited resources – too few social workers, and so on. So some people end up staying longer than they should. A success story is if someone leaves and we never see them again. Now, let me take you to admin so we can find you a bunk and by then you will find breakfast is ready." Breakfast. Food is something I know.

After this conversation, I forget about the whole asylum issue. I also forget a lot of other things – Geoff, Stan, Simon, Hazel. It's as if my past is gone for good. I have blanked it all, except for my knowledge of food. But of course, it isn't. At some point, the dentist drill will stop. Though it didn't for Harriet, I remind myself.

A member of the office staff leads me to the residential area, down a corridor past the showers. There are two doors and she opens one and ushers me in. "Take any bunk. Just don't fight over it if anyone else is picky." I suspect that there may be gender segregation, hence the other door.

My room has ten bunks. All are vacant when we get there, but most have obviously been slept in; I pick out one for myself that is unused. I am allocated a locker with a key and everything but my suitcase fits in. The suitcase disappears to the office, and I hang my damp clothes over the edge of my bunk, anticipating that I will find out later how to get them dry.

Then I get back to the dining hall. About 15 people are there already, shuffling towards the serving counter with no evidence of enthusiasm, for a breakfast that smells of overcooked egg and burnt toast. As I get closer, I see that this is an accurate description of the offerings. I get my share without words exchanged and somehow manage to eat the unappetising mess. No one is talking much – even the serving staff, who look as if they would rather be anywhere else. Some residents have every appearance of being hung over or worse.

I retire to the dormitory to find that my wet clothes have disappeared. I look around to see if they could have been moved and see nothing. One of the other residents shows up. I ask him: "I left a shirt and pants over the edge of my bunk to dry. Did one of the staff pick them up?"

"No chance. You will never see your stuff again. Use the locker. If you have wet clothes again, leave them in the office."

Lesson number one of many. I thank my informant (though he could easily be the thief). "My name is Luke. I clearly have a lot to learn."

"Harry. Believe me, you do. I thought I knew a lot before I landed on the street."

I go out to the office and ask if there are rules or some kind of guidelines for residents. No one can help, other than to point out a list of hours. When the front door is open. When meals are. I ask about my missing clothes and get the same answer as Harry gave.

I decide to check out the neighbourhood. It is mostly pretty seedy but, a few blocks away, there is an island of relative prosperity – decently-stocked shops, nice houses, even a few restaurants. I find a coffee shop and get a passable espresso – a luxury I need to ration if I am too mentally spent to seek work. That is the last time I think of COSAWR for far too long.

At 11:30, I find my way to the kitchen and try to offer my services. It is decently equipped with big gas burners, good-looking commercial-grade pots and pans, an impressive array of knives and ladles and large commercial fridges.

I ask who is in charge. An imposingly-large woman announces herself as the boss. I introduce myself. "My name is Luke. I was thrown out into the street by a friend. I would like to show my appreciation for being able to stay here by helping with cooking."

"Good day, pretty boy Luke. My name is Martha. Do I look like someone who needs help?"

"Well, no. But an extra pair of hands surely can be of use. I really like cooking and would be happy to do anything to help out."

"Don't try those puppy dog eyes on me mister. I've seen everything in this place. More than once. Tell you what. Show up at the serving station at 12:00 and show us how handy you are with a ladle. Then we can talk again." I don't think I have the puppy dog eyes thing, let alone that I have tried it on her, but I think better of arguing. Not for the last time, I take the win.

Chapter 18

The Cook

It's lunch time for the homeless and here I am with my ladle. I don't know what I am serving and am not sure I want to know. It is hot and greasy, with an unsavoury glint and an odour that demands hunger to put it in your face. It is served with a chunk of rather ordinary bread and some quite decent butter.

If I ever had pretensions of swapping my literary hopes for the culinary world, this isn't it. Nonetheless the residents shuffle through the serving area taking their portion and perform oral insertion, though with no sign of enthusiasm.

Martha is standing next to me wielding her ladle with aplomb. I match her swing for swing but with no enthusiasm. As the last plate is served, I ask: "Would you eat this yourself?"

"Why, pretty boy? Do you think I belong here?"

"No one belongs here! But as long as they are here, they are entitled to dignity!" Faces turn my way. I had not intended to shout. I lower my voice. "Look, I am sorry. I don't want to make a scene. But really, is this slop the best you can do? You have a well-equipped kitchen. Surely you know how to make better food than this."

"Of course I bloody well do. But do you know how little money they put into this place?"

Martha stares me down but something in me has snapped, the way I took a swing at that bully in boarding school so I do not back down. "There are shops and restaurants not far from here. Sometimes they must have food that goes to waste. How about I go to them and see if they have anything they can donate?"

"Fine, pretty boy. But if you come back with nothing, you eat slop like the rest of them."

Challenge accepted – so I set out, after an interval to avoid hitting the restaurants when they are busy.

My first stop: the nicest-looking restaurant in the area, Chez Henrique. It has just finished serving lunch so all is quiet. I walk in and am accosted by a waiter. "Apologies, but lunch service is over."

"No problem. Can I see someone in charge?"

"That would be Henrique, owner and head chef. Wait here."

Henrique shortly emerges from the kitchen, chef's whites immaculate. He is tall and moves confidently, a neat beard flecked with grey hinting that he has been around for a while.

"Henrique. And what can I do for you ...?"

"Luke. I am helping with cooking at the homeless shelter and they serve indescribable slop. I was wondering if you have any excess supplies that would otherwise be thrown out. I can't bear to see people living in such..." I stop, almost in tears. "To me food is not just something to keep you alive, it is how we show appreciation for others." I explain my cooking philosophy, as developed up to my San Francisco time. Basics done right, best possible ingredients, seafood and vegetarian. Classic technique but minimalist. I toss in my vegaquarian label.

"You know, we can't afford waste here, but I may be able to help. Do you know how to cook salmon? We had a slow lunch service and could have one too many."

"That would be great."

"Come, into the kitchen."

Henrique opens a large fridge and there are several whole salmon there. He pulls out one. "Do you know how to fillet a salmon?"

"Of course. You start at the tail end, cut with a smooth motion, not going deep so you don't rupture any organs..." I gesture with my hand where I would start the cut.

"Right, we can manage without one of these. I am sure we have some veg in excess." He opens another fridge. "Plenty of beans. May not be good by tomorrow."

Should I push my luck? I decide no. "That alone will be magnificent. I can find a bit of cash to buy a few more things. If I want cream, potatoes and shallots, is there a shop near here where I can get them?"

Henrique gives me a thorough once-over. "Tell me Luke, are you staying there or working there?"

I realise that I have given the game away so I give him the whole truth. "I landed on the street yesterday and when I saw how awful the food was, I had to do something. Not for me, for the regulars. I can get on my feet in a few days and even buy my own food for those few days. But they are treated with such lack of dignity. I can afford to pay for a few extras but nothing as wonderful as what you are offering me. So where can I go shopping?"

"Luke, I will give you what you need. There is always waste not matter how hard we try. I have an opened cream, plenty of shallots and potatoes and, if you want, an opened white wine to deglaze the pan,"

I am speechless as Henrique assembles everything. As I prepare to go, I have another thought. "Is there a place here that sells pin-boning tweezers?"

"I have a spare that I can lend you but I want it back."

"Absolutely. We serve at 6pm and I will bring it back right after." The expression on his face tells me who I now am in a way that I can never forget. "No, the embarrassment – not during your service – what am I thinking – I will bring it back before lunch service tomorrow."

I get back to the shelter with my haul and seek out Martha, expecting delight. Instead, I get horror. "How do you expect me to cook that thing? This isn't a dinner party for a few friends. We have to feed 20 people."

She takes a closer look at what else I have brought. "Wine! You crazy kid! People here have all kinds of addictions."

"Relax. I cook out the alcohol. I know how many portions you get out of a whole salmon. It will be a small serving per person. But plenty of veg. The only major food group missing is slop. Now, let me get this stuff prepped and if you don't agree it's going to plan, take over."

Martha is clearly not used to someone standing up to her and grudgingly backs down.

I find a nice big knife that is too blunt to cut butter, and work the sharpening steel on it, then quickly remove the fillets, with practice born of a dozen San Francisco dinner parties. I flip the first one skin down, run a finger over to make the pin-bones stand up and start pulling them with the tweezers. The kitchen staff including a still reluctant Martha settle in to watch, with the odd exclamation at how fast I get it done. I stop counting after 20 portions; a few extra is a bonus. Next, I start dicing potatoes and toss them in water.

Martha has seen enough. "OK, pretty boy. I can't argue with a man with a knife. Let's get the job done. Come on you lot! This isn't a football match! Pitch in."

Soon all the veg is prepped and the last thing is finely dicing shallots. With teamwork, that is all done with alacrity. Then we steam the beans, to the point where we can reheat without overcooking, and we are ready to finish cooking just before service, with 30 minutes to spare. "Wow, I've never worked with such a great team." I exaggerate slightly because I've never worked with *any* team. "Let's take a break, and do the final cooking at quarter to, so it's all fresh." I outline tasks and Martha gives a show of being in command, echoing what I say.

As the residents file in, the shuffling suddenly stops. The dining hall is different. Then there is a rush to get served. Harry gives me a sharp look. I wonder what is going on. Does he relish slop? But no, he tucks in like everyone else. Then someone else is at the door: Henrique.

I call out: "Hey, everyone! Look who's here! Henrique runs a fancy restaurant down the road and gifted us his spare supplies."

Henrique looks a bit disconcerted as applause rings out, and approaches me. "Please, it is nothing. That would all go to waste. Service today is quiet, which is why I can take a few minutes to see how it is going here. If it is as good as it looks,

I am happy to have helped."

Martha pushes a plate in his direction. "Here, we have a spare. Have a taste." I am surprised, as this is the first sign that she's an enthusiast. "Go on now, I am sure you want to see if we measure up."

Henrique finds a fork and samples the salmon and veg, then clears the plate. "Magificent! I would pay good money for this."

Before I can think it through, I grab an empty bowl, thrust it in his direction and say, "Nothing is stopping you." As he pulls out his wallet, I pull back. "Oh, no. That is so rude of me. You gave us so much and..."

"*Non, non.* I want to pay. You have turned food into love and that is what I aspire to do every day." He puts in £10. Suddenly the hall is abuzz with demands to put in money. The bowl is passed around. It comes back to me, mostly with coins. I notice when it goes past Harry, he puts his hand in his pocket, then withdraws it empty, looking sheepish. I wonder what that is.

"Henrique, let me get you your tweezers..."

"You keep those. I'm sure you will have another use for them. Please, visit me any time. Not during service when I am busy. Busy, not embarrassed. I must apologize for letting you think that. I was impressed by your idea from the start, and I will talk to other restaurants and suppliers. It may not be a whole salmon every day, but there is always something to spare."

Chapter 19

Harry

That night, I climb into my bunk, happy and tired — but something is not right. Then it hits me. I had totally unintentionally recreated the family dinner that didn't rescue me from Hazel's mother. Except for the macarons. I didn't pay close attention to the label on the wine bottle. I wouldn't be surprised if it was a New Zealand Sauvignon, to add insult to injury. But I dismiss the negativity — even if I can't dismiss a wave of pain at losing a friend. Despite that pain, for the first time since I was out in the street, I feel that I belong.

I look around for familiar faces. "Where's Harry?"

A voice I can't place says: "Probably out getting high. Or drunk."

On that sour note, I am drifting off to sleep when Harry shows up. He goes to me and says, "I found your clothes." My shirt and pants land on the end of my bunk. I get up and put them in my locker. They seem clean.

"Thanks."

"No problem."

I decide not to ask.

Late that night or in the early hours I am wakened by screams. "What's that?"

"Harry," says a disembodied voice. "Withdrawal or bad trip."

"Those aren't the same thing."

"I'm not a doctor," sneers the voice.

No one else is doing anything so I go to Harry. In the semi-dark, his face is contorted and he is clearly struggling. I don't know what to do so I just hold his hand until it subsides, and he falls into a fitful sleep.

The next morning I am up early, and in the kitchen as the staff arrive. I am greeted by Martha in her usual style. "Well, pretty boy, are you going to show me up again?"

"There's a good cook buried in that harsh exterior," I offer. I genuinely believe this as her work on dinner had been just fine. She gives me a hard look, so I let her have the victory. "Tell me what you would like me to do. You're the boss."

"Do you know how to stir porridge?"

"I am sure you will correct me if I get it wrong. Then, do you mind if I forage for lunch? I have nearly twenty quid from the collection, which should help a lot with getting started."

"As if you need my permission. Come on, less back-chat. We have people to feed."

So it goes for the next week – word slowly gets out that gourmet cuisine is available even for people who aren't homeless, as long as they are willing to wait their turn and put in some cash. Each time, the residents put in some too. I notice that Harry is regularly contributing but still don't ask what the clothes thing was about.

I decide to approach Harry indirectly one night, and get

chatting about my literary pretensions and how no one is interested. "English lit? Interesting in its own way. But my favourite is Russian. You have to read it in the original language to really understand. Russia is a land that revels in misery and is good at achieving it. You lose register and idiom in translation. Both so critical for extracting meaning."

I feel small and insignificant. My understanding of the literature of the UK, the US and African authors seems so small against someone who has mastered a completely foreign language. He goes on: "Ukranian is something else. The Russians hate Ukraine because it has an older culture than they do. The languages look similar to outsiders but there are even variations in the alphabet. A lot of differences in pronunciation and vocabulary; they're not just dialects."

"How many languages...?"

"I don't know, I lost count after ten. Literatures of other cultures are so fascinating and translation is a weak tool. Now go to sleep. I am waiting for the day when they put you in charge of breakfast."

The next day at dinner, we have a few more outsiders than usual but there is enough to go around, thanks to generous contributions from Henrique and his favourite greengrocer, George, topped up with the collection bowl. As the bowl is going around I am talking to the other cooks and hear a sudden commotion. I go out to see what the problem is. One of the residents yells out: "Harry is stealing from the collection!" Harry's hand is in a fist. He sheepishly opens it and coins drop out.

"No, Harry, Your need is greater than mine. Take the money." It is clear to me now what happened to my clothes and what he needs money for.

Harry looks me in the eye, with a steadier gaze than I have seen from him before. "No." He reaches into his pocket and empties out all his money into the bowl. "I know *exactly* whose need is less than yours. My dealer." I try to refuse his money but he pushes me away. There is dead silence in the hall.

I am concerned, having seen what withdrawal does to him. "Are you sure you will be OK?"

"Never better."

I go to bed that night shattered. Harry is a person who would rate great respect if he had not fallen on hard times. Yet here he is, fighting off criminal tendencies to feed an addiction, with no friends or family to support him. Every time I think I have hit a new low, I find someone far worse off. I must stop thinking of myself as a victim. I drift off to sleep to be awakened by a sharp cry of pain. Harry. I go to him and his face is contorted in a new way and he is struggling to breathe. This looks far worse than his last withdrawal.

"Someone call an ambulance!" I yell. Holding Harry's hand is not going to do it this time.

I hear the door open, and running feet. Then one of the residents is back with Fred. "Don't worry, son. Help is on the way." This is a very different Fred than the one I encountered on my first night at the shelter.

Harry is looking pretty bad by the time the ambulance shows up. The paramedics waste no time taking him to the ambulance and putting him on oxygen. I ask if I can go with them. "Are you next of kin?" the driver asks.

"Yes. My dad." I surprise myself at what a fluent liar I am when the need arises.

"Get on board. No time to waste."

I don't remember much about the ambulance trip and what happened at the hospital. Harry is soon out of my sight and I am waiting. It is almost dawn when someone comes looking for me. He is wearing a crisp blue outfit. Something in his bearing tells me he is an experienced medic.

"Are you with Harry Whitmore?"

"Yes." This is the first time I've heard his surname.

"I'm sorry to say we couldn't save him. His heart was too far gone. Surgery sometimes fails because there is no chance of success but, I assure you, we did everything humanly possible."

I put my head in my hands. "This was my fault. He was saving up money for a dose and he gave it up because of me." The whole story comes tumbling out, starting with the missing clothes and Harry's decision to empty his pockets into the collection.

The surgeon sits down next to me. "He isn't really your dad, is he?"

"No. Am I in trouble for that too?"

"Son, the ambulance would have taken you if you were just a friend. And no, you are not in trouble for anything. His heart was badly damaged long before anything that happened last night. You did the only thing anyone could have done for him. You were there when he needed you. The most soul-destroying part of this job is losing a patient who has no one. When I am in surgery, everyone is equal. The only thing worse than giving bad news is not giving bad news because there is no one who cares.

"It's been a long night and I am headed home. Can I give you a lift to the shelter?"

I think of the crazy barefoot shirtless trip to Durban, so

long ago. The surgeon can only be mystified by the way my face lights up but he says nothing. My wry grin when I wonder if he will offer me half a pie also does not trigger a response. We certainly do not stop for food of any description. Like me, I suspect he is too tired to think of eating.

On the way to the shelter, I tell him more about my food project, and invite him to be our guest. I can't read his reaction as he says nothing and the car is dark but that evening at 6pm, he is there. I invite him to the front of the queue. "This is the surgeon who fought hard through most of last night to save Harry. He is my guest. Does anyone mind if I serve him first?"

I am startled by the applause. I had really thought that I was the only one who liked Harry.

Chapter 20

Chez Harry

After we close up for the night, I decide to take on the last hard hurdle. "Martha, one of the last things Harry said to me was he looked forward to when I was put in charge of breakfast. He didn't live to see that. Even if I never do it again, could you let me run breakfast just this one time? For Harry."

She weighs up what do do. Clearly, this is a hard question to answer. "I thought I was immune to puppy dog eyes. I can't say no. I can't even tell you not to mess up." I wish I had a mirror handy. I still don't believe puppy dog eyes. She parts with: "Be here 7am sharp. No laziness."

With this ringing endorsement, the next morning, I look at what we have. There is bread – pretty ordinary, but toasted nicely, it will taste fine. Plenty of butter, a couple of dozen eggs. And a hidden treasure: dozens of oranges. There is nothing to liven up the eggs, but with butter and a little milk you can make a pretty decent scramble. All oranges need is to be peeled and chopped. Or juiced.

"Martha, do we have an orange juicer?"

"Just this." She hands me a classic manual press, a corrugated cone sticking up from a shallow jug.

"Fine. This is what we are going to do. We are going to make toast on the grille, butter applied to both sides of each slice before we cook. Scrambled egg using all the eggs and a cup of milk, cooked to order, with plenty of butter. And I am going to juice enough oranges for 20 serves. That will take a lot of time, so I will get into it now.

"Harry got to be my best friend in this place after a bad start. This is what he wanted. So let's get to it."

It takes about 3 oranges to make a glass of juice. That means juicing 60 oranges. With one juice press, that takes a long time. Ten minutes before we start breakfast, I am far behind even with one of the cooks halving the oranges for me. Martha steps in. "Pretty boy, there is a less fancy way to do this." She wields a strainer over a bowl and, with a mighty squeeze, an orange half is emptied. "Leave it to me and you take charge of the toast and scramble." Definitely, this is a skill I lack: her hands must be super strong to make such short work of juicing an orange.

As the residents shuffle in, there is a different atmosphere in the dining hall. Everyone knows we have lost Harry, but the way the cooking is proceeding is clearly different. There is a row of glasses with orange juice and no smell of burnt toast. As we start serving, I call out: "Save the orange juice! We are celebrating Harry, and we need a toast!"

A voice from a table responds with: "Mate, we already have pretty good toast."

We are all still laughing when the last person is served. I pick up a glass. "To Harry! His last wish was for me to make breakfast for all of you."

"To Harry!" echoes around the hall. If only Harry had lived to see this. I even hear it from Martha. But as I turn towards her, her face is as hard as ever.

Despite her apparent lack of reaction, the Harry breakfast marks a turning point. Though Martha remains sullen, she increasingly lets me take charge even for breakfast. At first I stay conservative, cooking things I have practiced many times in California and when I was with Hazel. But one day, I make a small mistake that puts me on a new path. I slightly overcook some shallots. They taste good and are crunchy – not the effect I was looking for but it awakens me to texture.

I start experimenting and some ideas obviously work. Chez Harry, I now call the dining hall in my head, is attracting a growing group of foodies. As before, they have to wait until last, they get whatever is left and are politely asked to put in as much cash as they think it's worth. The residents also chip in if they can afford it.

What is interesting is the variability of these new arrivals – hippy-looking types, people in business suits and everything in between. Occasionally I recognize snatches of German, French and Dutch, languages I know enough to recognize if not to follow. Other languages are completely foreign to me. At times like these, I miss Harry; he would have not only recognized the language but been able to translate.

About two weeks after Harry's death, Henrique pays a visit, brandishing a newspaper. "Luke, did you recognize any top food critics here?"

"No. I don't know any food critics."

"Well, you need to read this review in the *Observer*. Jay Granger rates you highly. It is only a matter of time before you get invaded by the media."

I roll my eyes. "Don't they have better things to report on? Thanks for the warning. Chez Harry belongs to the residents. I won't have it turned into a circus."

"Chez Harry?"

I realise that I said the thing out loud.

"Harry died a couple of weeks ago. I was just starting to know him and his last wishes helped me get control of breakfast. No one else knows this; I now think of this place as carrying his name. I didn't mean to say it out loud."

"Ah. That is the sort of thing the media will go bananas over so best you say nothing about that."

"Thanks for the warning. Best I say nothing at all and hope it all goes away."

But that was not to be – that evening, the media scrum is there in force. TV camera, cameras, microphones. For once, Martha and I are at one. She is mighty handy with a ladle, as I know from way back. I start trying to push the media out, refusing to comment. A charging Martha with ladle finishes the job, but not before they get some photos and video footage.

"Martha, you're a star. Let's get back to our real job. I hope they don't make a big thing of this. Our people are what count, not selling newspapers."

For once, I get a positive reaction out of her – if only a glimmer. If I am hoping this will not be a big story, it's because I don't know the media. There is nothing like trying to shut them up to make a story explode.

Chapter 21

Revisit

I don't watch TV much especially after a hard day and, after dinner service, I am pretty tired and only want to spend a bit of time reading before a shower and going to bed. So it is only at breakfast that I pick up that my attempt at seeing off the media is a spectacular fail. Some of the regulars have been out already and are back with the tabloids. I am all over the front page, with Martha in the backdrop, charging forward with a ladle.

"Oh, for Chrissake!" I yell. "I don't want to turn this place into a circus. If these clowns show up again, can we herd them away?"

Martha says: "Our job is to cook and serve. You'd better talk to management about that once they get to the office." Fortunately, the media are not sufficiently frienzied to accost us at breakfast, so we get underway. Afterwards, I go to the office and find that management is already on top of it. No one is to be let in other than residents and those genuinely wanting a meal.

I go out to do the usual forage immediately, and stop at supplies from the greengrocer, as Henrique is not open that early. I also get rice, lentils and spices from the local supermarket. All seems to be under control at lunch as we have no interruptions; if the media are camped outside, they are not going to see me.

Dinner prep goes smoothly. I plan on something less exotic than average, a mildy-spiced lentil breyani, something my gran used to make – but with techniques I have since learnt to jazz it up. Martha looks at me quizzically. "Pretty boy, backing down now you are in the limelight?"

"Keeping it simple so the media horde can't disrupt if they get in somehow. Should we do a salad as well?"

"My opinion counts now, does it?"

"Martha, please. I respect you a lot. I wish you respected me a little."

"Hmph," is all I get out of her, but she starts rounding up the kitchen staff to make a salad.

As we serve, things are tranquil. We have a small number of outsiders – around the average. When I get to the last plate, I look up to see Hazel.

"What are you doing here?"

"You are all over the news. I have been so worried about you. I am so sorry about what I said."

I channel her words back at her. "You should go." She knows exactly what I have done and her face crumples as she turns and flees.

Martha rounds on me. "She hurt you and she is sorry. You hurt her back. Is that you?"

This is a side of Martha I haven't seen. "Uh, no."

"Then go after her and make it right!"

"But cooking here, breakfast..."

"You've trained us well. We won't disappoint you."

"But I thought you hated me. Taking over..."

"For someone so talented, you can be so stupid. This job could not have been more soul-destroying. Keeping people alive who don't care if they live or die by serving them slop. Now I look forward to waking up every morning. Sure you are a royal pain in the arse but you are my pain in the arse. We will cope without you. Go!"

I run out – noting no media scrum. Such a short attention span. Anyway the shelter and I neither need nor want the attention.

I look up and down the road. It is clear. Where can she be? Tube station! Even if she did not go that way, I know where she lives. I don't recall the train combinations that got me here, but I can work it out. As I step that way, the rain comes down. Hard. I run through the rain and get to the tube station. It is as I remember it, minus Mr Plod – but colder as it's now late September. There are a few people there but there is a figure on the exact bench where I sat, just as drenched, with her head in her hands – in the exact pose I was in. I go up to her, reliving Mr Plod's moves, and touch her shoulder. She looks up, her face as wet as mine was.

I say: "I am so sorry. You know, you were right. At some point, if I am a visiting friend, I would need to move on. It's just... it was so sudden. We were talking as if two years is nothing then suddenly – 'you should leave'."

"That's what I was trying to say. As soon as I said that, I knew it had come out wrong but you wouldn't listen. When you threw your keys at me and slammed that door, my whole world turned inside out."

"Funny, that's the way I felt."

"This is all so wrong. If only we could get it back to where it was."

"It can't be exactly like that."

"Not exactly the same. But why not better?"

"What do you mean?"

"Restart. This time we promise not to give up when there is a misunderstanding."

"But I live here now." I gesture in the general direction of outside, suddenly not sure where 'here' is exactly.

"A homeless shelter. You have a home as long as you want it. You can still work back there." She points roughly where I had. "Come on. Let's just go home and we can work it out later."

She stands up and my resistance melts. Why am I fighting what I actually want? "Tell you what. If we can get back in time to shop, I will make us pesto. Would you like that?"

"Very much."

"Do you still have that pasta I made?"

"No, all used up."

So she can cook after all, I think but keep it to myself. "Let's just use factory pasta this one time."

She pulls me towards the station exit. "Let's get a cab – that way we can get to the shops in time."

In the cab, we silently drip; being wet somehow is not as bad as it was on my Mr Plod night, and the cabbie has thoughtfully put the heat up without being asked. Things are still far from right, but I finally remember how good it is to be with her. I quiz myself apprehensively – have I forgotten everything as I did with my Harriet life? I try to think of the mundane. Ordinary meal times. Days where nothing much happened. It's all still there. She rests her head on my shoulder and I caress it gently. Can this be real? Surely it must be as it feels so different from after Harriet.

When we get to the flat, she suggests we go in quickly to change. She says: "Your stuff you left in the laundry to the rescue." I had completely forgotten those clothes.

As she opens up, I look around. My mattress is on the floor. I point it out. "Were you that confident that you would be able to drag me back?"

"No. It's been there the whole time. I couldn't bear to move it. I didn't touch anything of yours. Other than using up the pasta. I couldn't have it staring at me when I went to bed."

I decide I need time to process this and say nothing, as we close up and go shopping. I find linguine, basil and pine kernels, while she looks for other ingredients. "Do you have garlic, olive oil and Parmesan?"

She holds up a wedge of Reggiano. "I have the rest at home."

I suddenly realise that I need a toothbrush and razor and scoot off. She catches up at the dental display. "What are you getting here?"

"Toothbrush..."

"You left yours behind. I told you I didn't touch your stuff."

"Oh."

Back in the flat, she says: "Before you do anything else, you need to make some phone calls. Geoff and Stan. With all the emotional roller coaster of finding you, I forgot to say: they have been as worried about you as I was. Both have phoned at least once a day since you ran away."

I feel so guilty. In all that self-absorbed time, I have forgotten all the people who have been kind to me – at least, the ones still alive. I get to it at once.

Geoff answers on first ring. I spill the story fast and promise a longer chat later. It's 9am in San Francisco, so I catch Stan still at home. To his numerous questions, I have one answer: "It's thanks to you that I could make something of this disaster. We must talk again. I have to cook now."

There is a knock at the door. "Aha!" says Hazel. "Let's see who that is." She ushers in a sturdy-looking woman, about her age. Short dark hair, eyes you wouldn't mess with.

"Luke, I'd like you to meet Claudette. My best friend from way back. I need to let my dad know you're back. The two of you, get to know each other. I will be right back." Hazel disappears to her bedroom and shuts the door as Claudette and I settle uneasily into easy chairs. I wait for her to start.

"So you're the infamous Luke." This doesn't bode well. But I wait. I am not about to make another social blunder. "Hazel has been such a sucker for jerks. Each time she breaks up, she sees it straight off. We go out for a drink. She verbally flagellates herself. Then does it again. Rinse, repeat. When she told me about you, it seemed different. But then you ran out on her."

There is a silence. I don't want to make excuses. What Hazel said was only half of what drove me away. The other half was me: shutting down and not listening.

"So she calls me over here, and there is an empty hole you left filled with masses of pasta on clothes hangers so I say to her, let's invite all our friends over and get rid of this once and for all by eating all his pasta. So we did that. It was a great party. You could hardly move. This place was packed.

Afterwards when everyone left and I was helping her clean up, she collapsed in a puddle.

"So either you are the real deal or the best con artist of all time. If it's the first one, great. If not, I will, so help me, personally cut off your balls."

I am about to argue when I see that this is the sort of friend I never had. I get up and take the two strides to the kitchen – the place is that small. She is right behind me. I turn and face her. "I take it you know where we keep the good knives?"

She holds my gaze. "That I do."

We both run out of things to say and Hazel walks into the silence with: "Ah, I see you are in a culinary discussion."

Claudette and I burst into uncontrolled laughter at the same instant; Hazel goes on: "What? What? Am I missing something?"

Eventually Claudette calms down, and says, "You had to be there."

I nod. It's clear that we have an understanding. That is the prompt for Claudette to take her leave. She says to Hazel, "Don't wait so long next time; we need to have a proper introduction."

After Hazel shows her out I ask: "How did it go with dad?"

"Fine. Mum was out as usual and he is really happy you're back. Let's eat, more talk later. Just tell me what the hell was going on between you and Claudette."

After I fill her in, I add: "If I had a few friends like that back when..."

She stops me. "Then you wouldn't be you. But you do have friends like that now. Think of Geoff, your California friends, me."

"Why have we not spent more time with your friends? Maybe we should redo the party you had without me, without the tears."

She agrees. "Things have been so hectic – we need to make more space for partying and I have other friends you would like." I think back to how it was – she was at work every day. I was out looking for work. She was following up work opportunities for me with connections. Just a few rushed parties between all this, with me mainly in the kitchen.

That out of the way, I haul out the pestle and mortar. I shred the pesto ingredients then pound them while water is boiling for the pasta. Factory-made pasta takes longer to cook but we have linguine al pesto ready in short order.

Hazel grins. "There's a bottle of Chablis in the fridge."

"Not the same one? The one I almost offered your mother?"

"The same."

"Is she still so against me?"

"I told her I wouldn't talk to her again unless you came back."

"Did you..."

"She's my mother. I have to talk to her. I think she gets it." Her hands reach out and she grasps both of mine. "We are friends no matter what. If you want that."

I pick up my glass and we clink and both say simultaneously, "This is so nice." I don't have to answer her question.

When we finish, she looks serious. "Besides missing you and feeling like crap about the way you left, there is something really important. The COSAWR people have been onto me almost every day about your asylum application. There is a real danger that it will be turned down because you are not pushing it along."

"Oh, crap. I completely forgot about that."

"Promise me you will go to them first thing."

"Right after I serve breakfast."

"Here or at the shelter?"

"Both."

"Do you know what I would like now?"

I study her closely before answering. "Hot spring."

"Exactly."

"Would you like the mattress this time?"

"Let's do it the same old way before we think of changing anything."

So here I am on my camping mattress staring at the ceiling and she is next to me on the floor doing likewise. To anyone else it would seem bizarre but to me it is bliss. I feel for her hand and she grasps mine firmly. There is a silence. Then, she says: "If I was naked, would you look?"

I turn and before I can look she has turned as well and we kiss. I keep my eyes closed. Eventually it ends, and I open my eyes. "I am looking now. I don't mind if you are wearing anything or not as long as it's what you want."

We must both have been super tired because I remember nothing after that until waking up on a hard floor. I remember where I am and assume I rolled off the mattress. I look around and Hazel is on the mattress, also in the process of waking up. "You hussy! You stole my bed!"

She gives as good as she got. "You brazen thief! You stole my floor!"

We both can't stop laughing, until I notice the time. "Oh, crap. I totally missed breakfast service."

She pulls me close. "Let me remind you that we have a

few things that we agreed to sort out first.

"Number one, this is your home as long as you want it to be.

"Number two, the shelter is your job, as long as you want it to be.

"And number zero, before all that, we need to do something about your asylum status."

I hold her. "I remember it as 'we can work it out later'. But I am not complaining. I'm at the same place. I will visit COSAWR as soon as I have been back to the shelter to organize supplies for the day, then come home with my suitcase."

The word "home" nearly chokes me up. I cover up by switching focus. "Let me see if I can make that fancy cappuccino machine of yours work again. If it is not rusted solid and you have actual coffee beans." It's been a while and it is overly complicated, not a kind I would buy.

While I am working out the coffee situation, I remember one more thing that we did not sort out. "You have a harder problem than me. One parent to sort out. For me, zero. What are we going to do about your mother?"

"What do you mean, zero?" She looks concerned.

My whole unhappy childhood story spews out. She goes to me and pulls me around to face her. "No wonder you are so skittish about rejection. Fixing up with mum is nothing so let's put that aside. I thought the way you ran away was a bit of an overreaction to exactly one past bad relationship. I have been through several and losing you scares me, so I get it – close enough, anyway. So please, let us get this straight.

"I would never deliberately hurt you. You are the best friend I ever had. Is there anything else I need to explain?"

There is a contemplative pause; I use a few random gestures to convey deep thought. Then: "Where is the on switch on the cappuccino machine?"

She swats at me playfully. She was right. It is not exactly the same. It is better.

Chapter 22

COSAWR

COSAWR really is not a mellifluous acronym. It comes across as sounding a bit like cosy about war, which is really the opposite to its intent. I meet Jonathan Childs, an exile from South Africa, assigned to my case after my initial meeting. He seems pleased to see me though his news is pretty grim.

"The Home Office doesn't take kindly to refugees who disappear into the woodwork then pop up again and claim asylum. The fact that you have been in a homeless shelter doesn't work in your favour. They will see it as sponging off welfare."

"Even if I turned the place around and am all over the news for doing gourmet cuisine for the homeless?"

"It's hard to know how the political bosses will take this; they may take it as a positive, in which case, they could try to harvest it as a self-promoting media stunt. Or they may take it as making an example of you for flouting the rules."

"Neither is a win. I did what I did because the homeless were having their dignity denied. They were being fed indescribable slop and no one cared. I showed we could do better without costing more. But if the price is turning my people into a media circus, no. Send me back to South Africa and I will take my chances with doing time." Jonathan reacts as I say 'my people' but I don't feel the need to explain.

"There is absolutely no way I can join the military." I tell him about my early childhhod friends, how I feel for the way they were left behind when I went to school and university. For good measure, I add recent news reports. "I see stories of shacks being bulldozed in mid-winter. How can anyone support a system like that?"

"If you do go back and go to jail, it will be a big media win for the End Conscription Campaign. But jail is hard. You need to be ready for that. You have other options. You could move to a more amenable country. Our office in Amsterdam..."

"No. I am not running again. The shelter needs me and I have a friend I can't walk out on. I don't want to lose her. If I go to jail, I can be out again in a year, and then try find a way to get back here with legal residence."

"Tell you what. We will pursue the legal route aggressively. We will take the angle that you have done wonders for the shelter, and hope that they accept that without trying to create a circus. Let's not over-anticipate."

I pick up some pamphlets advertising anti-apartheid events and thank Jonathan for his help but I do not leave with a great sense of optimism.

From there, it is back to the shelter, to plan dinner with Martha, and go foraging, as lunch has used up all their fresh supplies. Martha says: "Why don't you take Jill with you? it's time someone else learnt where all our food comes from, so you can spend more time with your girl." I think of protesting that Hazel is 'just a friend', but she is somewhere in the big space between that and 'my girl', so I decide to take the win. Another person foraging is long overdue and it's better that the idea came from Martha than from me.

I walk out with Jill, happy that Martha, despite her usual grumpy demeanour, is definitely on the same team now. Jill is a great choice. Though she doesn't talk much, she is usually the one who takes command when Martha is away. Now I think about it, I don't know of any instance when both have had a day off at the same time.

Chapter 23

New Start

I visit Henrique, who offers me a nice fresh halibut, even bigger than the salmon he gave me on the first day. I look at it in trepidation. All I know about halibut is it's expensive and highly regarded. The cost of the donated salmon didn't trouble me as I have plenty of experience with it from San Francisco.

"I never cooked one of these before. How complicated is filleting?"

"There is more to it than salmon. Come on, I will show you."

Henrique gives me a masterclass in dissecting halibut, as Jill looks on fascinated, and some hints on how best to cook it. I leave with it in pieces, along with a good selection of veg.

On the way back, I take a swing past my favourite green-grocer to introduce Jill. "Hi George. Jill is going to be doing the rounds when I am not available. Same deal as before – anything too good to throw away not good enough to sell to-morrow."

George shakes her hand. "A pleasure to meet someone who works with Luke."

As we walk back, Jill says: "I don't know if I will ever get the respect you do."

"Respect comes from what you do, not who you are. You have mine already, as do the rest of the staff. All of you are special people."

"Why don't you tell all of us that then? We had a suspicion from the start that you were trying to show us up. We are all working people and many of us know someone whose life has gone off the rails. We see those people in the residents."

"I sort of had that conversation with Martha. Do you remember that?"

"Yes. That was the first time I really believed that you were one of us and not a do-gooder planning to show us up to get his face on the telly."

"I hope you saw when I chased away the media that I don't care about that. I am not good at talking about this stuff. Do I need to tell everyone, or will you help me?"

"Don't worry. We are all with you now. I just had to get that off my chest."

Back at the shelter, I find Hazel waiting for me. I ask: "Is there a problem?"

"No. I want to see your other home and the people who live there, if I may."

"No problem – but we have to respect their privacy, and I can only show you the dining hall, because everyone but the media scrum is welcome there. I can't go into the dormitory myself anymore and wouldn't ask to."

"Of course."

Jill calls out on her way to the kitchen: "Is your girl staying for dinner? We have a halibut to cook and you are the only one who knows how."

Hazel looks at me. "Your 'girl'? What have you been telling them?"

"Nothing. They assume..."

She plants a kiss without looking around to see if anyone's watching. "Huh. It's up to us, not them. Go cook. I will come back at dinner time. When is that?"

"Six." She disappears before I can say anything more, so I follow Jill into the kitchen.

As Hazel walks in, most of the residents are at the ready. Before anyone can say anything, I announce: "Some of you may remember my very good friend, Hazel. She is my guest tonight. But as I know her, she would be embarrassed to jump the queue." The non-residents' queue is not long enough to exclude her; it is a *big* halibut.

Martha is having none of that. "Well, I would be bloody embarrassed if she missed out, so I suggest the other guests let her go first." Before anyone can protest, the other guests are applauding, followed by the residents.

That evening, we go home together on the tube. We talk about her work, books I want to read, the weather, how happy the dining hall is, and the potential for more of the work to be done by others. Everything, in short, but the hard subjects.

When we get in through the door, we hold each other tight. Eventually, I say, "What a day. After COSAWR I was depressed, but seeing Jill for the first time as an individual rather than as just one of the kitchen staff really woke me up. There is a lot more to the changes in that place than just better food for the residents. And I nearly broke it all by being so arrogant at the start."

"Well, you didn't. Come on, sit down. A nice glass of Sauvignon Blanc won't do us any harm while you talk about COSAWR."

"New Zealand?"

"Yes. I was saving it for mum, but what the hell. It is actually pretty good."

We sit at the table and clink glasses. "OK, so here is the deal. I have actually hurt my chances by not working on my application. They think what I did for the shelter may help but the politics of it is unpredictable."

"Is there anything we can do right now?"

"No. It's a waiting game until we hear from the Home Office."

"Then let us not worry about it. There is however one bit of unfinished business. Mum. Dad has invited us over for lunch on Saturday. He very much wants to fix things up. I am not sure about her."

I contemplate Hazel through the wine glass.

"Can we do anything about it now?"

"No."

"Let's finish our wine then take a nice soak in our hot spring. And I promise not to look…uninvited."

Saturday dawns – a bright sunny day for a change. I am up early and lie on my "bed" reading until it wouldn't be inconsiderate to be noisy. Hazel emerges from her bedroom at the sound of the coffee grinder and heads to the bathroom. I work the cappuccino machine with no feigned ignorance. Her cup is ready at the table when she emerges and I offer toast.

She holds up her cup and says, "To us!" I tell her about

the Harry celebration breakfast, and how the same joke had worked there. Another small slice of history shared.

The day is starting well. We head out to the local park to catch some sun, and chat about random things. It's great to have some time to ourselves, without worries like getting food ready on time for the shelter, being thrown out of the country or dealing with a difficult parent. Then we hit the time when we must take the tube to Greenwich.

We sit together on the train, noting the stops quietly, and changing trains a couple of times. Outside the station, Hazel's dad is waiting for is. "Come on, it's a short walk home. Nice weather to be out."

We arrive at a compact house, on two levels. Heather's mother is in the kitchen. "Make yourselves at home!" she yells, which is a promising start.

"Dad, let's show Luke the layout."

"Good idea. Son, we have two bedrooms and a bathroom upstairs, bathroom, kitchen and living room downstairs." He shows me the various spaces. It is compact and neatly furnished, in a combination of old and new styles – more about comfort than fashion. He leads the way out of the back door, where there is a substantial garden, neatly divided into decorative and edible. There's an outdoor furniture set, the table laid for lunch.

Once back inside, Robert offers drinks. The inevitable New Zealand Sauvignon Blanc, an Australian Merlot and beers I have never heard of. "In deference to the warmth, I would like to try a beer." I examine the selection and choose a lager. Hazel takes the Australian red, as does Robert. I wonder if the fact that we have all avoided the mum's favourite tipple presages anything, as we settle down in garden chairs.

Then Carol emerges and announces, "You know, I am short of a few things I like for the salad. Luke, how about you go shopping with me?"

This seems an invitation to be an insider, so I jump at it. The greengrocer is just down the road and she starts talking as we walk. "Luke, I hear you are in trouble with your application for asylum. Is this true?"

"Yes. I shouldn't have let it lapse while I was at the shelter, but the work I did there could help."

We reach the shop and she clearly does not need my help, so the asylum conversation is the actual intent. I let her pick out a cucumber, various sprouts, some heirloom tomatoes and radishes, without intervening, to make clear that I see through the pretext.

On the way back, she tries to restart the conversation, but I don't respond. This clearly is not going to plan, not mine anyway.

Back at the house, Carol makes short work of finishing the salad, and emerges to the back yard with a quiche to go with it, as well as her own glass of wine. We fall to eating; the quiche is not half bad and the salad is fine. I keep very quiet while everyone else exchanges pleasantries, expecting a bomb to drop. No one else notices except Carol, who flicks pointed glares at me regularly.

Eventually we are through the meal and the carefully conserved bomb drops. Carol looks at me then at Robert, avoiding Hazel. "My daughter has been through too many manipulative relationships for me to stay quiet. I know what this is about. Luke is on the point of being thrown out of the country because he messed up his asylum application. So,

Plan B. Get married. I will not have it."

I am ready for her this time. "I won't have it either. We haven't even talked about getting married, so I don't know where that comes from. Let me make this totally clear. I would rather go to jail than do anything to hurt her. If I lose out on my asylum application, it is on me and no one else. She is a good friend, and proved it by going to bring me back when I walked out on her. I was too terrified to try and she wasn't. It was a terribly hard thing for her to do but she did it anyway.

"I know what it is like to have parents who never back me. I am so disappointed in you."

I get up. Hazel does too. We walk out together. I don't look back, but she does. It is, after all, her family. We say nothing as we walk to the station. As we wait for the train, I say: "I have clearly blown it with your mother."

"No. She has blown it. When I looked back, you should have seen the look on dad's face. Let's phone them when we get home. I am too angry to talk to her now."

Back home, there is a message on the phone. Hazel plays it. It is from Robert, short and simple: "Talk to me." She looks at me. I nod.

"I will use my bedroom phone. You can eavesdrop on this phone if you like. If mum answers, though, I am not sure if I can talk to her. Not now." She goes to the bedroom, and I lift the handset as she dials.

"Hi dad? Is mum home?"

"No, she went out to have tea with her friends."

"Good, then we can talk. I'm sorry to tell you, but your wife is a manipulative cow." I nearly drop the phone but clutch it tigher in case there is more like this.

"Do you think I hadn't noticed? Where do you think all that good advice, that you mostly ignored, about dealing with manipulative relationships, came from? It came pretty close to divorce several times, the closest the day she pushed you to throwing Luke out. The idiotic cliché about staying together for the kids actually worked this time. I was there to see her do it again and I am not going to stand for it.

"What are your thoughts?"

"Luke and I have never been even close to talking about marriage. Things are great the way they are, close friends who get each other and have learnt how to stand up to abuse the hard way. There is no need to rush into anything new and I really believe he would go to jail if that was his only choice and there is nothing I could do to change that."

"I hope he has not run off again, because I want him to know that I have a spare bed for him anytime he needs to get away, and if Carol doesn't like it, she can sleep on your floor."

I see the humour in this and can't resist adding: "Or..." then realise I have given the game away.

"Luke! You naughty lad! Giving away your eavesdropping then not sharing your obviously profound thought. Out with it!"

"I'm sorry, I really shouldn't."

There is a pause. Then Robert says: "Let me help you then... Or, this city has one very fine homeless shelter, where they serve gourmet meals. Was that it?"

I ruefully admit it was. Everyone has a good laugh.

"But seriously, Luke, we need to work on your problem, otherwise I have a fear that my daughter may also end up in jail. She is even less to be persuaded than you. I have a few connections at the Home Office who could pull some strings. Much as I detest the old boy network, it's all that I have. Would that be acceptable?"

"I can't say no to any help."

Chapter 24

Good Old Boys

Hazel and her dad talk regularly. I follow my routine of ensuring that the shelter is well catered, while leaving more of the actual work to the staff, and dropping in regularly to share ideas on making the food more exciting. Part of this duty is trying ideas on Hazel and her friends, resulting in some fun dinner parties that take the sting out of anticipating what the Home Office might do.

As with California, though the kitchen isn't far off, I am saved from exercising social skills in my role as chef. And anyway Hazel and her friends talk so much, I don't feel the need to chip in – unless directly addressed. I talk mostly to Claudette when she's there. After our first encounter, I feel comfortable in her presence.

I also pay a few visits to COSAWR, and add new details to my application but after two weeks of uncertainty, Robert's enquiries finally pay off, just as we are starting to feel the growing chill of October. It's Friday evening, and Hazel is out seeing friends, when the phone rings. "Hazel is out," I say, without waiting for the caller to speak.

It's Robert. "It's you that I need to speak to, Luke. I am by no means in the inner circle, not having been to a fancy public school or a top university, but I do have friends who have. One of them has a connection at the Home Office and managed to persuade them that it could be an embarrassment to the government if the person famed for bringing gourmet food to the homeless ended up in an apartheid jail – particularly as the country is gearing up for an election."

"What do I have to do?"

"My connection has set up a meeting with the Home Secretary for you on Monday at eleven. It is exceptionally rare that someone in your position is invited to meet a cabinet minister."

"Gosh. Does your connection have any advice on what would carry weight?"

"No, but you will have ten minutes with the Permanent Secretary before you meet the minister, so you could air ideas with him."

"I'm not sure what all these titles mean."

"The Home Secretary is the cabinet minister responsible for matters like yours. The Permanent Secretary is the top civil servant in his ministry."

"I see. When Hazel gets home, I can rehearse arguments with her. Is there no one else who could help?"

"You could do that with me too, though I am not very political. Shall we all meet for tea over the weekend? I am sure we can find a time when Carol is otherwise engaged."

I agree, and when Hazel gets home, we set it all up. We meet Robert at a coffee shop near our home on Saturday morning. We discuss the matter from all angles, and agree that the Harry story is most compelling – I gave a person, who had fallen far, dignity in his final moments. "Surely even a seasoned politician has heartstrings – it is a matter of finding the right bow to play them," I add, pleased to have found a musical allusion. Robert unexpectedly high-fives me. I didn't know it was also a British thing.

Monday. 2 Marsham Street is about a half-hour trip by tube, but I leave at nine to be sure I am not late. I find the building at 9:45, with no problem, then look for a coffee shop. I find one a short walk away, and uneasily review my arguments. Appealing to a cabinet minister is way beyond my life experience. I am to lead with the Harry story, mention how uncomfortable I am with the South African military and how I will be jailed if I refuse conscription, then go back to the shelter and how I could do so much good if the idea takes off, and close by mentioning Harry again for good measure. Everything that seemed so clear on Saturday is now a blur. I am almost in a panic when I present myself in the building, and announce that I have an appointment with the Permanent Secretary in ten minutes.

I am ushered to his office and find the Permanent Secretary's secretary is rather aloof and unhelpful. "I see you have an appointment with the Home Secretary in fifteen minutes. I am terribly sorry, but the Permanent Secretary is with the minister and can't be called away."

This adds to my growing sense of unease. Will I even see the Home Secretary? But a minute before the appointed time, an official in a very conservative suit bustles out of the inner sanctum. "Follow me. The Home Secretary will see you now. You have ten minutes, so no waffle."

"And you are?"

"Second Permanent Secretary, Julian Holmes. Permanent Secretary is Sir Charles. I am sure you know the minister's name." In my panic, I have forgotten it, but resolve to address him as minister, as I am ushered into a large office, smelling of dust that has dust.

Which one is the Home Secretary is self-evident, as he addresses the underlings. "Thank you Holmes, can you brief us quickly on the issue before us?"

"Certainly, minister. This is Luke Fredericks. The South African draft dodger who doesn't know how to file proper paperwork and wants to be excused because he can cook."

"Oh, right. Fredericks, what do you have to say for yourself?"

I completely forget my planned opening. "Minister, I grew up in an intensely unfair society. I went to a school with great teachers. Going to university was no financial challenge. In the early years of my life, all of my friends were Black farm kids. We ran around barefoot, scaring each other with snake sightings. We had fun, we laughed, we cried, we scraped knees. We spoke Zulu. Yet once I was out of that, I could go to a good school, I had many career options open to me. They had nothing. Even if they could go to school, it would be substandard. By design. I wish I knew where they are now. All I can say is that if they are fighting for their freedom, I am not on the other side."

"I see. Is that all?"

"There is so much unfairness there. A single mother living in a shack trying to do the best for her family, and it gets bulldozed in the middle of winter."

"Terrible. We know all that, it is all over the news."

I suddenly wake up. I have messed up my pitch. Instead of appealing to reason and to his constituency, I am all but hectoring the Home Secretary. "Minister, what I want to tell you that is different is the homeless shelter where I brought people hope and dignity. Let me just tell you about one person, Harry. He was obviously highly educated but had fallen on hard times. He stole my clothes for drug money but bought them back when I showed him he could have dignity.

"More than that, the day he finally had a fatal heart attack, he gave up all his money to help buy food for the other residents, rather than spend it on drugs.

"This highly intelligent person would have died alone if I had not taken him to hospital.

"This is my home now. If I go back to South Africa, there is a good chance that I will end up in jail because I can't fight for a cause that is clearly unjust. But if you let me stay, I will fight for the poor right here and work hard for their dignity."

"Is that all?" Despite his studied politeness, the Home Secretary allows a hint of impatience to slip out. Sir Charles glances at the minister and glances at me, then shifts his gaze to his watch. I don't need to be an expert on body language to read this.

There is no way this has been ten minutes. I have a sinking feeling. I am not getting through to him and surely his Permanent Secretary knows this better than I do. "Thank you for listening, minister. I value your time."

Holmes ushers me out. He can see by my demeanour that I see this as failure. He leads me to his office and offers me tea, which I accept.

"A top tip, if you get to supplicate to a minister of the crown again – if ever. Don't go in spoiling for a fight. I'm afraid the minister is not moved by stories of a Black single parent having her home demolished. Sad though it is, it isn't his problem to solve."

"I know I messed up. I was expecting to have ten minutes with the Permanent Secretary before we started, and that was cancelled on me without notice. I had this carefully prepared pitch and got nowhere close to delivering it. The last-minute change when I was already nervous left me totally flustered."

Holmes sympathetically sips his tea. "Sadly, our time is not our own. If our minister demands our attention, that is where we need to be. Look, your only real chance is this Harry story. Closer to home. Perhaps if you could tell me a little more...?"

I give him the whole Harry story, up to his death in hospital. When I mention his linguistic proficiency, Holmes's eyebrows lift. When I get to the end, he looks thoughtful. "Perhaps if I can verify this story, it may help. I would need details of the hospital. What is his surname?"

"Whitmore."

"Good god! Not Harry Whitmore! We were at Oxford together. The most brilliant person I ever met. He could pick up a language faster than I can pick up a drink. I often wondered what happened to him. I expected big things. Academia, a high position in the Foreign Office. Then he dropped out of sight."

"My story should be easy to check. I am a bit hazy about dates over that time but the hospital will have a record and the surgeon will remember. Around mid-September..."

"Will he?"

"He specially thanked me for being there for Harry and

drove me back to the shelter. I invited him to be our honoured dinner guest."

"Did he arrive?"

"Yes. He will not forget the reception we gave him."

"Leave this with me. If your story checks out, this puts a whole different complexion on things. I am afraid that the fate of an Oxbridge graduate cuts a lot more ice in Whitehall than that of a poor Black woman in South Africa – much though this may pique your sense of injustice."

That Wednesday, I am back home from helping with lunch at the shelter, and am now preparing dinner for Hazel and her dad. I have heard nothing from COSAWR or the Home Office and am just living in the moment. There is a knock on the door. A person who looks late fifties to early sixties is there, in a rather expensive-looking jacket and tie. "Are you Luke Fredericks?"

"Yes."

"I am Arthur Whitmore." I see a resemblance to Harry, and invite him in. As he enters, he adds, "Harry's brother." I usher him to an armchair. "I am so grateful to meet you after what you did for him. Unlike my brother, I have done rather well for myself, and have the means to show my gratitude in a meaningful way."

"What do you mean?"

"I believe the Home Office is giving you trouble over your asylum process. I don't think it is anything that an accomplished barrister can't overcome."

I know enough about British law to know that this is a very expensive option. "Arthur, can I get you a drink while we talk this over? This sounds to me like an extremely generous gift."

"Not at all. I can spend my own time any way that I choose,

and I really have no need to make more money at this stage of my life. But a drink will be most welcome. What can you offer?"

As we are talking, Hazel gets home and I do introductions. She is curious. "I presume you learned of this arising from Luke's approach to the Home Office? If so, why do we need to fight them?"

"Ah. We don't. All we need is for them to *fear* that we *will*. The mere suggestion that I am involved will be enough to trigger the entire Oxbridge old boy's network against them and they won't want that."

I nod sagely. "You wouldn't happen to know one Julian Holmes by any chance?"

"I do believe he was in the same college as me at Oxford, but we didn't cross paths back then. Different eras. But yes, he is the one who informed me of my brothers' fate."

I sit at the table facing our guest. "There is one thing I would like to ask you. After his death, I started thinking of the food service as Chez Harry, because no one had been influenced more by my attempt at bringing dignity to the residents. But I thought it would be disrespectful to do that openly without his consent. What do you think?"

Arthur chuckles. "That is so Harry, mixing the pretentious with the informal. He would have loved it. You don't need to seek anyone's permission but I appreciate your sensitivity."

Hazel sits down with her own drink. "So, where next?"

"Luke, keep plugging away at the official process, and I will ensure that a letter lands in the hands of the Home Secretary that will concentrate his mind on the need to do the right thing. It won't hurt to influence a few people in the Foreign Office to lean on him. The South African government does not actually deeply favour jailing draft dodgers – while they do it sometimes for deterrence, they also don't like the negative publicity. So they quite likely are putting out feelers to the Foreign Office to try to make this thing go away."

Hazel looks shocked. "Does our government really take direction from the apartheid regime?"

"My dear, a lot of dark things go on behind the scenes. Right now, we are playing the old boy network, a thing Harry rightly despised. Yet I am sure he would have approved if it gets the job done. The two of you live to fight a most worthy battle another day. I will let you know if anything transpires."

He stands up to go, leaving a card on the table with his contact details. "Get in touch if anything changes on your side. And, by the way, if you officially rename the place as Chez Harry, I would be delighted to be your guest for the renaming."

Shortly after he leaves, Robert arrives. As Hazel lets him in she says, "Dad, we just had a visitor."

"Harry's brother," I add. "Apparently he is a top barrister and has the right connections to make things go my way."

"What is his name?"

"Arthur Whitmore. Do you know of him?" asks Hazel.

"Don't either of you read the news? Arthur Whitmore, QC. Wow. He has won some huge cases. This is like having Muhammad Ali in the ring for you. What's for dinner?"

Chapter 25

Starting to Win

The week starts off low-key. Sunday, we pretty much chill at home. Monday, I spend much of the day at Chez Harry – still only a name in my head – and work through meal options with the staff, increasing the trend of putting them in control. That night, we have a light supper at home and have a brief chat about the weekend.

"Saturday was pretty intense. What do you make of our new QC?"

"Dad is right. I was not paying attention. He has won cases that no one else could have won. Anyone up against him should be rightly terrified. It's a pity something as archaic as the old boys' network is what you need to get justice."

"Absolutely – this is why the single parent in a shack has so little chance. I wish I could fight for causes like that."

"One thing at a time. Let's get you safe, then take on the world."

"What is happening between your parents?"

"I don't know. I am giving dad space to sort things out."

"I never heard anyone talk about their mother like that."

"As in *manipulative cow?*"

"I was thinking more: calling her your dad's wife."

"You did say you have zero parents to sort out. This is hard." I gesture towards the floor. We clearly need time in the 'hot spring'. I offer her my side. She says: "No, I like the challenge of swapping with you in your sleep." I just laugh. I don't care if that thing happened on purpose.

Tuesday – I get to Chez Harry early and make sure all is in order for the day. Nothing exotic on the menu, but nothing is in short supply. I leave when lunch service is ready and I head out to COSAWR; I need to progress my application, as advised by my new QC. Jonathan Childs is champing at the bit.

"I've been leaving messages on your phone all morning."

"Apologies. I've been at the shelter and Hazel is at work. I'm here to see to any outstanding paperwork. News?"

"Pretty good, actually. The Home Office has written us a letter asking us politely to take it easy. You are being given permission to work and to reside in the UK pending a final decision on your application. This bit, however has me puzzled. It says: 'We are predisposed to consider this application favourably, taking into account the applicant's sterling work for the homeless; we therefore suggest it is not necessary to employ the expensive services of a highly-regarded QC.'

"What is that about? I hope you aren't expecting us to pay for that?"

"Oh, no. Someone who relates to what I have done at the shelter volunteered to influence the process on my behalf."

"I see. Perhaps you should have told us, so we don't work at cross purposes."

"Thoughtless of me. I do very much appreciate your hard work. I can introduce him to you so there is no further misunderstanding."

"Please do. In the meantime, I'm very happy it's going well. Let's continue with the next step of the paperwork and not leave anything to chance."

Just as the QC ordered, I think but decide best not to say it out aloud. As I am about to leave, Jonathan asks: "By the way, who is the QC?"

"Arthur Whitmore."

He whistles. "No wonder you have them rattled. I like your shelter project, but I didn't realise it had attention at that level."

"It doesn't generally. He happens to know someone I helped." I decide not to go through all the string-pulling involved. It gives me a dirty feeling that I am getting all this help when the real victims like the single mother in the shack get nothing.

Even so, I head home with a spring in my step. For the first time since I left gran's farm, I feel that life is heading in a positive direction. I unlock the door, and see there are messages on the phone as I walk in. Since it is not my phone, I wonder if I should check and decide I should, since at least some are from COSAWR. The first few are, and I delete them as they are nothing new. Then there is one from Hazel's mother. I stop after recognizing her voice. This is not for me.

I check out supplies, and decide to do a bit of shopping. When I get back, Hazel is on the couch crying. I think of the phone and wonder if it was that. "What's the matter?"

"My mother. Phone message. She says she will disown me if I don't get rid of you. She says you are driving me away from her."

I go to her. "Is that true?"

"Of course not. I already said she is a manipulative cow."

"And talked of her as your dad's wife."

She wipes her face. "I don't know why I am crying. I saw this a long way off. It's just hard to accept someone who has always been part of your life can turn on you like this. But of course, you know..."

"No, this is different. My parents never showed any interest in me. The big question is whether you want to reconcile. It has been better before. It never was with my parents."

"I wish there was a way. But I don't know how. Let's talk to dad though, he knows her better than anyone else."

"I got us some nice bread. Let's just have something simple for supper and not worry about things we can't fix right now. Why don't you talk to dad while I get it ready? Use the bedroom phone. I don't need to be involved."

As I start cutting bread, I realize that I never called Robert dad before. Something has shifted, not only the nastiness of Carol reaching a new level. That train of thought triggers another thing I had forgotten. As she reaches her bedroom, I stop her. "Wait, it's not all bad news." I tell her about the letter from the Home Office. "I can now legally work. I clean forgot about the script-writing opportunity up to now. I am sure that is long gone."

"Almost certainly. But I will ask again, and I am sure my boss and his contacts will be very understanding. Now let me chat to dad. That good news has lifted my mood."

Hazel is back as the food is ready, looking a lot happier. "What happened?" I ask.

"Dad told her straight. You are the one if that is what I want, and if you are not, he will support me too. She had better be on the team, or she is out.

"There was some pretty loud shouting but I would bet good money on dad for the win."

I hold both her hands as we arrive at the table. "Did you notice, when I suggested you talk to him, I called him 'dad'?"

"So you did." We lock eyes as we sit.

"Here is the thing. I never called anyone 'dad' before."

Chapter 26

Rename Reset

It's lunch at the shelter. As the weather warms, the homeless are more inclined to stay on the street. It is an aspect of homelessness that I don't get. Perhaps it is a residue of pride, of the need to be independent. We don't turn people away if they aren't residents and we get a few paying customers but still, the pace is relaxed. As we clean up, I decide this is the moment to clear up a few things with Martha.

"Martha, once we have cleaned up, could we have a chat?"

"Why not, pretty boy?"

As the others leave, she opens with: "Would you like a cuppa?"

Not one to dismiss an opening, I say, "I would love that. No sugar, no milk." That results in a bit of a frown, but she returns with two steaming mugs, stirring hers pointedly. She produces a pack of custard creams and I take one. I crunch mine; she dunks hers. This is an aspect of British culture that is new to me but I decide not to follow suit. It would seem too much like imitation for the sake of it.

I sip my tea slowly, as it is very hot, then put it down.

"The Home Office has given me permission to work. No one ever paid me to do what I am supposed to be qualified to do, creative writing. Now I can look for opportunities."

'You mean this is goodbye?" She looks genuinely sad at this thought.

"Oh, no. I will never walk out on you. I am just sharing good news. In any case, I have been taking a back seat more and more. I would love the opportunity to keep sharing new ideas. The days when I was the only one pushing change are long gone..."

She puts a hand on mine. The first gesture of affection I have seen from her. This helps me to open up. "Just a few things I would like to clear up. First, the 'puppy dog eyes' thing. Do I really do that? I hate to be manipulative."

"No, pretty boy. That's just me not wanting to admit you're right."

"Ah. And pretty boy?"

"Well, look at you. When you walked in here, you didn't look like someone who ever lived rough. I genuinely thought you were here to stir. Bring the tabloids down on us. Whatever. Well, I was wrong. But look at you now. You eat all this good food and you don't get fat. How do you do it?"

"The French secret. Eat good food made well and walk a lot. That's it. Really good food fills you up. Junk creates a craving for more. Too much sugar, too much salt." She looks into her tea cup. "Yes, that's one thing. It took me a while to get off sugar in tea and coffee. My gran put me on that path and I never went wrong following her advice. Cut back a little at a time. Now it tastes weird if there's even a tiny bit of sugar."

"Is that why you never make dessert?"

"Oh, no. That's just me making do. Once I've rounded up ingredients for one good course, there's no time to find more. And also no time for the kitchen to cook more. A bit of sugar in the right place is great. It's sugar with everything that's the problem."

"Do you really mind being my pretty boy?"

"I once had a girlfriend who said the most wonderful things about me then dumped me cold. It's what you do that counts. Call me what you like. You have more than earned the right."

She laughs, then shakes her head. "Is that why you are so slow with that nice girl of yours? Scared she will dump you too? This is not the first time I called you stupid..."

"Nor will it be the last. No, it isn't that. I like being with someone where we don't need to talk about boundaries. We both just know. When things shift, we will both know."

"Well, don't wait for a bloody earthquake. I see the two of you together. You are both missing what I see."

I nod. "I hope you're right. But that is not the main thing I want to talk about. You remember Harry?"

"Of course I do. I taught you how to make orange juice without dithering after he died."

"Correction, you showed me you could do it better than I *ever* could. I could never match the strength of your hands. Anyway, the point is, I met his brother and asked him what he thought of naming this place 'Chez Harry' and he thinks Harry would've loved the idea."

"Chez Harry?"

"Like at Henrique's – French for 'home of'."

"I know what it means. Isn't that a bit fancy for a

homeless dining room?"

"That's the thing. *Chez* makes it fancy, *Harry* is an ordinary name; it is the sort of language joke Harry would have loved."

"OK, I get it. But why are you asking me? You never asked my permission before."

"Because I now understand how much you care about this place. I was wrong to believe you didn't. I can stroll into a place like Chez Henrique to beg for ingredients exactly because I do not fit in here. All I needed to do was to open that door. It was wrong of me to disrespect all of you by taking over like that."

"Pretty boy, never apologize for trying to do right. Even if you get it wrong, it's better than not caring. I was angry with you at first. When I saw how you handled Harry and the money, I knew you were all right."

"So, name OK?"

"Fine with me. Just one thing: don't ask the management. Just put up a sign and let them complain if they don't like it."

"Harry's brother would like to be invited to the official name change."

"So we need a proper party."

"No. I think he should see it as Harry did. A good meal, like we usually do. Only difference, like the surgeon, he's guest of honour, served first."

"Then you must run the kitchen, if it will be the same as Harry saw. Don't argue, I insist."

"Thank you." I would've been hesitant to ask, but that is exactly as it should be. I have a spectacular menu in mind – something to remember. Even if I have to buy ingredients myself.

As I head out, I am accosted by Carol, who is waiting at the entrance. "What do you want?" I ask brusquely.

"We need to talk."

"I am not sure we do. You need to fix things with your daughter and you made me the obstacle to that."

"She won't talk to me." She actually does do the puppy dog eyes thing. It is so pathetic that I almost tell her to shove off. Then I remember: Hazel has only ever cried twice in my presence. Once, when she thought I couldn't forgive her. The second time when she thought she had to write off her mother.

"There's a coffee shop nearby. I've only been there once but they make a decent espresso."

We walk there and as we enter, I see the waiters conferring in the back. One darts into the kitchen and emerges with someone I take to be the manager or owner, by her bearing. She is slim, dark-haired and has a volatile look to her.

"Luke Fredericks. I am so pleased that you have finally graced us with your presence." I am not sure what I have done wrong.

"Actually, I did once get an espresso..."

But there is no stopping her. "We are the closest restaurant to your shelter and you never visit us. I know we do not have a fancy name, but we are as keen as anyone to join your project.

"Order what you like from the menu. On the house of course."

"Now, wait a minute. You are running a business. We will pay."

Carol interjects. "Correction, I will pay."

I go on: "We are not cutting anyone out. Once I found

a few suppliers it was easier just to go to them. If they have anything good enough to use now that will not be good tomorrow, that's it. I'm done. That is the only rule. Sometimes, they did cheat a bit and give us good stuff they knew was still good for tomorrow, but that was their choice."

"So can I show you what we can offer today?"

"No. Jill has taken over foraging and it's not my place anymore to do that. I will send her over when we are done. Who should she ask for?"

"Eleni. Now, what can we get you?"

"We just want a quiet space to talk over coffee. Or tea. Depending on what Carol wants."

The coffee shop has a small courtyard at the back that is not otherwise in use. I ask for a Greek coffee, much to the pleasure of Eleni. Carol orders a cappuccino.

We sit in silence until the coffees arrive. Once we are alone, I start. "Hazel is very upset about the rift with you."

"Do you think I'm not?"

"I don't know you the way I know her. I never had a relationship with my parents, so I am not the one to ask for advice."

"Surely a mother should be concerned about her daughter. Especially after every boyfriend has been a disaster."

"Of course you should care. But she has to be responsible for her own mistakes. As am I. We put no pressure on each other. You saw where I sleep, on that camping mattress on the floor. Do you think that is for show?" I wait and she knows that I know her answer, and she doesn't have to say it out loud.

"Do you know how often I've been in her bedroom?" Another pause, another non-answer that hints at a clear preconception. "Exactly once. I made fresh pasta and we needed a space to hang it to dry. She led the way in. We hung the pasta to dry. And that is the last time I went in there.

"Do you know why I didn't even go in to retrieve the pasta?" Another silence. "I could've done that earlier in the day you visited. The day you set her up to make me run away. But I didn't want to go into her space again."

She starts to say something and I stop her. "No, it is time you listened. Both of us have reason to be scared of relationships. I was the one who fled in terror. She must have been really scared of what would happen if she tracked me down, but she did. I know exactly how hard that was for her. Your daughter is an incredibly strong person. Her bad past relationships haven't broken her, they have made her careful.

"Now, are you going to stop messing up and trust her to know how to look after herself?"

"You've given me a lot to think about."

"Good. It's not my problem to solve but I care about your daughter a lot, so I really hope you do get this right. For her. You can be as horrible as you like to me, but save the choice rants for when she is not around."

I leave Carol to collect her thoughts and to pay. I drop back in at the shelter and find Jill and Martha discussing dinner options. "I could have a solution for dessert." I repeat the sugar conversation for Jill's benefit. "Eleni, who runs the coffee shop down the road, is terribly disappointed that we leave them out for foraging. How about checking what they have when you go out this afternoon? It's not a big place, but I am sure on the odd occasion, they will have treats that will be good for dessert."

Then, it's back home. I find Arthur Whitmore's card, then

decide to hold off on talking to him until Hazel gets back. She should be part of the Harry celebration. In any case, I am more likely to catch him at home past office hours. So I kill some time wandering the streets. The flat is in an area with curvy streets, not much of a rectangular grid, so it is easy to get lost, but I know the landmarks. It's the first time I have just been for a walk, with no purpose in mind – no shopping, not heading for the tube. It's a good feeling – exploring my home patch aimlessly – so I don't notice the passage of time.

By the time I get back, Hazel has been home for a while. She wraps herself around me with an enthusiasm I've not seen before. "Great news! BBC 2 has a series starting a new season, and they are open to a new writer. They know you have no experience, so they need a few episodes to see if you can do it. No promises, but it is an opening. Are you free to meet the producer?"

"Of course I am! Does a crocodile have teeth?"

"Is that a South Africanism?"

"No, I just made it up. I just know they have a *lot* of teeth. Did he set a date?"

"I need to get back to *her*. To get you started, she has given me the last three episodes for you to read. She suggests that you rough out the first three of the new series. She has a few options. Friday at 11 is the first one..."

"I'll take it." Two days should be more than enough time to read the scripts and come up with my own ideas. "Also, good news from my side. There is no resistance to renaming the shelter dining hall, so we need to set up a date that suits Arthur to be the guest of honour. I had my first really nice chat with Martha, and she insisted that I run the kitchen for that."

"Great. And I had a call from mother. She sounded really contrite and would like to make up."

"Ah." The way I say this gives something away.

"What did you do?" Hazel looks deep into my eyes.

I do my *hope I am not in trouble* look; this one I know – unlike puppy dog eyes. "She visited me on my way out of the shelter, and we had a good talk. Actually, it was mostly me talking. I hope I set her straight. I really am not a relationship expert."

"Leave her to me. It's not your problem to solve."

"That's what I told her. What I didn't tell her is that my asylum application is looking good. Let her think the worst of me. I don't care – she must make up with you."

"What else?"

"Funny, a thing that came up in conversation with Martha helped a lot. I never thought this through before. What I like about us is we never have to talk boundaries. If something changes, it just changes. I never feel I have invaded your space, and vice-versa. Both of us have had relationship disasters. What's wrong with being careful?"

I find her nose on my nose, a surprisingly comforting thing, and go on, as she shifts to a tight hug. "One thing I never tell anyone is the hot spring. That's our special thing. That is where it really started. If I had looked, everything would be different." She is still holding me, and her grip gets tighter, almost to the point of pain.

We set up a date with my QC for the renaming. He's free Saturday evening, plenty of time to plan something really special. So the rest of my week is set: two days to read scripts and write my own trial episodes, then Saturday to do a top-class meal to honour Harry.

Chapter 27

Rescripting

I don't waste time getting into reading the sample scripts. But it doesn't take long to feel that reading them *is* a waste of time. I walk out of the study to find Hazel watching TV, something we rarely do because we like talking to each other.

She switches the TV off as I have a good rant. "This stuff is dross! Did they really pay good money to someone to write it? The characters don't stay in voice. Each episode has a surprise that is completely contrived. There isn't a clear flow – no basics like clear start, middle and end."

"Well, the producer did say they need something fresh. But: marching in there and announcing the old stuff is dross isn't a great opening. It may make the producer feel you are attacking her for signing off on it. I don't know if she was in charge of the last series but why risk it? Just write your own, and let it speak for itself."

"OK, I suppose I need to learn 'polite'. That nearly cost me with the Home Office. This really should not be too hard. My gran was an Agatha Christie fan. I used to be too but when

I reread some a few years back, it is terribly dated and not as well written as I remembered. Racism, plot surprises that aren't possible to anticipate because details aren't disclosed. To me, a good mystery story should have enough clues for it to be possible for the reader to solve if you are wide awake."

"There you go, some ideas already. This crime series has been running forever. Gina Gibbons is a top producer and I am now wondering if she inherited this thing and why. She is quite the feminist. A bumbling male detective possibly doesn't appeal to her. Feminism isn't about celebrating male dysfunction, it's about equality."

"Aha! You've given me an idea!"

I rush back to the study, then return sheepishly. It's been so long since I wrote anything, I don't know how to turn on her computer. We have a good laugh about male dysfunction as she shows me the basics. It's a thing called a Mac that didn't even exist when I was last writing seriously. I wasn't informed that a mouse had ceased to be a rodent over the last year or so.

It takes a while to get the hang of it, but by midnight, I have my first episode. Hazel shows me how to print it, and I am about to sit down to type the next one when she says: "No! Hot spring!" I feel like I am a dog being ordered to my basket, but I comply. I fall asleep with her affectionately nuzzling up. I vaguely recall ordering her to bed and wondering if she will comply.

When I awaken, I am on the floor but there is no one on my mattress. *Trying all variants*, I wonder. Then I see her bedroom door is closed but there is a light on, visible at the edges. I get up and try to remember where my script is. The printed copy is not in the study. I decide to start coffee to signal wakefulness. As the grinder starts, she opens her door. "You are no longer the proofreader of the house. I thought you might appreciate it, even if my own job is not in drama..."

"I do. Would you appreciate some coffee? You can tell me after that what I got wrong."

As I put the cups on the table, she hands over my script. It is awash in red ink. "Oh, cripes. I never proofread as savagely as that."

"You haven't been around typical families much, have you?"

"Does it show that much?"

"Check what I marked up. I have – or at least had – a functional relationship with a mother and you, sadly, didn't and it shows. Just one example. The more banal aspects of the dialogue have to work too."

Much of her corrections are indeed of the boring routine connecting dialogue. I ruefully admit that her corrections read much better than the original. Key points of the plot are untouched. I point this out. "At least I got one thing right."

"Come on. That is the essence of the thing. I fixed the boring bits. Your life has never been boring. It takes practice to write total fiction. Stuff you've actually lived is easier to write."

That gets me thinking. "Maybe I should write more dysfunctional people. Misfits. People with substance abuse or mental health problems. Broken families. You may notice that the character I added, Genevieve, is heading that way a bit..."

"No, no, no. That is not this series. It's about an ordinary person who solves crimes, not a misfit. Someone close to him who is slowly going off the rails to add human interest should be enough." *Good, Genevieve lives* – but I keep that thought to myself as she goes on. "Anyway that stuff is too close. It will burn you up to write it. Learn boring. Write that. Then liven it up with things you know – observations from life can go that far. Think of it like cooking a French classic and adding Caribbean spice."

"That's it!"

"What, how you will write?"

"No, the Chez Harry opening. I've been borrowing a lot from French technique but we have some interesting things in South Africa as well. Perhaps something cross-cultural to celebrate his linguistic prowess? I will have to think about what that is, but there's time. I need to get back to writing."

"What about breakfast?"

"You can do that for once. Toast."

I rewrite my episode based on her corrections, but add in a few choice details to hint that one of the characters, Genevieve Mullins, is on the verge of going off the rails. Even if it's not the main theme, I still feel it will add interest. I print the episode for review then I start the next one, taking over from the first, in which that theme gradually develops.

"Your toast is cold."

There is a piece of toast next to me, covered with con-gealed butter. I take a bite. It tastes exactly like cold toast should. I get up with the toast, and pass Hazel the rewritten first episode. I walk to the kitchen and find marmalade, to liven the toast as Hazel reads. But the toast is still dead. She is looking quite intent and lightly wielding her red pen, which is either a good thing or a bad thing, so I make more coffee and a fresh piece of toast. By the time I finish mine, she hasn't touched her coffee. I venture a question, with some trepidation. "Better?"

"Much. You have done a great job of building on my corrections and putting your world into the story. Just enough. I can't wait to see how Genevieve turns out in later episodes. I didn't like the idea before but I'm sold. That adds to the tension of solving the mystery in this episode. I do think Gina will like your reformed detective character, clearly tilting towards feminism. Too few male roles are like that."

"But I mustn't write any of my shelter people. So please do keep tweaking the Genevieve dialogue in case I had done that unconsciously."

The rest of the day, I work on the last two episodes, with multiple drafts going between Hazel and I, each time with less red ink. After the last round, Hazel says, "You know what? I never took you out. You always cook for me. There's a really nice Indian place around the corner. Let's go there."

I pick up my scripts, intent on another round of review. She is having none of that. "No! You need some down time to present yourself coherently tomorrow. Not like when you spoke to the Home Secretary. Leave that stuff here."

Chapter 28

In the Game

Hazel leads the way to Gina Gibbons's office. She gives me an affectionate kiss on the cheek. It's me versus the lion's den. A formidable feminist somehow is not frightening to me. Gran surely would count as such. So I stride in confidently, with my pile of paper. I announce myself, and am politely asked to take a seat.

I'm five minutes early, and determined not to mess up. This is not the Home Secretary, it is much more my turf. A place where writing is valued, one of the major cultural broadcasters of the world. If I am rejected, at least I tried. No one has ever offered me such an opportunity before. So I am properly steeled when the inner door opens.

"Ms Gibbons will see you now." This form of address, not quite pronounced like 'Miss' is new to me but I am determined not to be fazed. I walk in, thanking the assistant on my way in, and walk up to the desk. Gina Gibbons is imposing, even sitting down, with a strong gaze that would wilt anyone not sure of themselves. I think of gran and approach her with a smile. "Pleased to meet you. My name is Luke."

"Gibbons," she says unsmiling, and points at a chair. I am determined not to be intimidated. "What did you think of the sample scripts I sent you?"

I remember Hazel's admonition. "I would prefer that we look at my work. I don't like to judge others."

"Well, I must. It's my job. Your honest opinion please."

"Uh, it is not... fresh...."

She stands up and is alarmingly tall, especially to a modestly built person sitting down. "Mister bloody Fredericks. I do not do platitudes! Now your honest opinion, or I won't so much as look at your scribblings!"

This wakens my inner anti-bully and I try to hold that in check. And fail. "Your really want my opinion of those episodes? Dross."

Her eyebrows go up, but weak skills at reading body language again fail me and I read this the wrong way, as I soon discover. I dump my pages on her desk. "One thing missing in your office is a shredder. I will buy you one. If that is what my writing rates, that is where it will go. Now, do you want to read it or not?"

"You know, you should have stopped at 'dross'. That is right on the money. Why else do you think I am looking for new talent? For a brat who has never sold a word, you have a nerve." I stand up. "Where are you going?"

"To get your shredder."

"Sit in the bloody chair. I haven't read anything yet. And keep your damn mouth shut, otherwise I will get a shredder myself and put *you* through it."

Martha meets gran, I say to myself, but sit back and wait, suppressing a smile. She barely flicks a glance my way, so I hope I get away with it. She is intensely reading, flipping back and forth between pages. She drops the first episode and picks up the second, which gets the same treatment. Then the third. She is clearly a quick reader.

After putting the third down she fixes her eyes on me. I hold my nerve. Just. Martha has taught me well. "I saw a little smirk on your face. What was that?"

"Ah, I meant no disrespect. I have been around strong women a lot of my life, and you reminded me... sorry, this is hard to explain."

She sees I am struggling. "OK, we can have your life story later. Clearly, you have never written a screenplay before. There are lots of technical details that are wrong. But we can fix that. The dialogue pops. Each character has a voice. There are clear alternative routes to solving the crime. The surprise in each episode is there, true to the history of the series, but it works.

"And I would love to see where Genevieve ends up. How soon can you write ten more like that?"

I miss a beat. Have I just won her over? This most definitely is not the Home Office. I think through the time these took – three in two days. "About a week. But what about the technical stuff I got wrong?"

"A week? My. You like a challenge. I'll introduce you to one of our most experienced writers before you leave today. He should be able to give you some hints. We don't expect anything close to finality at this stage anyway. Now, tell me about the strong women."

I tell her about gran, who was my only real parent, how I did everything I could to be with her after she sold the farm, how the one good thing my parents did was to put me in boarding school where I could be near her when she died. Then I tell her about Hazel, starting from running away to the homeless shelter and ending with how she helped with editing. Finally, I go to Martha. How she was so hard on me but ended up teaching me so much.

"So we got your life story as well – at least the condensed version. I won't ask whose memory I invoke. I should add as well, I really like the way you develop the lead role. He starts as the same misogynist asshole as in the previous series but learns better ways in tiny steps. Feminism sold subtly. I would also love to see where he ends up."

She picks up her phone, and dials a few digits. "Bill? I have a very green writer here who has promise. Do you have a few minutes to show him the ropes? His dialogue is good, but he needs some help on the basics of a screenplay... Yes, yes, I will send him over."

She ushers me out and her assistant takes me to see Bill Locke, who goes through my episodes with a red pen, explaining as he goes what I have wrong. "I don't have much time to go through everything in detail; this should however help you with some of the basics." I thank him, and head home.

I get home that afternoon with a lot of red ink on my screenplays, wondering if that cancels out *green*, and start fixing the technical issues right away, building on Bill's notes that turn out to be more sketchy than appeared while he was marking up my pages. *Did I hear 'has promise' right?* I am well into episode four by the time Hazel gets home. She sees immediately what is going on and stands behind me, watching me type. "What should I order in? Indian or pizza?"

"Whatever you like. I must get this done so I am free to start planning for tomorrow." This is the first time I have put her in charge of culinary matters. It feels right. A boundary has shifted without an earthquake.

Chapter 29

Celebrating Harry

Saturday morning. I have a dinner to plan, and have left very little time to do so. On the plus side, I have completed episodes four and five, as well as correcting the first three. So I only have eight to go, but am confident that it will go much faster. I have a rhythm – I know where my characters are going, so I only need to invent a new murder mystery every episode. Or do I? Murder mysteries often overdo it – multiple murders in a tiny village are surely a rarity.

We're heading for the shelter to get the dinner plan together. On the way to the tube, I say to Hazel: "Just a thought, but do we have to have murders every episode? Can't it sometimes be there *appears* to be a murder, but the person is actually alive and defrauding their insurance? Or it was natural causes, and just looked like murder?"

"Interesting ideas. Try that in a couple of episodes. If Gina doesn't like it, you will have to rewrite, but you are being paid for a fresh approach, if they take you on. Be brave!"

"Have you seen her close up?"

"No, but I know her reputation."

"Believe me, I've already done 'brave'." I have been so busy writing that I haven't shared what happened in Gina's office yet. This is the moment. I tell her the whole thing, including the shredder and who or what could have ended up in it.

"Seriously? You got into a fight with Gina Gibbons and walked out alive?" She puts a comforting arm around me as we wait for our train.

From the last stop, we go straight to the shelter. Lunch is finishing as we arrive, and I tell Martha the plan. She looks interested, and says: "We will be right there for you."

Next stop: the coffee shop. I'm relieved to find it open, as this is not a busy neighbourhood for Saturday coffees. I call for Eleni. I explain the whole Harry situation and tonight's celebration. "I should've spoken to you before but I have been rushed off my feet. Do you have any phyllo pastry to spare? I am also looking at making desserts. I can't ask you for help at such short notice, but I was wondering where you get your ingredients from."

Eleni looks at me sharply. "Why don't you think I have capacity to help? My kitchen is at your disposal. I can make baklava, easy. Tell me how many serves. I have lovely pistachio ice cream. Easily enough serves. Just tell me when to bring."

"You are a marvel. I'm aiming for 30 serves. Has Jill used you yet?"

"Couple of times. Very happy."

"I am too. Can I just take some phyllo now, or do I need to go shopping?"

"No problem. I have a couple of packs thawed and plenty

in the freezer. Dessert will be no worry." We exchange a few more details, then Hazel and I leave with the thawed phyllo.

Next stop: Henrique. I explain the plan, with the same concerns about being late. Again, no problem; he has much of what I need including some spices and a selection of veg. I thank him profusely, and mention Eleni's dessert contribution in passing. All I need from George, who is as obliging as always, is carrots and onions. Finally, I go to the grocery store to buy still more spices, lentils and rice. The grocer, who usually charges full price, asks me what it is for this time, as the mix is different. I explain the Harry story. He refuses to let me pay. This is a first.

Hazel helps carry everything, now quite a sizable cache. As we leave the grocer she says: "As someone who claims to have no social skills, you are remarkably good at getting people to part with ingredients."

"Interesting point. Somehow I always do better at presenting the plight of others than at presenting myself."

Back at the shelter, we get under way, as Hazel sets out on other errands. The menu: lentil breyani, made using a sweet curry in Cape Malay style, veg samoosas and salad, followed by baklava and pistachio ice cream. A cross-cultural mix of Greek and South African. And more than one South African culture: Indian with Cape Malay influences. Unlike the 'samosa' from some parts of India, common in the UK, the 'samoosa' in South Africa is made with a very thin pastry, accurately shaped into small triangles. That extra 'o' makes all the difference. Phyllo is not the exact same kind of pastry, but close enough.

I don't know how I learnt to make breyani or sammoosas; perhaps part of my lost year? At least the methods come back, though I have no idea from where. Cape Malay-style curry comes from my gran, who liked spicy but not hot.

I set the kitchen staff to making two curries: a mild, sweet one with lentils and non-hot spices like cinnamon, and another a bit hotter, based on a mix of finely-diced vegetables. The Cape Malay style favours sweeter, less fiery curries; Durban Indian is especially hot, but I tone it down a bit. The breyani has to be layered from precooked ingredients, so I ensure that its curry and rice are in progress first. Once they are on the go, I start the other curry, which has to be stuffed into samoosas. As a side for all this, we make a large pot of rice, generously dotted with raisins and coloured with turmeric.

As I finish layering the breyani and set it to cook again, Hazel arrives with a banner proclaiming the new name. So all is set; it is just a matter of filling and folding 60 samoosas, aiming for two per person. Most of the kitchen crew helps with this, with Martha making a salad on her own. We are frying the last batch of samoosas as the residents start filing in, closely followed by our guest of honour.

"Everyone, please welcome Harry's brother, Arthur Whitmore, QC. He is here today to celebrate our sadly lost resident, Harry, who showed his appreciation in the best way possible. He put in money he couldn't afford for the common cause. Does anyone mind if I serve our guest of honour first?"

I look around – maybe half of those present were in the shelter in Harry's time. But all applaud warmly. We have become a community.

Arthur, protesting, nonetheless gets the first plate. A serving of breyani, two samoosas and a healthy pile of salad.

As we are serving the last plate, Eleni arrives with Henrique, carrying between them a big tray of baklava and a large container of ice cream. George follows them, carrying more ice cream.

"Listen everyone. Today's theme is a celebration of diversity. The main course is South African. A sweet curry in the Cape Malay tradition in a breyani and samoosas in the style our Indian community like – petite triangles. Dessert just in is Greek: baklava and pistachio ice cream.

"I would like to thank everyone who made this possible. Henrique and Eleni, who have generously supplied most of the ingredients and brought the dessert that Eleni made. Also George, as usual, filled the gaps in veg.

"All of this is in honour of all of you, and we are renaming this eating establishment Chez Harry." This gets a loud cheer, even louder as Hazel and I unfurl the banner.

Arthur joins us. "My brother was a wonderful person. He fell on very hard times and mistakenly believed that his family was ashamed of him. I want you all to know that falling on hard times is no reason to be ashamed and I thank you all from the bottom of my heart for giving him a place that he could call home, and that recognized his humanity. I am pleased to see this place called Chez Harry."

From the floor a voice rings out: "It's a pity you didn't cook us toast, otherwise we could say 'To Harry'." This seems a fitting close to the renaming.

I return to my station and yell: "Dessert is served!"

Once the residents are out of the hall, Arthur approaches. "Luke, a most delightful meal. Your reputation is well deserved. I would like to invite you and Hazel to my home. We have a few loose ends to tidy up."

He leads us out to his Jag, rather out of place in the shabby surroundings. We sit contemplatively as he navigates to a smarter part of London than any I have seen before. He parks outside one of the more modest dwellings and leads us inside. The furnishings are a mix of antique and chic. The walls are decorated in similar fashion, with a mix of classical and modern paintings.

He leads us to the living room. "Please make yourselves at home. Cognac? Scotch?" I take a Cognac and Hazel asks for water.

He sits down with a large Scotch. "Right. Here's something none of us knew about Harry. When I was winding up his affairs, I discovered that a book he wrote was modestly successful – very successful for such a specialist work. Apparently it is the standard text on comparative Slavic literature, and the only one written by someone conversant with all of the major Slavic languages. It has never sold in huge numbers but, over twenty years, royalties have accumulated. Enough to be the kernel of a trust for charitable works.

"As the last person who knew Harry well, I would value your views on what this charity should support."

Hazel looks at me. I nod. "I can't say I knew him very well. I know that fighting addiction was a big problem for him. I really did not know how to handle that. But that is not the worst thing. We had a few people with serious mental health issues. None of us had any idea what to do about that. A fund to put more mental health care into homeless shelters would be great, and that could cover addiction. Maybe also an angle of using food as a way of affirming the humanity of the homeless?"

Arthur takes a generous swig of his drink. The ice clinks. "Yes. I think Harry would have appreciated that. Let me work on the detail."

Hazel turns to me. "You don't talk about any of these mental health cases."

"I try not to talk about them because it felt like a failure at the time, though I know better now. But also, I feel freer talking about Harry because he isn't with us any more. Arthur, do you think I am out of line, telling people about him?"

"Absolutely not. As I knew him, he would have wanted his plight to help others and, as you say, he is not with us any more. I completely agree that you should respect the privacy of the other residents. A shelter like that should be a place of safety, not a zoo. So it's decided. I will match the funds arising from Harry's royalties and I am sure we can find other generous donors. Would it offend you if we called it the Chez Harry Trust?"

No one is offended.

Arthur changes the subject. "The two of you are clearly a pair. The Home Office would love a quick solution to Luke's asylum application, without obviously cutting corners. Ordinarily, marrying a British citizen in such circumstances would arouse suspicion. But not in your situation, as they want the problem to go away."

There is a silence. He adds: "My apologies if I was out of line."

Hazel grins. "You are providing expert legal advice free of charge. There is no need to apologize for that."

Chapter 30

Scripting

We get home late that night, after swapping stories about Harry and expanding on my life in South Africa. I am torn between writing and falling asleep. Hazel decides it for me. "You can write pretty fast but you will make more sense if you are awake. You have 8 more screenplays to write. If you do two per day, as we know you can, you can get it done in four days."

I count on my fingers. "Let's see. Sunday tomorrow, Monday... I could be done by Wednesday, two days early."

"Exactly. Shower. Bed."

"Yes, boss."

Neither of us mentions Arthur's suggestion of getting married. My guess is that Hazel is where I am. We will talk about it when we feel something shift, not when someone else pushes us that way. It's our decision, not someone else's.

Sunday dawns wet and windy. I think. I get wakened by a loud peal of thunder, long past dawn. I go to the study to look out of the window and the rain seems well set. A good writing day. I check my watch. Nine o'clock already. I immediately sit down and start writing. I am two pages into the next episode when I sense Hazel behind me.

"Coffee?'

"Yes." Then I remember. "Oh, that's my thing. Let me do that, then think about other food."

She looks past me to the window. "Not a great day to go out."

We walk together to the kitchen. We find an apple and an orange and some nuts. There is some milk and a little Parmesan left in the fridge, and a search reveals the last of the factory pasta and a clove of garlic, plus a handful of coffee beans. I make coffees. A cappuccino for her, espresso for me. We sit down with our small haul of fruits and nuts. I grin. "You know, cooking for other people is such fun, I forgot that we need to cook for ourselves."

"This should keep us going for a bit — as long as you can write, I'm happy. Just pass me each episode when you want it checked."

I go back to writing. I print an episode for Hazel to check and get my head down and finish the next one in short order. As she gets out her red pen again, I see the first is not bleeding much, and do the edits before she finishes. "Lunch," I announce. I reach deep into a cupboard and find olive oil, missed on the first search. So it's pasta tossed in olive oil and garlic with Parmesan. "Believe it or not, this has a name: Aglio e Olio."

Hazel says: "I don't care what it is called. If the name was edible I would eat that."

We eat hungrily, and I go back to writing.

By the time it starts to get dark, with no let up in the rain, I have finished the fourth episode of the day, complete with corrections. I collapse in my chair, too tired to think of food. Hazel pulls me up and supports me. I look at her, no permission needed, wobbling on my unsteady legs. "The weather is terrible. I am too tired to stand up without help. We have no food. But I have never been happier."

That is the last thing I remember, except a weird dream involving lying in a hot spring with the rocks replaced by a springy bed. Which is what I wake up in, feeling absolutely ravenous. I turn but Hazel isn't there.

I jump out of bed. The flat is not big; it takes only a minute to find she is missing, as is a shopping bag and her keys. I scrape together the last of the coffee beans and make an espresso, which helps me wake up but not with the hunger.

Then the lock turns and the door opens. She brandishes a paper bag. "Croissants!" I devour mine too fast to think of butter or jam, both I know to be missing from the fridge. "Wait a minute! I bought you these too." She produces butter and a bottle of raspberry jam. "Perhaps I had better sit down. Look at all the crumbs you messed on the floor."

I look contrite. "Oh, never mind." She puts the shopping down on the table. "I like the new savage you. As long as the old one is still there."

I hold her tight. "I don't remember getting into your bed."

"You didn't. You were so zoned out, I had to put you to bed. Now let me eat, I am also starved."

I check through the shopping bag for things I can use now, then make us both cappuccinos while she starts on her croissant, and fish out yoghurt and an apple each from the bag, before putting the rest away. As I sit down, she says:

"My chef is back. You know what? You're ahead with your writing. Why don't we have a quiet day, and just swing past the shelter? If you write another episode, that's half the job done already."

So the day is planned. We're too late for breakfast, but we get to the shelter before lunch. All is under control. The menu is planned and Jill has had a successful forage, and she is running the kitchen that day, as Martha has the day off. Jill invites us to stay for lunch, but I decline. "We need some time for ourselves."

Asks Jill: "Still taking it slow?" I say nothing. We amble back to the tube. Neither of us says much on the trip home. We're both pretty tired from that hectic Sunday.

Once home, I lie down on my mattress. "Back to the hot spring." She lies down next to me as I add: "Martha keeps going on about us taking things slow and it has spread to Jill too." The late sun sneaking through the study blinds is catching her hair, reminding me of the first time I saw her in Yosemite. I study her eyes. It's a moment I don't want to lose.

She nuzzles closer and continues my train of thought: "Why rush, when we know it can only get better?" I like that and grin coyly. But she is not done. After a beat, she adds: "Except... if ..." she tails off, looking expectantly at me.

So I finish the thought: "... we want to?" Before I know it, we are in her bed and our clothes are all over her bedroom. Once it's over, I look. Clearly, I have permission and she is looking too. I know I will never again need permission.

Chapter 31

O Mother

I wake up in Hazel's bed for the second time. This time, she's there, still sleeping when I wake up. The phone rings, and she reaches for it, clouting my nose.

"Aargh! We aren't even married yet and I'm already getting abused!" I hold my nose but there is no harm done; she sees that and with an affectionate kiss picks up the phone.

"Hi dad, what's happening?" She listens. "Yes, he's right here." I hear dad's voice but not clearly enough to discern words. "No, he isn't going anywhere. His asylum application is on track and our QC keeps us updated." He talks again. "All right, I will ask him. Luke, mum would like us to visit again and promises this time to be nice to you."

"I don't need nice. I need her to respect you."

She relays this to her dad. "Tonight at seven? We are working hard and Luke has a deadline..."

"No, it's fine. I am ahead. Let's do this." As she drops the phone, I add: "Let's write some episodes. Right after I bring you breakfast. You stay right here."

We sit in bed with coffee, muesli and fruit. Hazel takes a break from eating. "Do you know what mum's problem is? She's jealous."

"Why? Dad is wonderful."

"He nearly walked out on her several times."

"True, but I didn't walk out on you, I ran."

"Is that ever going to happen again?"

"No. You're the strongest person I know and I made you cry. You can't imagine how bad that feels. Even now. And no, the solution is not to run harder next time. You are stuck with me whether you like it or not. Well, not unless you actually do throw me out. Is that going to happen?"

"Eat your muesli and stop being a fool. What are we going to do about mum?"

"Easy. Be ourselves."

That morning, I write two episodes. Without Hazel there to edit, I mosey over to the shelter and get there as lunch is finishing. I help out with cleaning up. Martha looks at me suspiciously as I finish. "Pretty boy, thanks for the help. But cleaning is not your big thing. Would you like to talk to me about what this really is over a cuppa?"

"No hiding anything from you. Yes, I would like that very much."

Once everyone else has left, she fetches two steaming mugs. Neither has a spoon. She pointedly brings out her custard creams. "Like something sweet with my tea."

"Can't say I mind too much, either." She offers me one and I crunch while she dunks.

"OK, pretty boy, out with it."

"You remember how you keep going on about us being

too slow?"

"Of course. You won't hear the end of it either."

"Here's the thing. Yesterday, we did fast."

"Ah. And you're scared."

"No, and that actually *is* a bit scary. I have never been so sure of something. But I know nothing is perfect. I need an honest person I can talk to if something goes wrong."

"I wonder where we will find one of those?" We clink mugs. It is not a question to answer.

"How's the tea without sugar?"

"Not as bad as it was last week. Getting there."

On the way home, I do a bit of shopping. I replenish wine supplies, buy some nice cheeses, a piece of cod and some veg. Once this is all packed away, I start another episode. It's done by the time Hazel gets home. She finds me at the study.

"Been here all day?"

"Oh, no. I visited the shelter again."

"And? Out with it!"

"I wanted Martha to know she should stop nagging about 'slow'."

"Isn't that a bit private?"

"Of course it is, but she's almost family."

"There is something else, isn't there?" It's eerie how she reads me.

"Things are going scarily well and I wanted to know if she would be there for me if I break something and need a friend to talk to. There, now you know everything. Am I in trouble?"

"No, of course not. You don't have a mother to turn to. But then again, I am not sure if I do. If she's going to adopt you, does she have space for one more?" We have a good laugh. "Anyway, how many scripts do you have for me to read? We need to go out in about an hour."

"Oh, cripes. I forgot about that. I bought food on my way home."

"Anything that will be off by tomorrow?"

"No. Anyway, skip the reading. I've completed three today, so I am still ahead. Only three more to finish by Friday and it's only Monday. I have a better idea to fill the time before we go."

"Oh?"

"The shower is big enough for two."

Despite the big day yesterday, as we head for the tube with a bottle of Chablis (too bad about New Zealand Sauvignon), I feel as frisky as a teen on a first date. Judging by the chatter from Hazel, she is not far off that.

An hour later, dad meets us. I hand over the bottle. "Hi dad, this has warmed up a bit on the train. Can we put it in the freezer for ten minutes or so?"

"No problem. Let's get to the house and see what else is on ice." This does not sound super promising, but we follow him, and try to keep the conversation upbeat.

At the house, Carol has the meal ready as we walk in. We sit around the table in the living room, passing around plates and salad bowls, as Carol digs a serving spoon into a large bowl of lasagna. Hazel peers at the now-revealed layers. "Mum, I thought you knew we don't do land animals. Vegaquarian."

"Oh, really? We had fish that time we visited you. I didn't think that was *vegetarian*."

Dad interrupts. "My fault entirely, I remember us talking about that now."

Hazel turns on him. "No, dad, it is not your fault. Anyway,

I am sure the salad will be fine." I keep my mouth firmly zipped. This is not the opening I hoped for. We eat in silence, then I remember the Chablis. I lean over to dad and remind him, discretely.

Carol pays close attention. As he returns with the bottle, she eyes it out. "French. Pretentious. But I am willing to try." I shush Hazel with my eyes. I am usually the one under attack, but Carol is not directing any of her remarks at me.

After the main course is cleared, Carol offers ice cream, a perfectly fine commercial brand that I would happily buy since I don't have an ice cream maker. I react with enthusiasm as I am still hungry after the depleting weekend and the light main course. Now it's my turn; Carol swings around to face me. "Well, I am sure it would be better if I made it myself, Mr Gourmet Chef."

This is too much. Making good food became my happy place, starting with gran, through my San Francisco friends and now Hazel. Why is she attacking me like this? I stand up, nearly upending the table. "What the hell is wrong with you? You have a great husband and a fantastic daughter. Get a grip. No one is judging you except yourself. Stop bloody apologizing for yourself by attacking other people and just be."

There is a dead silence. I take some ice cream and taste it. "This is pretty good." I take another scoop and pass it around.

Chapter 32

Finishing the First Round

I am not sure if much more is said, as I retreat into my head – a trick I should patent. Dad leads the way back to the station, before I snap out of it. "Gosh," he opines, "wherever did you learn to do that? I've been trying for years and I never seem to get through to her."

"You can't spend time around Martha without learning a few tricks."

"Martha?"

"Head cook at the shelter."

"Oh, right. Look, the two of you are welcome here any time. Carol will need a bit of time to process this. It's high time she had some therapy and she has been resisting up to now. I hope this pushes her over the edge – I mean to therapy, not the other way."

As we get to the station, Hazel hugs her dad tightly. "I just want her to be the mum she used to be, supportive, funny, caring. Is that a lot to ask?"

"No. And I will pass that on to her."

We get home by 9:30. Hazel is keen to get into editing but I block her path to the study. "This has been a tough day for you. If you're still hungry, I can cook us some nice cod."

"I am guessing you are still hungry too? I had clean forgotten that we didn't eat much. Yes, go for it. And any other nice nibbles you have handy. I didn't pig out on ice cream the way you did. Was that just to get to her?"

"No. I didn't see a reason to punish perfectly good ice cream." I turn to cooking.

I put two plates of cod on the table, along with some julienned carrots for colour, and a plate of cheese. While my back is turned, she has disregarded instructions and is reading the next episode. "Hey! I said no work!"

"Do you see a red pen in my hand? This isn't work, it's fun." She puts it down and at the rate she devours her cod, clearly she is right about who is hungrier. Then she levels her gaze at me. "What was that thing where you shut down, just when things got heated? I never saw you do that before."

"It's a trick I use sparingly. I put myself in a dental chair and listen to the drill. It is so relaxing."

"What? That's not relaxing!"

"I dealt with fear of a trip to the dentist by putting myself somewhere else. After all, there is nothing I can do when my tooth is being drilled into, so why not relax?"

"You really are a weird boy." She gets out of her chair and pulls me out of mine to give me a solid hug. I count that as approval of weird. "But why didn't you use that trick on the Home Secretary and on Gina?"

"Different problem. I couldn't just switch off on them. Besides, there are times when I need to be engaged." I explain how I lost most of my Honours year by over-using the dental drill solution.

"So Harriet turned out to be a toothache?"

"I wish I could have replaced her with a filling."

The next day, I am up early starting the next episode, having carefully exited the bed to let her sleep on. The day had been more draining for her than for me. When I judge it to be her wake up time, I operate the coffee grinder. She is up soon, and I sense that I am in trouble. "What have I done now?"

"Are you used to waking up with me?"

"No. I need a lot of practice at that. A skill I hope to develop over many years,"

"Here's the thing. I want to wake up with you. Instead, I wake up with the coffee grinder."

"It loves you as much as I love you." This does not seem to be the thing to say as I get no response, so I add: "Tomorrow, if I am awake before you, would you like me to wake you up?" Did I pick the wrong moment for the L word?

She contemplates. "How much before?"

"Aha, these things do not come in absolutes. I scored today because I woke up with you. Don't you remember not that long ago, I woke up alone because you went shopping? And yesterday, you bashed my nose..." That actually covers the entire history, so I stop there.

Minor battle resolved, I set to making breakfast, while she starts reviewing my next screenplay. When I am done, she brings it to the table, this time red pen in hand. It's a quiet breakfast; she marks up steadily, while I check the time to make sure she won't be late for work. She is almost done before she checks her own watch and pronounces: "Damn, I should leave now. I will catch up tonight."

That, I doubt, as she leaves. I have the last three episodes ready in my head, and pour them out as soon as she has left. I completely forget lunch and by 3pm, I have them all in first draft. *Wow – the whole job done by Tuesday tea time.* I correct myself: editing to follow. With that thought, I make tea and wonder why we never buy custard creams. We will have to do that before we invite Martha over, is my next thought. I also wonder why we never do that.

On a whim, I phone Geoff, hoping that he is home. I catch him on his way out. "Luke! Long time no hear! I have an appointment, so I gotta rush. What's the news?" I fill him in on Chez Harry, my progress on asylum, my writing and Hazel. "Great! How much is this writing going to pay?"

"I am a bit hazy on that. I don't have a contract yet. I expect that will show up on Friday, when I present my screenplays."

"How many in total?"

"My first three, plus ten more. Last batch awaiting Hazel's input."

"Fantastic! Tell me more later when I don't have to rush."

Since it's still early in the afternoon, I go out to buy bread. I make myself a sandwich to substitute for lunch, and walk out with it – another stroll around the neighbourhood. By the time I am done, it's before Hazel is back from work. *Wow, actual spare time.* I lie down on my old mattress and doze off.

I wake up with Hazel standing over me, in mock dismay. "What's the matter? Is *my* hot spring not good enough?"

As I make supper, she is reading intently, wielding her red pen. She takes a break to eat, and I put in corrections as she works through more episodes. We get through four more, leaving another three to go. Pretty good progress for someone who has never sold a screenplay and a proofreader who has never worked in drama.

I go to bed feeling content, happy that I will wake up in good hands.

Early the next morning, there is another phone call that wakes both of us. Hazel answers, and passes it over to me. "It's for you."

I take the phone. Someone with a heavy Afrikaans accent is on the other end. "Is that Luke Fredericks?"

"Yes."

"I understand that Geoffrey Fredericks is your uncle. I am afraid he has been killed in a car crash."

"Who is this?" The phone clicks off.

Hazel sees me looking tearful and I relay what happened.

"That's ridiculous. Why would they phone someone's nephew, then cut the call? Phone Geoff."

I do exactly that, and he answers on the fourth ring. "I have never been more relieved to hear your voice." I tell him what happened.

"The bastards. This is the government punishing you for being a successful draft dodger. I am just fine. They are probably tapping my phone and heard that we spoke yesterday and I was rushing out. Promise me this, Luke. If anything ever happens to me, don't let them get to you."

With that sombre issue out of the way, I am wide awake, despite the early hour. Hazel is too and decides to get back into editing, while I make coffees. By the time she leaves for work, she has left me two episodes to correct. I go out with her, and take the tube to the shelter. I need comfort from someone familiar.

At the shelter, Jill is about to go foraging, and I ask if I may tag along. She is cool with that and I mostly do carrying. She has developed the right skills at loosening stock from not only Henrique and George, but a few smaller retailers and restaurants. We end up at the coffee shop and Eleni recognizes my voice and rushes out. "Luke! I will not let you refuse a coffee on the house!"

"First, talk to Jill. I am her beast of burden."

"That I can see. Come, Jill, let us see if we can spare you some dessert today." They go to the kitchen and emerge with an enticing-looking package. "Not a lot," Eleni says, "but no one will send it back. Now, your coffee."

"Your best Greek, but let me get this to the shelter first."

Freshly charged with friendship, I am ready for what the world will throw at me and head back home, to sit out the last few minutes before Hazel is back.

By Thursday morning, we are all done. As Hazel leaves, she says: "You know that print shop just down the road?"

"Yes."

"Make it look as good as it reads. They have decent printers and you can put a binder on each episode."

I look at my stack of episodes. They do not look pretty. Even if I tear off the perforation, you can see – despite Apple's best efforts – that I have used a dot matrix printer. So I spend the morning learning about how to copy my episodes over to a disk that the print shop can read, and get them neatly printed with nice binders.

Job done, I head out to the shelter again, and share ideas with Martha on the next menu. She has started to get quite creative, sometimes thinking of ideas I wouldn't have thought of. At lunch, I am impressed to see a couple of people in upmarket suits show up. I say to Martha: "Chez Harry is thriving, and doing well without me."

"Nonsense. Every time you pitch in, you lift the level. Don't you ever think of excuses to walk out on us." I remember the conversation with Hazel – how I run rather than walk, but decide best not to say that.

When I get home, it's a new high. Hazel is paging through the episodes. "I can't believe you did all this."

"And you. My only worry is you are not getting enough credit."

"I am just an editor. You credit me when I add a new character, or think of a plot."

"Deal. But now you are committed to doing that."

"There was I thinking of taking you out again, and you now make me feel like I need to work." Before I can argue, she grabs her keys and pulls me to the door. We go to a nice Italian place not far from home. I like this kind of fight.

Chapter 33

Contract

I am back in Gina Gibbons's office. I hand over my completed screenplays. "Here you are, the original three plus ten." Gina takes the screenplays from me, hefting the pile.

"Neat. Professional. Now lets hope substance follows form." She quickly flips through the first three, checking that technical details have been fixed. "Good – Bill seems to have set you straight on the main points. Still a lot to get right I am sure." This sounds a little discouraging, but she is still reading. She puts the first three aside, and starts paging through the others. Four more episodes in, she pulls a document out of her drawer. "While I'm reading, you can start reading this. But first, you said your girlfriend helped with editing. Isn't she getting any credit?"

"I went through that with her. She insisted that she was only an editor but I will insist on crediting her if it gets beyond that."

Gina nods. "You had better be right. As a precaution, we can add her consent to the contract. I will check with legal on how to do that." She hands it over. "This is a draft, and we can discuss terms once we decide whether we want your work."

I page through it and feel totally out of my depth. I wish I had a lawyer... But don't I? I wonder if Arthur is willing to check it. I can only ask. As she carries on reading, so do I. I know what a few words mean; *advance* is the most promising. This means money up front.

Gina looks up. "I have done a quick read of enough sample episodes. I notice you have a few non-murders; I will have to think through whether that is a good idea. I must admit that I am startled at your speed. Normally, we allow a new writer two weeks to complete their first draft. You wrote ten episodes in a week. What I was expecting was a rough outline, an indication that we should pair you with an experienced writer to get your first episode right. We will still do that, and need at least one finished episode to sign off the contract."

"Why did you give me this impossible task then? When I offered to do ten in a week, I had no idea that it wasn't supposed to be possible."

"Because you came across as arrogant. You have never done a screenplay and you expected to be hired on the spot. Your first three had promise. These have promise."

"Luckily this is about my writing, not my ability to present myself. That's a big fail if it looked that way to you. I really didn't mean to come across that way. I tried to be respectful and you didn't like it."

"There's a difference between respectful and groveling."

I mention my other big fail, not impressing the Home Secretary. "Aha. *That* Luke Fredericks. The homeless gourmet. Where is Genevieve going to end up? In a homeless shelter?"

"Absolutely not. I need to research mental health to treat her sympathetically, but I will never write about anyone in a homeless shelter. Too much chance that someone could mistake fiction for reality. The residents I met have a right to respect of their privacy."

Gina nods. I sense approval; I hope I am right this time. "Chat with Bill on your way out. He may not be the writer you pair up with, but he can give you a few more hints. I will let you know when we are ready to move forward."

Bill helps to put it all into perspective. Yes, I had knocked out 13 screenplays in record time. Yes, the basics were pretty good. But they would need a lot of work to be good for TV. "You lack essentials like understanding how the camera frames a scene, transitions, and so on. You need a better idea of what a set is, how many we can practically use. All things you can learn – but learning to write good dialogue and a good story, not so much. You have those. We can get you there.

"Let's see who Gina decides to use as your mentor. If it was up to me, I would start by taking you on set so you can get a feel for the camera's view, why we design sets the way we do and so on. You can't do a good screenplay without a sense of camera."

I go home with mixed feelings. On the one hand, it looks like a definite sale. On the other hand, I annoyed one of the biggest names in British TV, and had been perilously close to losing the opportunity.

When Hazel arrives home, I am for once sitting frozen in an armchair. She goes over to me. "What's the matter?" I point out the contract on the table. "Wow! Are they signing you up?"

"Maybe."

"So why the long face?"

"Because Gina made me realise that I am a jerk. I walked into her office the first time, thinking I knew everything. I am now starting to understand how much more I need to learn. I nearly blew it with the Home Secretary because I didn't fit there. I thought I fitted with her and I screwed up anyway."

"But she gave you a contract."

"Yes. I need to read it, and they will amend it to mention your contribution, even if you don't want the money. But there is a lot more to writing a screenplay than I realised and she put me in my place."

Hazel points at the spot where my mattress used to be. "Oops, we shifted your sleeping place to my bed. Come on. Let's put the mattress back and do our hot spring thing."

I lie on the floor this time. She holds me gently. "You aren't perfect. Repeat that after me."

"You aren't perfect," I intone.

She cuffs me. "That's the funny boy I love. Stop letting setbacks get to you. You have been to hell and back. You can handle this."

She leaves me there to unwind. I contemplate life for a while and suddenly it hits me. Whenever I try to do something I love, things fall apart. Where did that come from? I was bullied by my brother and at school. I thought that was just because I was bookish and not sporty. But was it because they resented my easy mastery of schoolwork?

But Martha seemed to hate me at first, then got to like me. Maybe Gina would too. Or was I supposed to aim for mediocrity, just so people would like me? Suddenly the stress of dealing with everything catches up with me. Then there is a presence. Hazel is lying next to me, and pulls my wet face out of my hands. "My poor darling. What is going on?"

"I just don't know. Whenever I do something I love, people hate me. They see me as an arrogant jerk."

"You mean like when you pissed off the Home Secretary?"

"Well... Like that, but that was out of my comfort zone. I mean Martha. When I started cooking in the shelter. Gina, when I made such a hash of pitching my screenplays. Cooking and writing are my things. How do I get this so badly wrong?"

"You know, my biggest problem is fear of rejection. Silly, I know, when I haven't been through what you have, but look at that string of bad relationships. Some sleazeball would behave in a slightly flattering way and I would be sucked in. Happened every time."

"But you aren't like that now, right? I have always seen you as a very strong person. But I can't escape this. How did you do it?"

"I got careful. Or to be honest, scared. When you eyed me out at Yosemite, I went through the usual *looks tasty* reaction, then I decided *no, not again*. Then you walked up to me and talked about doing a trail. I thought, *Yeah, right*. And guess what? We did a trail. No bullshit, just friendly chat. Some other guy tried chatting me up afterwards and you didn't mind at all. I kept giving you glances while you were eating your messburger and you were just eating. You know what? I thought I could relate to someone who respects my space."

"Is that why you did the naked spring thing?"

"No. That was strictly spontaneous. I didn't lie about that. But once we were lying together, I couldn't help feeling that I wanted to do that again. From there on, I was determined to reel you in, but not so as you'd notice. I was so happy that you wanted to visit."

"Oh. Even before you asked me if I was gay?"

"Lukie, as I was then, I would've taken a gay boy sharing my life over what had gone before."

I like *Lukie*. I wonder if I will get that again. "So there was never any risk of a boyfriend moving in?"

"No. Did you mind when I said you would be fine if that did happen? Back when mum was pushing us into a corner?"

"My stupid head said I was fine with it, but I had you marked as mine back at Yosemite when I saw how your hair caught the sun."

"Really?"

"No, actually it was your eyes that finally caught me. But seriously, the first time we met, I was too scared to imagine anything more than a fun trail walk. When you paired up with that other guy, I thought that was it. I never know the moves, and it seemed that he did. And anyway, we aren't fixing my problem. I am so happy I fixed yours though, and I was the one to benefit."

"Did it all really end so badly? Martha really likes you now and Gina is almost ready to sign a contract."

"I know. But I don't want people like that to hate me. What if it starts like that and I don't fix it?"

"It hasn't happened yet. Get to know Gina better, then ask her advice. Meantime, you are close to your first sale. Let's celebrate. I will take you out. No argument about where, my choice this time."

Chapter 34

Legal Advice

We are at breakfast when the phone rings. Hazel picks it up. "Arthur? Good to hear from you. We were just thinking of you... No, not asylum. Let me pass this over to Luke."

"Hi Arthur. It would be good to talk further about the Chez Harry project. Also, I have a contract from the BBC and was wondering if you could take a quick look at it, if you aren't too busy."

Arthur isn't too busy and is in fact inviting us out. "I can afford to take you to a good restaurant, which I am sure that *you* can't afford, and it's about time to show you your competition," he adds. "However, as regards the BBC, are you trying to form a long-term relationship with them, or squeeze out as much as you can on this one contract and disappear?"

"Long term, I hope."

"As I advise clients too ready to rush headlong into litigation: you can sue for divorce, but not for marriage. So: do you want to be the person who forces the BBC to rewrite their screenwriter contract, or the person they want to use again?"

"I see what you mean."

"As long as the contract does not lock you out of any other opportunity, I wouldn't worry too much. Bring it along and I will take a look. But later. This time I want us to enjoy ourselves, and have a think about what to do with the culinary side of your life."

We arrange to meet that Sunday at 7pm, at one of Arthur's favourites, Notting Hill Place, a restaurant that builds on classic French with Chinese touches.

A couple of tube swaps, and we are there. Arthur arrives shortly after, and ushers us in – clearly a regular, as he doesn't have to ask to be seated. The place is absolutely humming – plates of mussels, lobsters and oysters pass us as we reach our table. Odours are interesting – hints of soy, ginger and garlic, not quite the combination you would get in a French restaurant. Our table seats six. Arthur sees that I note the empty spaces as he parks his briefcase. "I hope you don't mind, I invited some friends who are interested in your project. They will be a few minutes late." We don't mind.

Menus are handed around. I study mine. The prices make me feel faint. I pass Arthur a copy of my contract and he files it in his briefcase.

"Luke, you will love this place. Classic French technique, with influences from China. They offer the option to serve a meal banquet-style in the Chinese tradition, with numerous courses that we all share. Would you like to try that? Much easier, your first time. Banquet #3 is my favourite."

I look at Hazel and she nods. I take another look at the menu. I don't know what everything is, but it looks interesting. "Let's go with that then. Or shouldn't we wait for your friends..."

"Oh, no. They always let me order here."

I look down the list of courses; some are completely unknown to me. "Bouillabaisse Shanghai style? Bouillabaisse is a classic French recipe. How do you make it Shanghai style?" This takes me back to bouillabaisse Pacific Northwest style – the seafood mix was different but not the soup base.

"I thought you would find this interesting. Shanghai has many traditional seafood dishes. Bouillabaisse of course has a very specific soup base, as well as fish typical of the Mediterranean. This dish is essentially a Bouillabaisse recipe with the French-style soup substituted by a traditional Shanghai recipe, with rouille on the side."

"Interesting."

A rather smart looking waiter approaches Arthur with the wine list. "Aha, my favourite sommelier. I suggest my guests should start with their preference for a wine to pair with the sort of robust flavours on the #3 banquet."

I look at Hazel. *Sommelier. Fancy.* I keep this to myself as she says: "We tend to have less strongly-spiced food at home, the kind that goes with a Chablis or Sauvignon Blanc." I nod.

Arthur turns to the sommelier. "Possibly something more robust? I think I had a rather tasty Syrah, Mourvèdre and Cabernet Sauvignon blend, the last time I was here."

"Definitely, I remember the exact one. However, we have an even better one from Spain, just in today. It is not yet on the wine list. Shall I bring the bottle out for you to inspect?"

"Oh, no, just bring it. And I see our other guests on the way in, so we shall want two bottles."

Just like that, Arthur is ordering two bottles of wine in an expensive restaurant without even checking the price. I am thankful that his services for me are free of charge; how much must he charge his clients to care so little about money?

The guests arrive; Arthur does the introductions. "Luke, Hazel, meet Hamish Leery, a broker for a large investment firm. Andrew McGill, runs a software company, payroll and so on for big firms. Judith Simons, runs an upmarket retail chain."

As everyone sits, the wine shows up. Soon after the wine is poured, the first of several small courses arrive. I ask Arthur what it is. "A Chinese empress was strictly vegetarian, so her chefs came up with recipes that were reminiscent of the sea. We start with a few of these, with French touches, to hint at what is to follow."

As the food is passed around, Arthur starts his pitch.

"As you all know, Luke has been in the news as the homeless gourmet. Fortunately, the media tired of the story quickly as it could otherwise have overwhelmed the homeless shelter. But it got me thinking: why not find a compromise, where you could have a smart restaurant allied to a homeless shelter, that would build on the goodwill of the Chez Harry story, without turning the shelter into a zoo?"

This takes me by surprise, as I wasn't expecting something like this. I decide to let him go on.

"Clearly the restaurant should be near the shelter, but not interfere with its function."

Hazel buts in: "There is one already. It's called Chez Henrique." I nod.

"I see the two of you have a soft spot for Henrique, as you should. Please just hear me out. No doubt you will want to talk to him as well about how it will work."

Simons weighs in. "The area where the shelter is situated is a classic example of urban decay. Ordinarily, one of my shops would go nowhere near there. As Arthur explained the idea, it would include urban renewal, which would create a space for more up-market retail."

Discussion goes to options for reviving the area and the potential for the sort of cross-over cuisine I explored at the opening of Chez Harry. I hold my hands up. "I'm sorry, this is too much at once. I need to think this through."

"Of course." Arthur pulls out a neatly-bound document from his briefcase. "I have a detailed proposal for you to study." The cover page only has a title in dramatically large letters: *Service!* "I am not pressuring you to do it this way, but opening up an opportunity. We have an enthusiastic group here with access to plenty of capital and experience. Take my proposal home, study it, and get back to me. Now, let's just enjoy ourselves."

I look around the table. Clearly, Arthur's friends are in on the surprise. I smile appreciatively, and nod at Arthur. "One thing at a time. I am learning a lot just from this menu."

At this point, the bouillabaisse arrives. Split over 6 people, it is a small serving but clearly rates my full attention. Despite my misgivings about being presented with an unexpected plan by a high-powered group, the flavour and odour combination is stunning and I lose myself in that. The rest of the meal is just as good, with one unexpected combination after another.

On the way back, I can see that Hazel is seething. Back at home, she finally lets rip. "What the hell was that?"

"An ambush. But let's read this thing. If we don't like it,

we can either say no, or offer another option. I'm tired. Hot spring?"

"My place or yours?"

The next morning, I get a call from Gina just before Hazel leaves for work, inviting me to meet over progressing my contract and doing further work on my episodes. I haven't heard from Arthur on the contract, but decide I am not seeking to divorce the BBC and Hazel and I set out for the BBC.

We part as I head towards Gina's office. "Good luck – and remember not to get in a fight," Hazel offers.

I am at the office a couple of minutes early and glance around the assistant's office. There are scenes from various TV shows decorating the walls, including one with a flying blue phone booth. Before I can inspect it more closely, I am ushered in.

"Good morning Gina," I offer, hoping to set a positive tone.

"Sit, sit." She passes a fresh copy of the contract over. "Legal insisted on writing Hazel in for 10%. If she has creative input, she must get paid."

Something in her manner prompts me to ask: "Did legal insist, or did you?"

"More to the point, why didn't you?"

I lift a hand, then drop it. I am not fighting today. "I wanted to give her a cut, but she refused."

"How hard did you argue?"

I feel deflated. "I didn't want a fight."

"You marched in here spoiling for a fight that could have cost you any chance of a career. The fight we are talking about now is not fighting her, it's fighting *for* her."

There is a silence. "You're right. I am an idiot. I would be happy if she got 100% but I know she won't take that. How much effort would it be to ask legal to up it to 50%?"

"None at all except they may ask why you are suddenly valuing her work so high when you previously valued it at zero."

"Bargaining position. If she won't take 50% then maybe we can negotiate it down to a reasonable amount. Would legal buy that argument?"

"I don't see why not, if I back it. Hold on, I will tell them right now." The call is short, with a few sharp words exchanged. It ends with: "Blame me then. He's pretty green. I should've advised him more competently."

I start thanking her but she stops me. "Don't thank me until we have you signed up. I still have a serious issue. I can't pair you with one of my top writers if you are a prima donna. I can give as good as I get in a fight. You have to be thick-skinned to get where I am. But I can't have you abusing anyone else.

"When a series closes as badly as this one, there are a few options. Drop it on some poor sap of a producer who is trying to make a name for themselves, find a fresh writer, or kill it. The first doesn't apply here. It was dumped on me as a challenge, but I don't need a new win. However there are others who do need the win, and if you are more trouble than you're worth, they would be happy with the challenge."

I hold back a rising feeling of panic. "Don't do that." She waits for me to amplify. "Please. You nailed my weakest point. Now you want Hazel to get a fair cut and helped me to see how badly I handled that. I want to work with you."

"And would I want some poor sap trying to build a career

to be landed with an anger management problem?" Her hands form a steeple and her hard gaze stares me down over the apex.

I sit back in my chair, again feeling lost. Then I have an idea. "I have a mental trick to shut myself down when things are out of control." I tell her about my dental drill thing. "The problem is, I can't just shut down. I need a way to remind myself to stay calm. How about I buy my mentor a shredder with my name on it?"

"That won't be necessary. A picture of such a shredder will suffice." For the first time, I feel that she is starting to get me. I say nothing. It is not a moment to spoil. "So," she adds, "to business. Bill likes your style and can fit you into his schedule. Pick up the revised contract on your way out and set up your first meeting with Bill for after you bring it back signed by yourself and Hazel." As I get up to leave, she adds: "Shredder." She mimes shaping a picture frame with her hands.

I pick up the newly revised contract from Gina's assistant, find Bill, set up a time for Wednesday, then head home. *This is going to be interesting*, I think. And add another thought: *Hazel and the contract, I mean...*

Straight from the Edgware Road tube stop, I go to the local print shop. They have a nice shredder on sale there and the staff clearly think I am more than a bit barmy when I ask if they can print a photo of the shredder about to eat a piece of paper with "Luke" in large letters. I get three copies of the photo: two small enough for a wallet, the other in a frame that can mount on a wall or stand on a desk. Thus fortified, I feel ready for meeting Bill... but Hazel?

I wander the streets until it is close to the time when

she gets home, then head there. She is not in yet, so I pour myself a nice glass of Spanish red – a Rioja, not as fancy as Arthur's restaurant choice, but a change from the usual. I leaf through the contract. Other than Hazel's 50%, it looks much as before.

I notice there is a message on the phone and check if it's for me. It is; it is Arthur: "Apologies for being slow to get back to you, but I am in the middle of a big case. I see no big issue with the BBC contract, except that the allowance for Hazel is vague enough to cause problems. I am sure they can fix that. I look forward to hearing your views on my proposal."

I pull out his proposal and am leafing through it when Hazel arrives. I greet her at the door: "Good news, I am two steps closer to a contract. I have the final version here to sign, and you need to sign too. And Bill is going to be my mentor."

"Why do I have to sign?"

"You are getting a cut."

She takes it from me, and pages through. "What? 50%? That's ridiculous. I only made a few edits..."

I hand her the first three episodes. "Read the dialogue again. Remember what you said? I don't know how families talk. Genevieve is a major role. I had her dialogue all wrong. And, also, you fixed Genevieve's progress towards going off the rails to be sure that I wasn't echoing anything I witnessed in the shelter."

She starts reading, looking ready to contradict me. After reading the first episode, she drops it sharply and yells: "No, no, no!"

This is a complete puzzle. "What did I do wrong now?"

"Not *you*. *Me*. I wrote my mother. This is exactly how she was before things went wrong. And if I read on, I am pretty sure it is exactly how things are now going wrong with her."

"There was I being really careful not to write the shelter into it; I didn't even think of whether anything connected with anyone else we know. But what are we going to do? Gina likes the character. I will have to completely rewrite her. Different voice, different unravelling."

Hazel is looking contemplative. "I wonder... What if I show this to mum? Maybe it will remind her of how things were?"

"She hates me already. How will that help?"

"Yes, but if we add my name to it and I tell her I wrote this character and want her review the dialogue... Maybe this will be a way to wake her up to what she is doing?"

"I don't know. How about we run the idea past dad first?"

Hazel agrees and dials his number. He answers on first ring. "Dad, we have a problem – you know mum better than anyone. Is this a good time to come around..." She puts the phone down. "She's out with friends, once again. We can go now." I pick up the pile of episodes, not noticing that Arthur's proposal is at the bottom of the pile, and we rush for the tube.

Chapter 35

Keeping Mum

We arrive at the family home, for once not met by dad at the tube station. He ushers us in. "She isn't here, but her gatherings with friends are a bit unpredictable. Is it something we can sort out fast?"

I put the episodes down on the kitchen counter to catch my breath, as Hazel explains. "We messed up. I helped Luke with his dialogue, and we only now discovered that I wrote mum." Dad points the way to the living room and when I pick the episodes up, I don't notice that I left something behind – three bound episodes is what I intended to bring, and that is what is in my hand.

We sit down and Hazel explains further. He picks up the first episode and says: "I see what you mean. This is so her, without the mean manipulative streak." He pages through the second and third episodes. "And here she is, turning into what she is now, in small stages."

While this is going on, I am trying to process the whole story. "Hazel, didn't you say she was OK with you up until recently – about when I showed up, but dad has seen this side of her for a long time? What could be causing this? I am a new factor. What else?"

Robert is thoughtful. "You know, it started around the time we moved to the city. Back when we lived in Ayelsbury, she was starting to develop a home-based business. Training people up in cooking. Some of them were quite good, went on to start restaurants. When I was offered the job in the city, we thought she could restart here, but it somehow never took off." He shakes his head. "Why didn't I think of this before? She never said she resented my new job. I thought the cooking school thing was just a hobby that made some money on the side and she didn't miss it that much."

"Except..." Hazel puts a hand up in the air "... she kept trying to push me into being interested in cooking. Then I acquired a live-in friend who not only bought me a pasta machine but actually used it. I wonder..."

Then we all turn towards the kitchen. Carol is there, holding a document. The Chez Harry proposal that I inadvertently brought with the episodes. She is not paying attention to what we are saying. I am sitting in a position she can't see from the doorway. She says, "You know, this is quite a good idea, but it's not quite there. I could..." She takes a pace forward while talking and stops, as she sees me. "You!" The document does not have my name on the cover. I wonder if she has paged past critical detail that identifies me.

I stand up slowly. "Carol, the author of that document has pitched that idea at me and there was something about it that didn't seem quite right. I would really appreciate it if you could help to make it work."

She looks at me levelly, as if she is sizing me up for the

first time. Hazel jumps up. "Mum! I want you back. You and Luke are the food people in my life. It would mean a lot to me if you could work together."

Carol looks around the room. "Surely this is not why you are here. What are those other documents?"

Robert passes her the first episode. She reads and looks up. "This Genevieve is me."

"Yes," says Hazel. "Luke needed help with dialogue because he has never lived with a proper family. So I fixed it for him. You can blame me – I didn't realise at the time that it was you. I missed the way you were so much and unconsciously poured it into the dialogue. But then I did a really bad thing. You don't want to read the next episode. Luke was writing a character who was gradually..."

Carol snatches the other two episodes and reads, shaking her head. "Is that how you now see me?"

I look her in the eye and break the silence. "I really didn't know it was you and Hazel didn't do it consciously. I am so sorry. I will rewrite the character entirely. It doesn't matter to the story, this is just a draft, and they want me to do a lot of work on it." I decide it's best not to mention that Gina likes the way the character is developing.

Carol sits down heavily. "I've been thinking for a long time that I need therapy. I booked my first session tomorrow. How about I take these episodes to my therapist and ask her how we can make this Genevieve part of the process?"

I nod. "It would be brilliant if this horrible blunder was of some use. I really cannot use this character like this. The rewrite will be a completely different person. But I do hope our mistake helps you. Do you need a therapist to be willing to work on Arthur's idea?"

"You mean this?" She holds up the proposal.

"Yes."

"Let me think about it. It's a lot to take in." Carol nervously pages through the proposal.

There's a silence. I wait for Carol to turn her attention back to me and go on: "Read that proposal in more detail, and let me know when you're ready to share ideas."

I'm not sure if a handshake or hug is the right thing and freeze. This is one time I really do need not to mess up. Hazel looks at me and looks at her mother and breaks the silence. "If the two of you can bury the hatchet – but not in each other – I would be so happy." Instead of a hug or a handshake, we end up with a group laugh.

On the train home, I ask Hazel: "Is this going to work?"

"I don't know." There's a pause as the train stops and people get on and off. "Mum has not been herself since you showed up and it was a shock to hear from dad how bad things had been between them. This is the first time in ages that we've all had a good laugh together. I am actually wondering if she is the only one who needs therapy."

"I am pretty messed up..."

"This is true..." she starts and I break in.

"Oh. Well, I suppose agreeing with me is being support-ive." I stare her down; surely she can't be that mean? My flight reflex is now well suppressed so I allow her space to correct.

"Once I again, I am not the great communicator I thought I was. That didn't come out the way I intended at all." I nod, acknowledging her correction. "We have to be honest with ourselves, and I admire you for that" – she puts an affectionate arm around me and goes on – "but dad has a lot to deal with. He totally missed the fact that mum felt undervalued after we moved to the city, and put the entire problem on her. I am sure it's hard for him to accept that he has had things wrong for so long."

"I suppose. Even when it's obvious to me that I am struggling with the world, it is still hard for me to confront my own flaws. I am sure it will be difficult for him. I mean, compared with me, he seems super-functional, and even you thought the entire problem was with your mother."

I have another thought. "Should we tell Arthur where we are with his proposal?"

"Good idea."

When we get home, I phone Arthur. He isn't in so I leave a message: "Hi Arthur. Luke. We are trying to work through options on your plan that work for us. It is a little difficult as it is a big step into the dark. We could have some ideas soon, so don't think we have forgotten you."

As I put the phone down, I ask: "Did that catch it well enough?"

"I think so. But let's do some brainstorming. If we can get mum on the team, is there some way we can revive her culinary school as part of it?"

I contemplate this option, then agree. "Maybe that could be a better fit than a restaurant. It could give skills to the presently unemployable and be a path to rehabilitation for the homeless, with the right support. After all, part of Arthur's plan is urban renewal. Another part is rehabilitating the homeless. This is a better fit than allying an upscale restaurant with the shelter. And less of a threat to Henrique."

"Not a bad idea. But will she want to do that?" Hazel asks.

"You know your mother better than I do."

"But do I? Everything that seemed so certain isn't. I didn't know she and dad had tensions. Then it appeared as if she turned on me."

I feel out of my depth, but surely Hazel must know her own mother well enough to find an opening. I offer one. "She did say she had some ideas. How about we ask her what those are? Maybe she is heading the same way as we are, but won't it be better if she says it first?"

After some discussion, we decide on a joint approach – without Robert involved to start with. Hazel can easily take tomorrow off work and I am happy to meet in the morning, as my preliminary meeting with Bill is at two that afternoon. So Hazel sets up the meeting with her mother for the next morning, in a coffee shop in Canary Wharf, near enough to her home for Carol to get there easily; not so near that Robert will bump into us by chance. Hazel and I get there first, and find a secluded table. It is not a busy time so a private conversation is possible. I have a copy of Arthur's proposal with me along with a few other items in my shopping bag. Carol arrives soon after, looking unsure of herself. Hazel waves, and she arrives and sits at our table. After coffee orders are taken, she looks at me, then at Hazel. "All right, what is it this time?" She sounds a bit defeated.

I look at Hazel, hoping she can open, and she starts with: "Mum, you said you had some ideas about how to make that proposal work."

"That was before I realised that your boyfriend was in-volved."

I am not sure if 'boyfriend' is an upgrade, and say nothing. Then I see Hazel looking ready for a fight and decide to intervene. "Carol, this thing was dumped on me by a high-powered group who want to help make something of our shelter project. One of them is the brother of Harry, who died while I was there, and he appreciated the way I related to Harry. The problem is, I don't see how it can work as they proposed it. I would really value your ideas and involvement. It's too much for me. I want to focus on my writing."

Carol exchanges glances around the table again. Before she can say anything, I add: "I am absolutely going to completely rewrite that character. I had no idea it was coming out as you, and Hazel is really sorry that she did that. It was an honest mistake. I have no experience of family dialogue and was afraid that I would write in someone from the shelter inadvertently."

There is a silence. Eventually, Carol looks at Hazel. "Is that really how you see me?"

Hazel struggles to speak. "That first episode is you, the way I remember you. I don't want to think about how it develops after that. I want you back."

The coffees arrive, a welcome break. Carol appears to wake up. "Luke," she says, pausing – the first time she has used my name – "what is it that you keep saying about no experience of a family?"

I give the quick summary of the rejection by my parents, my early years with gran, how I never felt at home when I had to move back in with the parents, how I always gravitated back to gran even when she was too ill to know I was there.

There is another silence. I note that my cappuccino is getting cold and focus my attention on that. Finally, Carol speaks. "This is all very hard to process. Do you mind if I don't try to understand it all now?"

"Not at all," I say. "I can't say I understand it at all either, and it is the only life I've known. Can we talk about your idea?"

Carol starts hesitantly, then warms to the topic. "Before we moved to the city, I ran a culinary school from home. I thought I did rather well. A few of my students are now running good restaurants. I planned to restart it when we got to the city but somehow it did not work out. Perhaps I had too few social connections." I nod, urging her to go on. "It seems to me that learning culinary skills would be a good fit for both rehabilitating the homeless and for uplifting the unemployable."

I look at Hazel. She looks at me, as if passing me the initiative, but I say no with my eyes. This is *her* moment to grasp, so she plunges in. "Mum, that is a great idea. How would you feel about running the school?" I stay quiet, but try to look approving.

Carol looks my way but I gesture to her to respond. "I don't know much about poverty and homelessness, it's just an idea."

Finally I feel I should talk. "I know enough about these things having seen them first hand to know that we need expert help to make this work." I explain about the Chez Harry Trust and the plan to bring in the missing resources to make urban renewal and rehabilitating the homeless work.

I check my watch. "It's still a couple of hours to go, to get to my appointment with Bill." To Carol, I add: "Bill Locke, senior BBC screenwriter. He's going to show me the ropes. Why don't the two of you go home to work through more details?"

Chapter 36

The Ropes

The tube is a good place to unwind. I want to meet Bill with no preconceptions. I don't even have my sample scripts with me: I want to learn from him, not go in with what I already know as a start. He has, after all, seen them already.

I find my way to his office, and he is waiting for me. "Ah, Luke. Good that you are punctual. I don't anticipate a long meeting today. I just want to get to know you better before we start on the substance." He gestures towards a chair. I sit.

"Now the first thing," he pauses, "is your anger problem. I don't take kindly to abuse and if you try that on me, that is the end of my involvement."

I reach into the bag and produce my framed picture of the shredder eating a page with my name it. I explain how this works and end with: "If things are going in a direction you don't like, just point at the picture." I decide not to add: I don't think it's anger management, it's taming my inner anti-bully, but calling Gina a bully is not helpful. And anyway, the whole thing between us was a misunderstanding.

"Interesting idea, but we are not going to work exclusively in my office."

I hand him a wallet-sized version of the photo. "Just pull this out and show it to me. I want this to work more than you do. I've been through some difficult times and I am not good at reading body language so I can take things the wrong way. A reminder like this will work pretty well, I hope – actually I am just hoping that giving you these things will stop it ever happening." I show him my own copy of the photo in my wallet. "This is a constant reminder that I need to keep myself under control. It really does not happen often and I am very motivated."

"A red card? Or just yellow?"

I look at him quizzically. "Do you know nothing about British popular culture? In a football match, a yellow card means you are sent off for a bad case of foul play. Red means you are out for the rest of the match."

This seems vaguely familiar. Soccer, as we call it in South Africa, is not something I follow much. I'm not sure if they use this concept.

Bill goes on: "Have you thought of therapy?"

"No. But maybe I should."

"You shouldn't have to live with a problem like this. If you had a difficult past, some professional help will definitely be a plus. For now, let's try it this way. The second thing is understanding how little you know about screenplays. Clearly, from your writing, you have no experience in the field. Have you had any courses?"

"No. I studied English Lit. The nearest thing to a screenplay that I studied was plays. Obviously, there are big differences. I never studied film but I went to a lot of movies, and was interested in how the written word does or doesn't adapt to the screen. But I admit to no actual formal training."

"That's where I come in. You have a feel for using dialogue to push along the story and for constructing a mystery plot. There is a freshness to your writing that is exactly what is needed to revive the new series. This is why I want to work with you. Much of what you are missing is technical but there is nothing like seeing filming for putting things into context. How would you feel about visiting the location where we are filming the latest series of *Dr Who*?"

"Doctor... who?"

"Oh my giddy aunt! Have you never watched *Dr Who*?" I sense by the way he said it that Bill has substituted the opening phrase for extreme profanity.

I ruefully admit that I haven't. "In South Africa, because of the culture boycott, we get no British TV and, since I've been here, I haven't had time to watch much TV. I'm afraid the American junk and apartheid propaganda back home did not feed a TV addiction."

"You found time to belt out thirteen screenplays, and you don't watch TV! No wonder we have some work to do on you. You really are getting ahead of yourself. Do you have big plans for the weekend?"

"No, just helping at the shelter, and they don't need me much these days."

"Good. I will give you a pile of *Dr Who* episodes so you know what we will be witnessing, as well as episodes of the last series of your show. Your assignment is to be back here first thing Monday for a trip to Wales to see how TV is filmed, with your TV-watching deficiency cured. Not just the tapes I give you; watch as much TV as you can. 8:30 sharp. Can do?"

I nod enthusiastically. That seems to be a dismissal but as I get up I feel the need to add the issue with Genevieve. "Just one more thing. I messed up the dialogue of one character. It will need a rewrite."

"What have you done? Plagiarised Enid Blyton?" This gives me quite a start, evoking as it does my Mr Plod moment, so he quickly adds: "Stranger things have happened. What is your actual problem?" I decide not to explain my Mr Plod reaction but instead explain that Genevieve is actually Hazel's mum – complete with going off the rails. And Gina likes her like that...

"Aha! You are by no means the first to write someone into a screenplay unintentionally. There have been all manner of lawsuits, even plagiarism cases – not Enid Blyton, as far as I know. Don't worry about it. We will work together on recrafting the character. I know Gina well. We'll make Genevieve someone she can relate to even better."

I leave Bill barely thinking about shredders and their new role in making my life less dysfunctional.

Chapter 37

Chez Harry Take 2

When I get home from my meeting with Bill, Hazel is looking upbeat and gives me a wraparound hug. "Mum has bought into the idea, and dad is really happy that she has."

"Good. Now all we need to do is sell Arthur and his financial backers on it. Should we set up a meeting?" I dump my tapes. "I need to get through this by Monday and watch a lot of TV. But I am sure we can fit in a meeting between all that."

Hazel looks at the pile. "Are you a *Dr Who* fan?"

"Well, I sort of got into trouble because I didn't know what that is. I admitted to not watching much TV, in part because we had such junk on TV in South Africa. So this is my catch-up homework. Bill is taking me to the *Dr Who* location in Wales on Monday."

"Exciting. I'm jealous." Hazel pauses to reflect. "But back to here and now. Shouldn't we bring mum in on the meeting with Arthur? If she's on the team, we should involve her, particularly as we have no good ideas on how to make it work."

"You're right as always."

"Except when I get it wrong."

"Badly wrong." My grin disarms her. "How about we see if she is free this evening? It's not too late yet. *Your* mother..." I point at the phone.

Hazel picks it up and punches buttons. It answers quickly. "Hi dad. Is mum in?... OK, what time?... We want to talk about Arthur's plan. Is she up for it?... Great, we'll head over there now."

I look at Hazel quizically. She responds: "She is out again, but should be back by the time we get there, as she promised to make dinner for her and dad. Let's catch the tube."

I am heading to check the fridge for a wine to take as we go out but notice a Rioja before I get there, and grab it as I pass. "Not Chablis or New Zealand Sauvignon, but that battle is over. I hope."

On the train, we chat about *Dr Who*, Wales, my lack of TV literacy and how idiotic my whole screenplay career plan was. "Yet, somehow," Hazel concludes as we near Greenwich, "it just could come together."

"It could. But right now what I really want is to end the war with your mum."

Robert is at the station this time, and walks with us. We don't say much but the mood is upbeat. When we get to the house, Carol has started preparing food and greets us. "Robert, you didn't say we were having guests. Luckily I am only planning a salad and there's more than enough bread and cheese to stretch it."

"It's only us," I say. "We're here to see you so anything will be good." She favours me with a smile, and I see what

Hazel means about her better days.

The meal is simple, but Carol has a way with simple salads that I hadn't paid attention to before. I offer around my wine, and she offers hers. I take some of hers. She takes some of mine, to everyone's surprise. We clink glasses. This is a big moment.

"These New Zealand guys really do a good Sauvignon Blanc," I remark.

She ripostes with: "I should be more open to red. This Spanish plonk isn't half bad."

After we clear away the plates, I lead the way to the lounge. "Carol, the more I think about this plan of Arthur's the more I feel it is totally beyond what I can do. I like your idea of shifting it to training but I have never worked with people with no cooking skills. I learned my craft from experienced cooks and the shelter cooks already had the basics. They just needed good ingredients and motivation. It would make a lot more sense to me if you were in charge. What do you think?"

Carol looks around the room, as if looking for an escape route. Then the reality sinks in. "Do you really mean that? After the way I treated you?"

"Carol, Hazel had been through really bad experiences. You were trying to protect her. A little too much, I hope. I mean, I hope there is no need to protect her from me. My parents never cared enough about me to do something like that. What you did was wrong but you meant well. That I can live with. Indifference, not."

Robert starts to speak but Hazel shushes him. "Dad, let's not overthink this. All of us need time to undo our assumptions about each other. Let's just become one team on this, then we can work out anything else we need to later. Agreed?"

We all agree. I phone Arthur and he is at home, and agrees to set up another meeting, this time at his home, on Friday at 7pm.

Robert offers to walk us to the station while Carol tidies up. On the way, he is clearly troubled and takes a while to express himself. Hazel and I hold hands in silence as we walk, giving him space. As we approach the station, he says to Hazel, "I have been so unfair on your mother. I didn't see at all that she was so down about losing her cooking school. If I had paid more attention, instead of assuming her bad behaviour had no cause..."

Hazel cuts in: "Dad, I also totally misunderstood her reaction to Luke. I don't think she understood it either. Let's not beat ourselves up. How is her therapy going?"

"Well. She has positive reports about her sessions. So much that I am thinking of having one too." We get to the station. Neither Hazel nor I feel the need to say more.

I stay up late that night watching *Dr Who*. It's amazing what a blue phone booth can do. The next morning, I get up in time to make a hasty breakfast – toast with cappuccino for Hazel, espresso for me. Between munches of toast, I ask: "I don't remember seeing blue phone booths. Have I missed them?"

"Ah, the TARDIS. They were ubiquitous around the UK when the programme started but they were phased out in the 1970s. The idea was that if it was something ubiquitous, you could park it anywhere, with a few mind games to stop people from actually trying to use it."

"What were they for?"

"Quick communication with the nearest police station. But once cops had personal walkie-talkies and most of the public had access to phones, they ceased to be useful and were withdrawn." She finishes her toast and starts working on her coffee.

But I am not done yet. "But surely even if the British were inclined to disregard such a box, what if it landed in a foreign country or another time?"

"The premise may have made sense in the 1960s to some extent. But look, almost all characters the Doctor encounters speak with British accents – no matter what the time or place or distance from Earth. But you suspend disbelief for SciFi, not so?"

I test my espresso; it's good. "Well, luckily I am not writing for that series, just viewing how they film."

She gets up. "Nearly my time to go to work. What will you do today? Just watch more *Dr Who*?"

"No. I want to go to the shelter to run the project idea past Martha and Jill. Then, if I have time, I will immerse myself in the wonders of daytime TV."

By 11:00, I am at the shelter and find that Martha has taken the day off. Seeing my disappointment, Jill asks: "Not happy to see the rest of us?"

"Not that. We have a plan to do something more with the Chez Harry idea and I wanted to talk to her about it. But I would value your opinion too. Could you talk to her when you next see her?"

"That would be tomorrow for breakfast."

"Great." I explain Arthur's proposal and see that it does not sit well with her. "Now, wait. I didn't like it either."

I go on to the culinary school idea, and she finds that

a bit more palatable but has misgivings. "Yes, I can see that working to some extent. For me learning to cook came naturally but some of our staff had a tough time at first. But people straight off the street will be difficult. Our residents are in a shelter for a reason."

"This is why we need to have support – social workers, psychologists, and so on, to find out what motivates people to stay on the street. But really, what I want from you, Martha and the rest of the crew is solid ideas on how to make this work. You know the residents a lot better than I do – I was only here a few weeks."

"You won us over by what you did back then. I am sure Martha and the rest will back you."

I thank her, then head home, feeling upbeat and even manage to survive a few hours of some of the more depressing TV that is broadcast in Britain. Some is not half bad, like *Eastenders* – other shows seem pretty pointless. I even hit some American shows, reminding me why I was put off TV in South Africa.

By the time Hazel gets home, I need a break. I am eyeing out the pasta machine. She looks at it and looks at me. "Do I have a rival?"

"No, it wants to be friends with both of us. Remember pesto?"

"How could I forget?"

"I need a break from TV." So we do some shopping and relive our pesto adventure, complete with hanging pasta to dry – this time in a room that I also sleep in.

Once we are done, I admire our handiwork. "Finally, I get to sleep to the odour of drying pasta."

She grins. "Finally, I don't have to deal with it without

you."

Friday is much the same routine, until we take the tube to Arthur's neighbourhood. We are a bit early, and wait outside for Carol. As we wait. Hamish Leery shows up. "Am I early?" He checks his watch. "So I am." As he says that, Carol shows up and I do introductions, without going into detail.

As Hazel rings the doorbell. Judith Simons shows up, shortly followed by Andrew McGill, so I decide to save further introductions until we are inside. Arthur opens the door promptly, and we all file in. Arthur looks at Carol as she walks in, but doesn't forget his manners, and ushers us into the living room before opening with: "Ah, I see you have brought a new person in. Shall I do the introductions, once you've introduced her?"

Hazel takes the initiative."Arthur, we studied your proposal and we all agree that it would be better to run a culinary school than a restaurant as part of the project. My mother, Carol, has relevant experience, and we would like to bring her into the project."

Arthur nods contemplatively, but does the introductions before adding: "Well, that is an interesting turn of events. Would you care to explain the reasoning?"

At that point, I step in. "The plan to revitalise the area is great. But there is already one good restaurant there and starting another may be premature, and I don't see how it could work with the shelter. The residents need stability. A small number of guests in their own space gives them a sense of belonging in the wider world. A smart restaurant would not work for them. They would feel out of place.

"A culinary school though could work for the project. The homeless could learn skills and, with the right additional support to work out what keeps them on the street, it could be a way out for them. None of this excludes the broader revitalisation project. Once the culinary school is off the ground, if things are going well, a new restaurant or two could work."

Simmons looks thoughtful. "This could work. Carol, can you tell us more about yourself? What is your experience in this area, and why are you available now?"

Carol recounts her history and how she was unable to get the same thing off the ground once they moved to the city. After that, Arthur offers drinks, and the discussion turns to detail, much of which does not include me – in part because I stay very quiet. As things are winding down and a plan is taking shape, Arthur notes this. "Luke, you are the one who inspired all this but you aren't saying much."

"Harry was a friend to the extent that someone can be in a place like that. It's about him, not about me. I don't have skills that work for the plan. I am happy to help out where I can, but even happier that others can do the real work. I really would like to focus on my writing."

Arthur looks at me in mock seriousness. "Ah, but my dear boy, I bought some gourmet ingredients just so you could cook for us. Please don't tell me you want to walk away from that to *write*?"

Arthur leads the way to the kitchen. I beckon Carol to follow. What greets us is a pile of sole, a big lumpy looking object I can't identify and a pile of interesting veg that I can mostly identity, including some good-looking mushrooms. There is also a bag of Arborio rice and a good wedge of Parmesan, as well as a fancy-looking bottle of olive oil. I look at Carol and she looks a whole lot more excited than I do. I look at Arthur. "Arthur, you have grossly over-estimated my culinary range. I have never dissected a sole and I don't know what all of this is. Carol, can you help?"

"I've never seen such a large truffle, for a start... "

"... Ah," I add, "I know *of* truffle. Do you know your way around a sole?"

"Absolutely."

"Then I will be your student. One thing I do know is how to make risotto. However, I would love to learn about truffles and sole. Arthur, do you want to watch?"

"Oh, no, dear boy. I will only get in the way. The two of you, make yourselves at home. Consider the fridge and larder to be in play as well, not just my latest extravagant shopping."

We start with the sole as soon as Arthur leaves. Clearly I would have been lost without Carol, as it reverses everything I know about salmon. You need to remove the skin, which you peel off from the tail end. Then you start filleting at the head end. Working with someone who knows more than I do takes me back to gran and my early days in San Francisco. Soon, all tension between us is lost. We are having fun.

After completing my masterclass in filleting Dover sole, Carol discusses mushroom options with me for risotto, since my usual approach of using dried mushroom would be too slow even if there were some to be found. We settle on using morels and truffle for the base and shavings of truffle added before serving; I start the risotto while she preps the veg and works on a sauce.

When the risotto is almost done, she asks: "Any ideas for pud?"

"There are some nice figs. What would go with that?"

"How about some crumbled honeycomb with Chantilly cream? Simple and we can do it quickly."

"Honeycomb?" I don't even know what that is.

"Easy. Caramelise sugar, take it off the heat just before it turns dark, add bicarb and pour out onto a baking sheet."

I finish cooking the risotto and she shaves on a little more Parmesan and a generous amount of truffle. We take it out to the dining room, where conversation is animated over wine. Arthur sniffs. "Smells wonderful. I forgot to say, there's champers in the fridge. Do bring it out with the main, when you must of course join us. I'm sure it will go with the sole."

We go back into the kitchen and I open the fridge. The only bubbly I can find is a couple of bottles of Dom Pérignon Rosé. I pull one out and show it to Carol. "Isn't this rather expensive?"

"Very. Luckily he isn't being extravagant. It gets even more expensive than this. But he's the boss."

Cooking the sole is a quick job so it's last; the fondant potatoes are almost done as are the various colours of broccoli when I start on it, under Carol's close supervision. We dress the soles with caper, lemon and parsley butter that Carol made while I was doing the risotto and we are ready to serve. Our own plates contain the last of the risotto.

As we sit, Arthur and his friends are already avidly sampling theirs. But Hazel is the first to speak. "Wow, mom. You never cooked like this for us before."

"I never had such an able assistant or such wonderful ingredients all at the same time. But we forgot one thing..."

"Of course..." I see the empty champagne flutes and fetch a bottle and present it to Arthur, sommelier style. "Is this the correct plonk?" This scores a good laugh.

As we finish the main, Carol and I get up. Arthur looks quizzical. "Surely there isn't more?"

"Absolutely," I say, following Carol. She sets me to whipping cream with sugar and scraped vanilla bean seeds, while she starts the caramel. Both are quick processes and I watch as she makes the caramel fizz before she pours it out to set. We work together on rinsing and quartering figs, setting a few on each bowl with a neat pile of cream in the centre. Carol splits the honeycomb and I work on crumbling it and, with that addition, dessert is ready to serve.

Everyone digs in. Then, once we are done, Arthur leads the applause. But something is worrying Hazel. I look at her quizzically and a light dawns. I leave it to her to see if she sees the same problem. "The thing that we've been aiming for is mixing cultures. We had Italian and French, but to do this right, we need expertise on other cuisines that are not well known, like African. Luke obviously knows about South Africa but is he going to have the time...?"

"No." I'm totally with her: this is a good point that we had not thought through. "What about other refugees, so we can add to my experience of being away from my old home, while trying to do good for our new home? I know a little about Cape Malay and Durban Indian, but am by no means an expert."

Judith Simmons weighs in. "This could add a breath of fresh air to my retail chain. We could identify new flavours developed in your kitchen and produce branded products, or add to our fresh food selection." There are nods around the table. She goes on: "We have a lot of expertise around this table; all we really lack is expertise in rehabilitation and in other exotic cuisines. This really could work."

When we get back home that night, I give Hazel a tight hug. "This has been quite a week. I'm not sure if I can wind down by watching TV..." She points at the floor. I point at her bedroom, leading to an impasse. Then I flash her a wicked grin. "I know! Compromise! Let's put the camping mattress on the floor of your bedroom."

Chapter 38

What the Doctor Ordered

It's 7am on Monday, and I am on the tube to meet Bill at his office. Even this early, the tube is busy – some people start work early, some may have a long way to go. I try to puzzle out each person's story. A person heading for an early shift looks awake. A person heading home from a late shift looks sleepy. Or is it the other way around? After a weekend of solid *Dr Who* and trashy crime series episodes, interleaved with the occasional bit of live TV, I'm not sure what is real anymore, and start fantasising about space aliens in disguise as droopy-eyed janitors.

I find Bill in his office already when I get there, a notebook and pen at the ready. He looks me up and down. "Do you have a photographic memory?"

"No. Why?"

"Where's your notebook? You're with me to learn." I look embarrassed and glance at the picture of the shredder. Bill laughs. "Don't worry, this is not my first time mentoring a precocious rookie. These are for you." He hands over the notebook and pen, and retrieves another well-worn notebook from his desk. Suitably chastened, I follow him out to his car, a Triumph Stag with the top down. As I stare at it – a car I had only before seen in pictures, a real beauty, he jumps in and says: "Apologies, it's not a TARDIS. Get aboard. Powys Castle is nearly 4 hours away in my modest conveyance."

The way Bill takes off, I am not so convinced it's an ordinary mode of transport. The burble of the V8, something new to me, catches my attention – in part because it is so quiet, a surprise in an open-top car. Then again, I have never been in one of those either. Bill glances my way. "A beaut, isn't she? But I was lucky, I got one of the later models when the problems were better known. I just need to top up the radiator regularly and she runs sweetly. Not quite the sports car it is supposed to be on the B roads, but I am more style than substance when it comes to cars. But the stuff that matters is good: the hood works well in wet weather and I like the fact that the engine noise isn't showy." As the near-winter air swirls around me, I am silently thankful that the hood works.

As we exit the city, Bill suggests I review the map. "Unfortunately we don't have time to stop but we go through some really interesting places on the way including Oxford and Stratford-upon-Avon. Plus also Birmingham."

"Isn't Birmingham interesting?"

"It is, in its own way. Most people think of it as an industrial city, but it has plenty of culture from ballet to Black Sabbath."

I study the map as we go, picking out landmarks. By the time we reach the castle, it's nearly midday, and filming has obviously hit a break. The camera crew are packing their equipment and the rest of the cast and crew are heading for a tent. Bill corners one of the camera crew and explains our purpose. "No problem as long as you don't mess with anything in front of the castle, where we are filming next. No continuity glitches, please."

Bill leads me to the front door of the castle, saying, "Let's see if anyone's home."

"Will they mind?"

"I hope not. The National Trust took over the castle in 1952, when the family could no longer afford the upkeep. Though the family still reside there, the castle is open to visitors. We will just have to see if they are open now."

We walk to the entrance and it is open; Bill pays the entrance fee. We walk around admiring the grand staircase, artworks and so on. I ask: "How does filming the interior work? Do they have to close it to visitors? Surely setting up the equipment, retakes and so on will take a lot of time."

"Aha! The first rule of film is illusion. What makes you think any interior shots are actually in this building? You film someone walking in a door. You cut. You film someone walking inside. Who is to say it is *actually* the same building?"

We go out, and find everyone in the tent, where lunch is in progress. Someone spots me and suddenly I am being mobbed. It seems food is not as good as some like, and the rumour quickly goes around that I am to cook for them. Bill pulls me out of the crowd and turns out to have a surprisingly commanding voice. "Back off! This one's mine now! He will be reworking a crime series and I am showing him the ropes. We are here to learn from you." To grumbles of disappointment, we join the food queue. There are two choices: Irish stew or veg curry; Bill takes the former, I take the latter.

When we sample ours, I say to Bill, "This actually isn't bad. Why all the fuss?"

Someone next to me hears this and answers: "Mate, it was good the first time but we get pretty much the same stuff every meal. Meat stew and vegetarian option, curried, no distinguishable difference, whatever it says differently on the menu."

"Including breakfast?" I ask innocently, pointedly staring at my plate, visualising veg curry.

"Different from this but as indifferent. Cornflakes and rubberised egg."

Others are paying attention, and I find a crowd around me once again. I look around desperately for support, but they have somehow separated me from Bill, perhaps when he got up to forage for dessert. This time, there is no getting away. I eventually manage to shout through the hubbub: "OK, OK – I will talk to the food crew if you all agree to spend some time with me talking through practicalities of filming and what does and does not work in a screenplay."

A tall figure grabs my hand and intones imperiously, "You have a deal!"

Bill finds his way to me with a bowl of custard that looks like puke as the crowd dissipates. "What did I miss?"

"I'm to talk to the cooks and they are going to give me some one-on-one time." I point out the receding figure who clinched the deal.

"Cheap at the price," Bill adds, after looking where I am pointing. "Quality time with The Doctor himself. Come on, let's talk to the cookery crew while they are clearing away."

As we get to the food tent, my heart sinks. What have I committed to? If this goes as well as my starts with Martha, the Home Secretary and Gina, we might as well go home now. But I have Bill with me, and he takes the heat out of it, while I start clutching at my photo of the shredder. As the head cook is about to give me a blast, he intervenes. "My young friend has a bit of a culinary reputation, but he also is not the best at first impressions. How about we take this slowly? First, I am Bill Locke, senior screenwriter, his mentor. I guess you know who Luke is; but to me, he is a green screenwriter who needs some practical help from a real film crew and they somehow expect him magically to make the food more interesting. That makes it my problem, so how about we be civil about it, and see how we can help each other?"

The head cook introduces himself. "Ian McLennan. Head chef, and my crew ..." he points each out in turn and does introductions. Bill and I shake hands with each of them.

Then Bill goes on: "I'm sure you all know your craft. Why is it that there are complaints?"

"Unlike your lad, we don't have smart restaurants to donate top class ingredients. We have a very modest budget, and we have to stick to nutritious and safe because we get in trouble if the crew get sick."

"So safe not sorry?" I ask.

"Exactly. Try 'sorry', if you want to lose your livelihood."

"I understand. But why not see if you can get donations of more varied ingredients? Surely there are food purveyors who would love to be seen in the credits of the next *Dr Who* series? It doesn't have to be fancy stuff – just variety. More interesting veg. A few herbs and spices. Free range eggs."

I see I am not entirely getting through, so I add: "Why is

this your problem? Shouldn't the BBC be concerned about the health and happiness of their film crew? If you give me a shopping list, perhaps Bill and I can pitch the idea to management?" I turn to Bill. He nods.

"Oh, and by the way," I add, trying my best to sound polite, "what exactly was the dessert today?"

The head cook rolls his eyes. "New cook. I asked for custard and he made something out of a packet, inexpertly – full of lumps. Now that was embarrassing. I'll give you the shopping list before you leave. Now get back to the film crew."

As we get to the car, the chill is starting to set in and Bill closes the hood before we move out. On the trip back, we start out in silence. After we pass Birmingham and it is starting to get dark, Bill opens with: "Well, I hope you learnt a few good lessons. You had quality time with some of the best."

"I learnt to bring you with me when I could get into a sticky situation."

Bill laughs. "Whether you like it or not, you're a celebrity. Big celebrities have minders. Here is a a very simple lesson for you, since you are not in a position to pay for one. When a conversation could take a wrong turn, deflect to civility."

It is thoroughly dark by the time I get home and, tired though I am, I have enough adrenaline to spill the whole story to Hazel. But not enough to cook or to stay awake long enough for her to order in food.

Chapter 39

New Cooks

For the next two weeks, my schedule with Bill is set; sessions going over lessons from the *Dr Who* crew, lessons from Bill, rewrites and more rewrites. Despite the intensity of the work, I have time to chase the Chez Harry project.

On Tuesday, I call in at the shelter just after lunch time and this time, Martha is there. She accosts me. "Jill tells me you have a new plan. Why do I only hear it from her?"

"I wanted to tell you first, but you weren't here. I thought it would be better to get it to you sooner rather than later, even if it went through Jill. After all, she knows you better than I do – or is she not so good at puppy dog eyes?" I grin.

Martha shakes her head. "Don't say you don't know how to get around me. Even without puppy dog eyes you do. Come on, let's have a cuppa and work through the details."

Once I am sure that Martha is happy, I head for COSAWR and find Johathan will be available shortly, so I wait and page through various pamphlets from other anti-apartheid movements. Once Jonathan arrives, he ushers me into his office, "Good afternoon Luke. We don't have any update from the Home Office but things generally move slowly at this stage."

"Thanks, Jonathan. But that's not what I am here about." I explain the plan of expanding Chez Harry to a culinary school as part of an urban renewal development, and how I would like to involve South African exiles to expand the range. "I don't know all South African cuisines, but I know a little about Cape Malay and Durban Indian, so I was wondering if you have connections with other parts of the anti-apartheid movement that could find people with those skills."

"Right, so not draft dodgers. As you know, those are all white people. They may have culinary skills in those areas but not based on their home life. And also, given the age group, probably not highly experienced even if they know how to cook. We do work with a number of organizations. How many people are you looking for?"

"I was thinking two to start with; we have one person already who has a lot of experience with training in European cuisine – French, Italian, and so on. A UK citizen, not a refugee."

"So a refugee skilled in Cape Malay and another in Durban Indian? Got it. I will ask around and let you know. To be clear, are you looking for chefs or trainers?"

"The main requirement will be training but experienced chefs who can learn how to train will be fine. We already have someone skilled in training who can add that if needed."

By Friday, I am wondering if this is not going to work out, when I get a call from Jonathan as I am about to head out to Bill. It seems he has two prospects, so we set up a meeting for 4pm, the earliest time that I can get to him.

As before, the session with Bill is intense and the first episode is now quite different from the start – similar dialogue, except for the reimagined Genevieve, who is still a work in progress, but fewer scene changes, more explicit camera directions and so on. By the time I am on the tube at 3pm, I need to clear my head. I pull out my tatty shredder picture, then decide that's not it. I visualise the dentist's drill but that doesn't work either. Then I look around at the other people on the train and try to imagine what they are doing traveling at this hour – not exactly when anyone starts or ends work. Tourists? People like me with appointments? I give up but my head is clearer. Perhaps, I contemplate, a single kind of scalpel isn't always enough on its own. Or sledgehammer. I am not sure at which end of the scale of finesse to brute force my tools are.

I get to Jonathan's office a few minutes past four and he has two guests already, one with relatively pale skin, the other dark. The first, Jonathan introduces as Abdul Hendricks; clearly the Cape Malay representative. We shake hands. Hendricks is skinny, with quick nervous movements.

The second, however looks African. Jonathan introduces him as "Shlaka-nee-file Zibbie". The second visitor examines me quizzically as I contort my face trying to get out a version of his name that makes sense to a Zulu speaker. Jonathan, notwithstanding his anti-apartheid credentials, has obviously not spent much time with African languages. Eventually I get to: "Hlakaniphile Zibi, *kunjani?*"

He shakes my hand, mirth barely disguised. '*Ngiyaphila. Wena unjani?*" He asks how I am, after responding in the positive to my similar question.

"*Kuhle nakimi.*"

Having established that we are both well and that I have successfully unmangled his name, I turn to Jonathan, who has turned a lighter shade of puce. I reassure him: "English speakers struggle with the aspirated form of *L* and *P*. What matters is we have two people representing South African cuisine. Abdul, I would guess would know Cape Malay. Hlakaniphile, I was expecting someone representing Durban Indian cuisine. You seem to me to be a Zulu speaker though the surname is unfamiliar."

"Well spotted. My family is from Southern Natal and we have some isiXhosa roots. But I moved to Durban to find work and learned my craft at the Royal. So I may not look or sound Indian, but I know my spices. And my friends call me Zibi, which is a lot easier for foreigners."

"The Royal Hotel? I've heard of it, but it was too pricey for me. I did my fancy cooking at home, back when I was in Natal." At least I think I did; during that pesky lost year, I at least learned how to layer a breyani and make samoosas. But I keep that to myself.

Abdul and Zibi share glances. I am guessing that neither of them eat out at fancy places either. But the point Abdul raises is: "Why this project? I read about you as the shelter gourmet but there wasn't anything about your history."

I relate my family history, with emphasis on the farm years and leaving my friends behind, ending with Geoff's stories about political trials. Both of the guests look doubtful. But Zibi breaks the uncomfortable silence. "These farm kids were your best friends yet you don't know how they lived. The only South African cuisine you know is from outside."

"When you are four, you take the world as you see it. I knew something was wrong but ..."

"And you did nothing until you were forced to run away." Abdul looks at me accusingly as he says this.

"You're right. I was too caught up in my own personal disasters to see the big picture." I am making a fool of myself and don't see a way out. Then I remember Bill's advice. Civility. "My apologies, I am making this about me and I had easy options. But I am willing to learn."

I am not sure this is working, when Zibi comes to the rescue. "Of course you had soft options. With a degree you could have had a desk job in the apartheid army. Exile is not easy for anyone. But perhaps if you hear my story, it will help you to understand.

"At the Royal, us Africans were skivvies but one of the chefs was pleased that I was taking an interest and started showing me the ropes. It got to the point where I could do all of the work on his most prized recipes, and he was treating me almost like a son. We got talking politics, and he took me to a Black Consciousness meeting, a small one, we had to be careful because The System –" he pronounced it in capitals "– has spies everywhere. After the movement was banned we had some contact with the ANC underground. Nothing serious. But I had a coffee mug with the ANC logo on it. I had it at my workstation. I thought we were safe there, we all knew each other. But there must have been a spy. It could only be the mug because we did not talk politics at work, except that one time. The cops raided when I was on break. I saw them taking my chef away but I hid. I thought, what kind of country is this where a coffee mug can get a man arrested? I contacted the ANC underground and they smuggled me out of the country and here I am."

I shake my head. "Just like that? Why him though? It was

at your workstation."

"They had to pick up someone and maybe the spy told them we were close. My chef was very wily. When they interrogated him, he asked them to show him the mug. He handled it, then said he'd never seen it before. They charged him with possession of banned literature but when it came to cross examining, his lawyer trapped the cops into admitting that they handed him the mug and had no way of telling if his finger prints on it were from before or after that event. But by then he knew I was long gone, so deflecting the suspicion didn't get me into trouble."

Zibi looks at Abdul, who takes up the cue. "I was born in District 6 and we were forcibly removed to the Cape Flats when I was training to be a teacher. We had a lot of resistance to the move. I too gravitated to Black Consciousness though my family had a tradition of supporting the ANC. A friend had some ANC pamphlets and I decided to help him distribute them, as we all recognised the injustice of banning our organizations.

"Someone must have spotted me. I was arrested but concocted a plausible story and perhaps they decided it was mistaken identity. I didn't know I was such a good liar. But they were still sure that it must be someone close to me, so they arrested my uncle who was completely non-political, the most innocent sweet soul you could imagine. They would not believe him when he told them the absolute truth that he knew nothing and tortured him. Can you imagine that? They believed my lies but not his truth. When they let him go, both of his arms were broken. I went to see him in hospital. When I was trying to say how sorry I was, he wouldn't have it.

"The only thing he wanted to say is that he was so scared

that he would say something to betray one of us, even if he knew nothing, just to stop the pain. After that, I had to leave. I could not put any more of my family through that."

This story affects me deeply. I can't imagine anyone caring so much about me that they would endure torture to protect me. I find myself crying uncontrollably, something that only happened once before, in my Mr Plod moment. Eventually, I say, "I am so sorry." I can't add to it but, from the reactions, it seems I don't need to.

Abdul gives me a hug. "At last, a real apology from a white South African. The rest of them are full of excuses. *It's bad but* I *didn't do it...* When do we start?"

Chapter 40

The Real Genevieve

That night, I am first home. It's been yet another intense day and I am ready to unwind the usual way, by cooking. So I check what we have and go out shoppping. By the time I get back, Hazel is home.

She sees the shopping bags and grins. "That's my Lukie – ready to cook and make me feel at home in my own home." I put the bags down and give her a super-tight hug. She pushes me out to arms length. "Another intense day? Put that stuff away and let's talk about it."

I put the shopping away in short order, except a nice bar of chocolate that we share. Then I relate the story of the new cooks, how much I feel the pain of people taking the hit for them, their pain at being so far from home. Hazel points at the floor. I unroll the camping mattress and we lie close, neither of us fully on it, neither of us on the floor.

We hold tight for a while, then I get up to cook. Hazel checks with her mother and Arthur and reports back that they are both free to talk about the project on Saturday, 3pm, two days off. I stick with something simple – a stir fry of veg with rice noodles, and some cashews thrown in for crunch. We eat slowly, exchanging glances. The silence somehow conveys togetherness more than words.

As we finish, she says, "You know, I've been rethinking your Genevieve character. Imagine someone who is terrible at reading people, gets all the social cues wrong. But sees everyone from the *inside*. In early episodes, she is just socially awkward. But it is increasingly she who sees inside the mind of the criminal, solves the crime no one else can solve. What do you think?"

"Interesting idea... but... you aren't writing someone else from your family?"

"You idiot! It's you! You are bloody useless at body language, social cues and so on, but you see inside other people's heads in a way no one else I know can."

"So I am Genevieve?"

"No, silly. You can create Genevieve in a way that does not mimic or ridicule anyone else because it is how *you* are."

I nod slowly. "I think Gina will relate to this. Genevieve is a misunderstood character who breaks boundaries. In some ways, like her. I want to do this. Are you too tired to work?"

"I'm not but you look as if you are."

"No. Let's do this. If you can do the dishes, I will make a start, then you can help with the dialogue. Your thing, remember?"

By the time we really are too tired to work, we have redone the first three episodes. Hazel looks at her watch. "Is that the time? I can take tomorrow off but don't you have a meeting set with Bill?"

"Oh, yes. Not so early, 9:30, fortunately – so let's get

some sleep. But I want you to go with me. It's your idea."'

Next morning we are on the tube together. I hold Hazel's hand. "It's so great to feel we are a proper team. Why did you resist putting your name on the screenplays so much? I would never be where I am without you."

"I don't know. Maybe I feel that I should be the one with a writing job, instead of doing backroom research. It feels so odd to be jealous, I didn't realise that was what it is. I'm sorry."

"Come on. Aren't we over apologies? We both screwed some things up so badly. We worked it out. Let's enjoy the moment." I remember that I have another bar of that good chocolate with me and offer some.

She grins and takes a piece. "Chocolate covers a lot of sins."

We talk about Genevieve, the plans for the Harry project, things I miss from South Africa, the new cooks and what they will bring to the project.

We are just past the worst of the morning rush so the tube is not crowded. As we get close to our stop, I start anxiously checking my watch. "We may have cut it a bit fine. Let's rush. Bill appreciates punctuality." We get to his office as my watch shows 9:31 and his door opens as I am about to knock.

Bill ushers us in wordlessly then looks at Hazel. "Hazel, your co-author I presume?"

"Yes," I say. "I took the liberty of bringing her in because she has thought of a creative way to rescue the Genevieve dialogue."

"Intriguing. Hazel, what's the idea?"

Hazel explains the new Genevieve, the person who has

terrible interpersonal skills, can't read body language, always takes things the wrong way. At this point, Bill interjects: "I think we know someone like that. But the original Genevieve developed, became increasingly neurotic. Do we want someone worse than that?"

"Aha!" Hazel ripostes. "This Genevieve becomes *more* not *less* functional. Despite her total lack of skills at reading the exterior, she has an unmatched skill at reading the *interior*, in other words, *empathy*. Her social ineptitude leads her to being grossly underestimated. From being a bit player, she gradually transforms to eclipsing the original detective and becomes the lead."

"What do you think?"

"Interesting. I wonder if Gina is in. This is a development worth running past her." He phones Gina's office and checks. "11:30? Fine, we will be there.

"OK, you two. I would like her input before we put more time into this. I have other work to do, so let's postpone Luke's session with me and meet at Gina's office in a couple of hours."

As we leave the building, Hazel stops and stares back at the entrance. "Wow. The great Gina Gibbons. I led you to her office what seems like a lifetime ago but now I get to meet her myself."

"She isn't as scary as you think she is. Far worse." Then I grin. "My useless people skills didn't destroy everything. You will be just fine. Don't forget, she pushed hard for you to get a decent share of the contract. She's in your corner."

"I know. But my own writing pretensions are far more thwarted than yours."

"Stop fretting. There is a decent coffee shop or two in

these parts. Stay in the moment or –'

"– dentist's drill or –" she adds, awaiting my follow-up. I end the thought by extracting my tattered shredder picture from my wallet.

The coffee break passes with pleasantries and we find ourselves back in the building in Gina's anteroom a few minutes early, when Bill arrives. He glances at Gina's assistant who says, "Just a minute, she's finishing a call." Shortly after, she ushers us in.

Gina glances around the delegation. "My, this is interesting. I finally meet Hazel. What is the grand occasion?"

I glance at Bill, who is having none of that. It is my project, so I must explain. I get into it. "Gina, when this whole thing started, Hazel spotted my weakness in dialogue from not having anything like a normal family, and did a brilliant job with getting that up to standard, and I am very thankful that you pushed us to give her decent credit for this."

"But...?" Gina is waiting for the punchline.

"But she inadvertently wrote Genevieve as her mother who has been having a difficult time. We absolutely can't leave it like that. But Hazel has another inspiration as to how to develop Genevieve. Hazel?" I want her to do this; it's her idea.

Gina frowns. "I hope this is good. I liked the way it was going."

Hazel looks nervous but it's her moment, and she hurries through her pitch. "My new Genevieve is a character who is terrible at reading people. Always gets body language wrong, misses where a conversation is going but has amazing empathy. She can't read the *outside* but is a master at reading the *inside*. So the series starts with her continually blundering, but her empathy superpower gradually transforms her into the lead detective. What do you think?"

Gina sits back.

There is a silence.

"Interesting. Do you have some episodes...?" – I hand them over – "Of course you do. I am going to have to spend a bit of time on this but I completely agree that Hazel cannot write her mother. That would be unspeakable. But tell me, Hazel, what else do you do? Do you have a job? Doing your part of this could take up a lot of your time, particularly as you have wholly conceptualised this character."

"I work at the BBC satellite channel, doing background research..." Gina purses her lips "... is that a problem?"

"I will have to check with legal but I am pretty sure you can't both be a contractor and salaried."

Hazel looks close to tears. "I am such a fool. I should have thought of that. I do so much want to be a writer."

Gina has clearly summed up the situation. "Don't worry. Let me know who you work for and we can make a plan. Possibly you can go part-time. Maybe we can second you here and you can do this as a staff writer rather than as a contractor. Are you happy to leave it with me?"

"Absolutely. Thank you so much." Hazel writes down her boss's details and hands that over.

"Not a problem. I remember how hard it was for me to break out of my first demeaning role. Bill, can you stay on a bit to discuss other issues?"

This is clearly a dismissal so I add: "Bill, should we stick to our schedule for our next meeting?" He nods, and we exit from The Presence. Back out on the street, I say: "Was that so terrible?"

"Actually, no – nothing as bad as the way you described your first encounter."

I laugh. "Never take what happens to me as a model. Come on, let's find a nice pub and celebrate. Things are moving our way. I saw some on the way here from the tube."

It's just before the Friday lunch rush so the pub Hazel picks out isn't crowded. We sit at a table just off the bar with drinks. I have a small ale; she has a glass of white wine. We clink glasses. "To us," we say simultaneously, followed by "This is so nice." As a writer, saying that triggers my inner cliché police – but it feels right anyway. I'm not going to be a pedant.

We are in the moment and there is nothing to say. As the glasses empty, Hazel asks: "Is there any update on your asylum application?"

"No. I almost forgot about that."

"What was it that Arthur said about us getting married?"

"Aside from apologising for speaking out of turn?" I look at her mischievously, knowing this is not the direction she is going.

"Idiot. You know what I mean. Remember, we decided that no one would push us into it, even if it solves your asylum problem."

"And we do not move fast unless..." I add, building on a memory.

"... we want to." She completes. "So do we want to?"

"Is that a proposal?" I ask coyly.

"Of course it bloody well is."

"Oh. We kind of constructed the thought simultaneously so obviously..." – as I say this, we both prompt with an index finger.

"Yes," we say in unison.

Chapter 41

Party Up and Down

When we get home that afternoon, the excitement has not worn off. But I feel the need to offload. I pour us each a glass of water and we sit down facing each other at the table. Clearly, I have conveyed the need to talk as Hazel sits expectantly.

"One thing I never talked through was that first night in the shelter." I pause to reflect. "No, more accurately, memories I relived on the first morning. I woke up on the floor and that took me back to a time I visited my gran where I slept on the floor. That was a positive memory. But it also took me back to the Harriet year, where I had a mattress on the floor. Not a positive memory at all."

I pause; she has the good sense to give me space to work this out.

"The thing is, I tried to remember that year and it was almost all gone – just some of the great highs and the great lows. I did know that I had blanked *some* of it. I remember finding a reading list and not remembering reading a single thing on it, though I must have read everything at the time. But this was the first time I really tried to relive that year and it was as if most of it never happened. I can't remember anything about the place I lived, making food, going out, going to class. Nothing. Just the highs and lows of the whole Harriet nightmare."

Again, Hazel allows me space to collect myself.

"So I did not dare think about anything that happened here before I fled. I was terrified that it was all gone. When Martha told me I was a fool and should chase after you, I forgot all those fears but everything came back to me on our trip back here in the cab. The thing is, my damaged head did not erase anything. It's all still here. You have no idea how much that means to me."

Before I know it, we are on the floor doing our hot spring thing again. She is doing soft moves on my back that relieve all kinds of tensions I did not know I had. Then she whispers in my ear. "Lukie, my lad. You have PTSD."

"PTSD?"

"Post-traumatic stress disorder."

"I know what it is. But I haven't been in a shooting war with people being blown up."

"Emotional trauma is also trauma. You were rejected by the people who should have supported you most. For a long time, you only ever had one true supporter – your gran, then your uncle. That would have completely wrecked most people. I researched the background on a show about this. It's a real condition and can be treated."

"I feel such a fraud. Remember what people like Abdul and Zibi have been through – relatives tortured, friends jailed."

"But that is what makes you special. You see their pain through the lens of your life instead of being immersed in your own. Let's talk to mum about her therapist. Maybe that can help. Just because someone else's pain is worse than yours does not put you beyond help."

She gets up and offers me a hand-up. "We're forgetting something. We need to tell everyone our news."

"And then organize that long-delayed party with all your friends. And this time, without using up old pasta. Let's make some phone calls. But first, let me call COSAWR and see if my two cooks can also make the meeting on Saturday."

Jonathan is in the office and promises to check with the cooks, so we switch to personal news mode.

A flurry of calls follows, with details blurring into one, except one jarring note. Geoff is clearly ecstatic but ends with a sombre tone. "As you can imagine, I am not close to government but if you live in Pretoria, you have contacts who have contacts. Mine tell me if I apply for a passport, all they will be prepared to give me is an exit permit. That means: don't come back. I would lose my citizenship and become stateless. Much as I would love to be with you now and have no fear of being a refugee, I am in demand again for political cases."

This does not surprise me as the news from South Africa shows protests heating up. "Geoff, Hazel has never tried to turn me into something else. I would never try to turn her into someone else. This is you, and I am proud of who you are. It will be as if you are here, I promise. We will send photos. Send us a nice one of you so it can be with us.

"Oh, and one more thing. If it hadn't been for you, I may have been sent back in a body bag from Angola."

"Angola? Interesting. Everyone is talking about our war in Angola but the local press is obviously being censored because it isn't in the news."

"That's crazy. I saw it on the cover of *Time* recently, so it's hardly a secret from our government's enemies. No apologies from you. I owe you everything. If you had not been there for me when gran died, I would have had nothing."

As we end the conversation, I think of the British tabloids. No censorship but much of what they publish is drivel. Is that what freedom is? Surely a big part of freedom is an informed population. Back in South Africa, the apartheid government totally controls what people know.

Phone calls out of the way, we start talking about The Party. But some things don't wait. There is a knock on the door. It's Arthur, with the biggest champagne bottle I've ever seen. He hands it to me and, fortunately, I grip it firmly as it's pretty weighty. He gives Hazel a hug. "My dears, if you want to buy the biggest possible bottle of champagne, a Jeroboam is the place to stop because it's not too big to pour."

"Gosh. You mean they get bigger than this?" I usher him in, following Hazel.

"Oh, absolutely, champagne comes in many sizes, down to a quarter of a bottle. A double is a magnum, which I am sure you know. A Jeroboam is this size, 4 bottles. Then you get a Methuselah, which is 8 bottles. A Salmanazar is 12 bottles, a Balthazar is 16 and a Nebuchadnezzar is 20. All biblical names, requiring a thirst of biblical proportions. Exactly how you are meant to pour out of one of those monsters is a puzzle that I do not intend to solve."

I lay the bottle down in the sink for want of a better place to put it. "There is another practical problem. How do we chill a thing this size?"

"Aha! You're way ahead of me. The sink would be an
option, with masses of ice. But I brought a suitable bucket
as well, and we can procure ice when it's needed."

There's another knock. It's Claudette. She engulfs Hazel
and I in a group hug. Then she looks at both of us in turn. "So
tell me about the proposal?" Clearly she already knows us
well enough to ask. There is no way it could be conventional.

Hazel says, "It was a simultaneous thing. No one proposed to anyone else."

"My, that is the most feminist proposal I've heard of. How
exactly did it happen?"

Hazel gives her a mischievous look. "You had to be
there."

Claudette turns to me. "I suppose you told her the whole
knife thing?"

"I had to. No secrets." I hold up my hands in an opening
gesture.

Claudette grins. "Then no secrets here either."

So we explain the whole thing.

After that it's a procession. I lose track of faces and names
until Martha shows up. I am stunned. "Martha! I don't even
remember phoning..."

"Of course you bloody didn't but word gets around, you
know." Before she can question whether she is wanted, I give
her a monster hug, leaving her looking embarrassed but for
once I don't care about social blunders.

Arthur glances around the rapidly-filling flat. "I will be
right back, ice, bucket and..."

Further people flood in – still mostly people I don't know,
then Carol and Robert arrive, closely followed by Arthur.

Between them they are carrying a large bag of ice, two large ice buckets, a crate of champagne flutes and another Jeroboam.

Champagne is flowing freely, happy voices fill the space and I am lost. I dart my eyes around the room to pick out familiar faces. Hazel. Robert. Carol. Claudette. Martha. Gina. When did she arrive? So many more than I know or can take in. The noise, the movement, the colours, the flashing cameras. I am closing up. I can't breathe. It is a blur. I am near the door. I open it. I am outside. I close it behind me. I breathe. Haltingly at first, then hyperventilate, then slow down. Do I have my key? Did it lock? I look up the stairs to the street. There is a street light. There are stars. I don't want to run. I am terrified to go back. I don't want to cry. Why am I such a failure? This should be the best day of my life. I cover my face with a hand. I freeze from the inside out.

The door opens. I barely take in the sound. There is a gentle touch on my shoulder. I turn my head slowly. It is Claudette.

"Are you OK?"

I thaw slightly, and grin coyly. "No knife?"

"Idiot. Did you really think I would do that? You are clearly in trouble. Tell me."

"I don't know. Everything suddenly got too much. I don't know if I can go back in there."

"Have you always had a problem with crowds?"

"I've been to lectures for big classes and to full movie theatres. But not so much noise, so much activity."

"Are you feeling better now?"

"Yes, thanks. Talking has helped. Even this little bit. Hazel thinks I may have PTSD. Rejected by parents, all the bad stuff that happened..."

"You need a proper diagnosis. You can't decide someone has PTSD just like that. Right now, what are we going to do? We can ask everyone to leave. I'm sure they will understand."

"This is a part of Hazel's life I haven't experienced yet. Big, happy parties. I want it to be good. I have a few mind tricks to turn off when something is too stressful. Instead of running outside, I should have gone to the study. It's not completely isolated but it's away from the main party,"

"Are you sure?"

"Let's say I am a motivated patient. I'll give it my best shot. I already have an idea for coping."

"What's that?"

"Visualise you defending me with the biggest knife in the kitchen. Only: please don't actually do that."

"Hazel is a lucky girl. There really is something weirdly special about you. Come on. Go to your hideaway and I will cover for you. Will it work to send people to talk to you one at a time?"

"I think so. Yes. Let's do it that way."

So we are back inside, and Claudette ushers me past the crowd to the study. I see her turn back to talk to others as I sit down and do my dentist's chair thing, visualising Claudette threatening the dentist with a giant knife – the Nebuchadnezzar of knives. After an indeterminate time, Hazel is next to me.

"Claudette says you are struggling to cope but want the party to go on. I don't want this to be bad for you. I can send everyone home."

"No. I want it to go on. I didn't even know I was bad with big happy crowds because I never had one before and I don't want to kill the moment. Send your friends to me one at a time. I may not have great interpersonal skills but one-on-one will be a lot easier and I want to get to know them. You never tried to force me to change and I don't want you to be anyone else. If you do big parties, we will work this out. Not 100% this time, but we will get there. OK?"

"OK."

As the crowd thins, I feel less overwhelmed. By the end of the party, I am drained but happy. I have met many new people and know so much more about Hazel and who she really is. By the time the last group leaves, I am back on my feet and with Hazel to see them off.

As the door closes, I turn to her. "Right, so when are you going to ask your mum to introduce me to her therapist?"

"Why don't you do that yourself? Aren't you forgetting what we planned for tomorrow? Project meeting."

Chapter 42

The Project

Hazel and I arrive at the shelter a little before the start time of 2pm, planned to be past the post-lunch clean up. Robert and Carol arrive shortly after, followed by Arthur and his associates. As he is parking his Jag, Zibi and Abdul scurry along the road from the tube. By the time they arrive, the rest of us are at the entrance of the shelter.

Says Abdul: "Apologies for being a few minutes late. We got a bit lost finding our directions out of the tube."

"So embarrassing, you will think we do African time," adds Zibi.

"No, not at all. The rest of us just arrived." I point at the entrance. "Come on, Martha and her team are waiting for us."

I lead the way to the kitchen where Martha, Jill and the rest of the team have already brewed tea. Martha has one ready for me and passes it over. "Right, I know how my Luke likes his tea. How about the rest of you?"

Tea orders complete and custard creams passed around

sets us up for business. I do the introductions. "Arthur you already know; he was here to celebrate his brother Harry. Judith runs an upmarket chain. Andrew is in the software business and Hamish is a money guy. Did I get that all right?"

They nod, so I duck the issue of not knowing Martha's team as well as I should. "Martha, would you like to introduce your crew?"

"Ah, you aren't so hot with names are you?" I look rueful but she goes on. "Jill is my second in command. Al takes care of supplies. Jen does pretty much any job the rest of us does and Bea is the general dogsbody and dish washer."

I nod; I would have used more polite job descriptions but not remembering everyone's name is not super polite either so I let it rest. "Martha, you know Hazel and I think you may remember Carol. This is Hazel's dad, Robert. Last but not least, Abdul and Zibi are experts on two kinds of South African food. Carol, over to you."

Carol looks around the room. "I am not sure where to begin. Perhaps I should start with what I do, what I *want* to do. Some years back in Aylesbury, I ran a cooking school. At first it was just a hobby but it got serious when some of the people I trained started opening restaurants. Then we moved to London, and somehow I could not get it off the ground again. The sort of cooking I do is European classics – French and Italian mainly. But Luke has opened my eyes to looking wider. So, when I saw the ideas that Arthur and his team put together, I thought that the best way to use that idea was to create a cooking school near the shelter, where the aim would be to build skills among the homeless." She looks at Abdul and Zibi. "Where the two of you come in is that we would like to build on ideas that Luke brought in of integrating cuisine of South Africa, to benefit refugees. So that ties together his two passions: using food to bring dignity to the homeless, while honouring his own roots.

"Oh, wow, that was a long speech. Did I catch everything?"

Carol's enthusiasm is showing. I sit back to see where this goes. I am really happy that it is not my project.

Zibi grins. "I can see where you are coming from though it may seem a bit odd that a Zulu South African is representing Durban Indian. That is the professional kitchen experience I bring in, though we have a Zulu cuisine as well. But the big problem is we can't get the ingredients. Samp, mealie meal in all its forms, for a start."

"Samp? Mealie meal?" Carol enquires.

"Samp is dried maize, partly crushed into big chunks. We usually soak it overnight with dried beans and cook the two together. Cheap, nutritious food for the poor and everyone has their own recipes to make it tasty. We call it *istambu* in Zulu; the Xhosa people have their own version and call it *umngqusho*." Carol's eyes cross around the click sound in the middle. I grin. I grew up with this stuff – I was fluent in Zulu before I was fluent in English.

"Mealie meal is finely ground maize, in various grades. I found polenta in the shops but it isn't the same," Zibi concludes.

Abdul shakes his head. "You give up too easily. My ancestors came from Malaysia as slaves and they made do even though they couldn't get all the ingredients. Your Durban Indian friends also came out as indentured labourers and had to make do. Durban Indian and Cape Malay are now totally separate kinds of curry, only distantly related to ancestral dishes."

"You're right," Zibi admits. "But my restaurant experience is Durban Indian. I would love to find ways to recre-
ate tastes of home as well. But I would have to start from
scratch." He looks wistful. "Zulu boy, rural upbringing. Cooking wasn't a thing for me before I landed at the Royal."

Arthur weighs in. "This sort of thing you can work out
between you, Carol and the shelter cooks. What my group
needs to know is whether we can craft a business plan out of
this. We have Harry's trust so it doesn't need to make money
at first, but it needs to be self-sustaining."

Judith takes her turn. "That's where I come in. I would
love to get some ideas from your cross-cultural expertise
that we can turn to supermarket products."

Martha has been uncharacteristically silent but eventually
weighs in. "Where exactly do we fit in? Lukie sold us on some
of his ideas, but we are pretty much meat and veg British
besides that."

I've become Lukie here too. That's a plus. But I look to
Carol to respond, since it's now her project.

She takes a while to respond. "You know, there are two
reasons to bring you in. Number one, you know the homeless
better than any of us so if this is to work, we need your
ideas and your ongoing involvement. And: Luke is part of
the package whether he likes it or not and he is our link to
you and the shelter." There is definitely a thaw there, which
emboldens me to open up on the issue of her therapist.

A bit more discussion on practicalities follows. The
finance part of the team have found a building a block away
that would be big enough. "Close enough to involve the
shelter, not so close that it would interfere," opines Judith.
As we are about to take our leave, I ask Carol if she can stay on

for a chat over coffee. And anyway, she should be introduced to Eleni properly at some point and this would be as good a time as any. Henrique we can meet another time.

As we arrive, Eleni greets me effusively. "Luke! Where have you been! I thought you had forgotten us!"

"You, never. I thought you would like to be introduced properly to my future mother-in-law who is starting up a project here," This is the first time I've called Carol that. Another boundary crossed. "You may remember we had coffee here once."

"Oh, yes, Everyone is talking about you getting married. Quite the celebrity wedding you know!"

"Actually, I don't know. I'm afraid I don't do big happy parties well."

Eleni takes coffee orders then returns to chat. She and Carol seem to get on well; that is a great start. The weight of the Chez Harry project is seriously lifting. But then I remember the other thing, as Eleni leaves us.

"Carol, what I really want to talk about is your therapist. Who is it? How well is it going?"

"Ah, your crash at the party."

"Exactly. I wasn't sure if anyone besides Claudette noticed..."

"Besides that you vanished outside, came back looking shaken and spent the rest of the evening receiving guests individually in the study... What was there to notice? Of course it was clear that something was up. And with your story of parental rejection, and your escape from Hazel to the shelter, obviously there is an issue."

She pauses. "Do you need me to tell you how bad I feel about chasing you away?"

"Of course not. You were not to know and Hazel had so many bad experiences before. Tell me about your therapist."

"His name is Richard Doyle. He's a great listener, doesn't look for instant solutions. It took a while to get to the bottom of my issues. These things are not always as obvious as you think."

I nod. "Yes, I have some ideas and have some coping strategies, but another meltdown like that party one is not something to look forward to. I would like to give this a try."

Eleni is back, offering baklava. "On the house!" That is not something to refuse.

Chapter 43

Refocus

The next few weeks are a blur. A lot of writing and rewriting is involved. There are project meetings that take the Harry project further and further from me, which is a great release because I want it to work in a way that I know is beyond my capacity. What really stands out is my sessions with Richard.

The first starts awkwardly. I'm not sure what to expect. I am ushered into the inner sanctum and look around. There is a skinny grey-haired man behind a desk. He stands, revealing himself to be tall. "Aha. You are looking for the couch. I'm afraid I don't do cliché. Take a seat."

I remember the glass-clinking moment in the pub that was "so nice" and can't help bursting out laughing as I sit opposite his desk.

"Well, that's a first," he says, as I get myself under control. "Richard Doyle, Richard to most people. Luke, you're in a jolly mood. What brings you here?"

I explain the glass-clinking moment and my lack of aversion to cliché despite being a writer. He grins. "It's always

good to have an ice-breaker before we get into deeper issues. Fortunately I don't have to contrive one. Let's get into
it. First, a little about your life history, then we can get into
what you see as the problem that brought you here."

That is not so separate, I think. But I launch nonetheless
into parental abandonment, life on gran's farm, the useless
but favoured older brother, how things went downhill when
gran's health failed, Geoff rescuing me, my (mostly) smooth
academic progress except for the bad patch when gran sold
the farm. I go on to Harriet and my blank memory of much of
that year, then on to my move to California, meeting Hazel at
Yosemite, ending up in London and what followed.

By the time I get to melting down at the party, I feel
drained. But I remember that Richard has said we should end
with what brought me to him. So I add, "Hazel thinks I have
PTSD. Can that really explain all this?"

He nods slowly, "It could explain some of it. But psychi-
atry is a very inexact science. We gather information and try
to classify. I have a few questions."

I sit on the edge of my chair and pay close attention.

"Have you ever had any other memory blanking incident?"

"None, none at all – when I ran from Hazel, I was scared
to think about it until she showed up, but I didn't forget
anything. I remember times with my gran well and with my
parents and at school all too well."

"Interesting."

He pauses, and makes some notes then looks up again.
"Would you consider yourself academically gifted?"

"I suppose. I never really thought about it. Other than
the time when I was scared of losing gran, getting top marks
seemed natural too me. Even in the Harriet year, though I

have no idea how, my results apparently were good."

He nods. "Have you had sensory issues before – reacting to noise, crowds, and so on, as you did at the party?"

"I can't really say. I am so socially inept that until Hazel brought me into that side of her life, I never did big happy crowds. A movie theatre full of people is quiet, except for the movie itself and the sound of popcorn crunching. Lectures are quiet except for the drone of the lecturer and the intermittent sound of snoring from the class."

Richard has a good laugh, then refocuses. "All right, we have a number of things going on here. We need to understand your priorities and be realistic about what can be fixed."

After a pause, Richard continues. "PTSD is a possibility, but it could be restricted to your memory loss over the affected time. The sensitivity to emotional trauma and sensory sensitivity could be related. But there is another possibility that could explain those things, given your social awkwardness."

He pauses to reflect. "There's a condition that has only recently been studied in the English-speaking world and is not a recognized diagnosis yet. It's called Asperger's Syndrome, after the Austrian doctor who first described it in the 1940s. German discoveries back then were discredited as Nazi science because, well, Nazi science. They did some particularly horrendous things that forced us to rewrite the book on medical ethics."

Richard writes briefly then looks up at me. "Anyway, Asperger's is characterised by difficulties with social interactions, but strong linguistic and cognitive skills. There is some controversy over whether it is a form of autism, which is also a poorly-understood condition."

"So it's an illness?"

"You mean something we can cure? No. It is a personality type. However, if you are aware of it and, as you clearly are, of above average intelligence, you can develop accommodations."

"Aha." I tell him about my dentist drill trick, my shredder gambit and how I turned Claudette's rhetorical knifing threat into a defense against my party angst.

Suddenly, Richard is looking at his watch. "Oh, my goodness. We are way over time. You are so fascinating. Look, for our next session, you need to think through how important that memory problem is. It seems that you remember the actual things that traumatised you, so we can work on those, and work through whether those have contributed to a form of PTSD. But an important question in any memory-loss situation is whether regaining those memories matters more than putting away anything they obscure."

Richard ushers me to the door and leaves me with a suggestion. "In the meantime, try to avoid high-stress situations and keep honing those accommodations. If you run into any issues before your next appointment, don't hesitate to get in touch."

When I get home, Hazel is still at work. I settle with a few episodes that need tidying up, but that doesn't take long. Then I decide: *the doctor didn't order me not to. A nice glass of Chablis will not do me any harm.*

I am settled in an armchair with my glass half empty when Hazel gets back. "My! Is that what the shrink prescribed?"

"Oh, no. This isn't prescription Chablis. Would you like one?"

Once she is settled with her glass, I say: "Put that down."
I put my glass down and so does she and looks expectant.
"Now wait for this...
        "... my psychiatrist finds me *fascinating.*"

Chapter 44

Making it

Things are starting to take shape. Carol and the new cooks have the basic planning for the cooking school in place. They and the financial backers have mind-numbingly boring conversations about business plans. I have many memorable conversations with Richard. So let's start there.

It is my second visit. He ushers me in and I need no reminder to sit facing him. He starts out looking apologetic. "One of the tough things in this job is maintaining professional detachment. Every now and then I fail. I shouldn't have said I found you fascinating."

"Ah. I was wondering if that was usual. Hazel and I had a good laugh over that. It's better than a pilot finding the way their plane flies to be fascinating. But: remember, you have one over me. I am a writer and I do cliché."

"Well, it isn't a contest, but I am happy if it keeps us on track. Should we talk about memory today?"

I close my eyes for a minute, then: "Why not?"

He nods. "Memory is a strange thing at the best of times.

If your memory issue is indeed PTSD, it may not be the only issue.

"Do you have anything at all that could remind you of the missing months? You mentioned a reading list. Did you keep lecture notes?"

"Actually, no. I generally attended classes I enjoyed and got ahead of the lecturer so I could focus on asking interesting questions. Particularly with English Lit, it was a matter of doing the reading in advance and thinking through how to analyse the text. If the lecturer did it a different way, which they usually did, that set me going."

"Interesting. Do you remember nothing of that in that particular year?"

There is a silence.

I slowly shake my head.

"Do your recollections of Harriet still bother you at all? Do you have bad dreams, think of her obsessively or see her in every day events?"

There is a very long silence. Then I start hesitantly.

"It was like that right up to the point where Hazel found me at the shelter. I would wake up expecting to see her there, see someone in the street that reminded me of her, feel deep inner pain when reliving..." Was it really like that? I find myself doubting even these memories. What mattered to me at the time was cooking, Harry, Martha.

There is another silence, then I go on. "I had forgotten all of that until you asked. I am not even sure I had those flashbacks. Why do I not remember my courses or most things that happened during that missing year? This is so confusing."

I shake my head and feel totally lost. "I'm sorry, I don't

feel like I am making sense at all."

Richard looks at me with concern. "These are memories you are trying to suppress. We need to work on that constructively so you put these recollections aside permanently."

He taps his pen on his desk a few times. "What I suspect is going on here is that these memories represent trauma. You are reliving them at the expense of other memories. There are many ways we can deal with this, but I suggest we work on letting this all go. You say this stopped after Hazel found you at the shelter. Do you mean completely, or have you had these thoughts occasionally?"

I look deep inside myself. I feel sure. "Yes, definitely. I have stopped having those thoughts entirely."

Richard nods encouragement. "Good, now we just need to be sure you have put them away, not suppressed them. Do you ever feel that what happened with Harriet was your fault?"

"I don't know. Maybe I did. I never had a relationship before and I was so terrified of a new one that I couldn't accept what was happening with Hazel at first."

Richard taps his pencil again. "Here's the thing. You are not typical. You have had difficult circumstances early in life. So it wouldn't be surprising if you had difficult relationships. But what you describe about Harriet is very atypical – for her. To drop a relationship the way you described is way outside social norms."

"So something wrong with her...?"

Richard shakes his head. "It would be most unprofessional for me to diagnose someone who is not my patient and whom I have never met. All I am saying is that we need to work on any tendency you may have to blame yourself."

And with that, the hard part is over. We discuss mental exercises to dismiss harmful thoughts, ways to put myself outside the picture and see things objectively and ways to re-balance myself in my current reality.

As the session draws to a close, Richard asks me one more thing. "How important is it for you to get back those lost memories?"

"It feels like a big gap. But I suppose I can learn to deal with it."

"You can. There are many ways to address memory gaps including hypnotherapy, but let's not even consider it until we are sure that you have fully put the bad memories where they belong."

From there, I have another session with Bill, who is happy with the first batch of episodes. "I would like to talk to Gina about signing off on the new Genevieve. How does that sound?"

I pull my extremely battered shredder picture out of wallet and give it a solid kiss to Bill's bemusement. "Did that thing really help you so much?"

"I don't know. But it is what got my foot in the door, is it not?"

"You're weird. Come on, let's see when Gina is free."

That turns out to be next Monday, so I head over to the shelter and arrive just as they've finished cleaning up from lunch. Martha greets me. "Hey stranger! We've been missing you here." I plan on a quick look in, then to go over to the school site to see how it's going.

"Judging from the tasty odour I picked up on the way in, you're doing pretty well without me."

"Never! Listen, have you thought about having a party

here? I know we can't do the whole wedding thing, champers and everything, you know, no booze but..."

For a while I can't talk. Then: "Of course. That will be wonderful." With that, I decide that the school site can wait. I need to go home to get my feet back on the ground.

A few tube changes later, I am walking downstairs to our door where I encounter Claudette. "Hi Claudette. Hazel should be home in half an hour..."

"'No, it's you I want to see."

Uh, oh. What have I done now? I say nothing though as I let us both in. I offer her a drink. She shakes her head. "Not this time, thanks. There's a thing we need to deal with before Hazel gets back."

I sit on the edge of my chair.

"You remember what happened at the big engagement party?" I nod. I hadn't thought of it that way before. "Hazel is very worried about the whole wedding thing. Her mum is very trad and has this grand scheme of a big party with Hazel wearing a super meringue and..." This cracks me up. I never heard a wedding dress described that way before.

Claudette looks at me sternly. "This is serious. Hazel wants to get married to you, not to her mother. A big formal event would be her mother's thing, not hers. But she also worries that a big noisy party wouldn't work for you."

"Ah." I contemplate her briefly. "I have no idea how this stuff is supposed to work. I mean, I've seen it in movies but I never actually went to a big family wedding. If there has to be some huge noisy occasion, just give me a bolt-hole. I can handle it just this once. And anyway, I have another idea – maybe more than one party, not only one big one." I tell her about Martha's invitation.

"Interesting. So we could have a sort-of formal thing for Hazel's mum that wouldn't be everyone we could invite, and a few smaller ones. Shelter, a party here, any other places both of you like."

"Yes. That is more us than a big formal thing."

"Great, will you talk to her, or should I?"

"I would love it if you were involved. I don't even know what a best man is. You're the best person I know who can help with this stuff."

"Best Person? I like it."

I hadn't actually been offering her the job. But why not? I don't know what the traditional thing is anyway.

Half an hour after she leaves, Hazel walks in. I grab her in a tight hug and say: "Guess what? Claudette is going to be my Best Person." Strangely, she is not surprised.

Chapter 45

Consciousness

The next day, a Friday, I am on a high. The scripting project is awaiting Gina and that can only be next week. There is a project meeting at 11:00 at the school site, so I decide to go there, much as I dislike all the money talk. I get there at about 10:30 and only Abdul and Zibi are there. They are moving furniture and cleaning up. The place is taking shape, though much is still to be done. I now have a clear picture of how masterclasses can be conducted in front of students and where the main kitchen is being installed.

I help straighten things up, but we are still early. I remember something from the first conversation. "You guys both mentioned black consciousness. I never really understood that."

Zibi looks at Abdul, who throws the initiative straight back. "OK," says Zibi. Have you heard of Biko?"

"Steve Biko?" I vaguely recall someone being killed to massive publicity. It was in my last year of high school, which was not a happy time.

"That's the one. He and his friends developed the idea after splitting with NUSAS." This was a bit before my time – the National Union of South African Students was under heavy attack by the apartheid security police while I was studying. "NUSAS had a meeting and the Black students were not accommodated on campus. They were expected to stay in township hovels. So Biko led a walkout."

"I think I may have read something about that. What is it about?"

Abdul takes up the story. "One of the key ideas is that white people – particularly liberals – believe they know us better than we know ourselves. Another important idea is that because whiteness defines exclusivity, all Black people should stick together. We should reject labels like Indian, Coloured and so on."

There's a pause. Zibi takes over again. "Biko taught us that the most powerful weapon of the oppressor is the mind of the oppressed. So he developed the idea of psychological liberation: you should not let others define you."

"That's so interesting. There are things about me that are different that many people don't get. When I let them tell me who I am, it destroys me." I think about the bullies and – yes – Harriet. "But please, go on."

"Aha. So you have some idea." Zibi grins. "But blackness is something that never goes away. In a racist society, everyone sees you only by your skin colour. I remember once when I was in a supermarket, I suddenly realised that someone was staring at me, as if I was a thief. I was only reading the labels to choose which product to buy. Are your differences like that, things that never go away?"

"Not exactly. It's the way I relate to people. I can learn to adapt so it is not so obvious."

"But you can never be un-black," Abdul concludes.

"I think I see but I have a lot to learn. But tell me, why do Black people not hate white people for all the pain they've caused?"

I look from Zibi to Abdul and back, when Zibi takes the initiative. "Some do, unfortunately. But it is not our way. Ubuntu. I am because you are." As he says the last sentence, he points at his eyes with 2 fingers, then turns the hand around to point at me with the same fingers.

I feel we are connecting but say nothing for a while, then: "Hazel says I have strong empathy. I may be bad at reading the outside of a person but I am good at reading the inside. Is ubuntu something like that?"

Before they can answer, Andrew and Judith walk in and are shortly followed by Carol. The meeting is convening. A deeper understanding of ubuntu will have to wait.

The project meeting goes relatively well – we are over most of the boring things about funding and financial sustainability. We end by agreeing that we should start working on how Martha and her crew can fit into the plan; that will involve me the next time we meet.

That night, back home, I share the conversation with Hazel. "That's so interesting. I wonder if you picked the empathy thing up from playing with farm kids?"

"I don't know – I suspect that ubuntu is an ideal rather than every-day reality. But: the apartheid cops killed Biko, so maybe he was onto something."

We switch to talking about wedding plans. It becomes clear that Carol will need careful management and then I hit on an inspiration. "Why can't Claudette be your Best Person too? I bet she can handle your mum."

Hazel bursts out laughing. "I can just imagine that. But no, it's unfair. Let's talk to her together. It's time we all started treating each other as family."

So Saturday morning we are with Carol in a coffee shop near her home. As we take our seats she looks from one to the other and says: "So, am I in trouble again?"

Hazel takes charge. "Oh, no, no. We aren't doing that again. Ever, I hope. We just need to be together on the wedding plan." She reminds Carol of my problem with noisy partying.

"Do you think I could forget that?"

I smile shyly and cast Hazel a look to shut her up, while we wait for Carol to go on.

"I really like a traditional wedding but I do realize that I am not the one getting married. Can we compromise?"

This is a very different Carol than the one who was fighting me at the start. My confidence in my own prospects for therapy takes a big step up. I look outside and see something I've never seen before. "Wow! Snow!"

Chapter 46

Putting it all Together

Monday morning. The snow has not let up. It's nearly eight and the sun is barely showing, making for a gloomy look as I find my way to the study and fling the curtains open. The snow has an increasingly cheery glow as the sunrise slowly develops. I'm not sure how long I've been looking at it when the phone rings. I grab the phone next to me on first ring, hoping it hasn't woken Hazel. She has a late start today and I have no plans and am contemplating going to the shelter to help with lunch.

It's Bill. "Luke, how soon can you get here? Gina has a break in her schedule."

"If you don't mind if I am unshaved and I don't have to wait for the tube, about 9:30."

"Fine, see you then." I don't pick up much from his tone – when do I ever? – but I rush back to the bedroom where Hazel is actually awake, give her a goodbye kiss, pull on some clothes including a heavy jacket for the snow and dash for the tube.

Running through snow is not as hard as I imagined. It isn't deep and isn't falling hard. When I get to Bill's office, breathless, about thirty minutes early, he eyes me up and down. "Did you run the whole way?"

"Well, only to the tube on my side and from the tube to here."

"Luckily the snow is fresh. You don't want to do that after a thaw. Black ice."

"Oh?" I enquire.

"When there is a thaw and the water freezes over a surface, sometimes you can only see it as a more shiny version of the surface. Super slippery. Come on, Gina said she would be ready as soon as you get here."

We arrive in her office with me looking a bit rough around the edges and still breathing heavily. She favours me with a stare. "Let's hope this signifies eagerness and dropping everything to be here." I've learned enough to keep my mouth shut when I can't be sure what a person's reaction signifies. She points to chairs. We sit.

"Luke, this is a radical departure from where you started. Usually, you would rectify something like this with a minor tweak. A big rewrite like this is quite a risk as it deviates from what we signed you up to write. But: I did give you the go-ahead to try the new angle. I like someone with integrity and, as it happens, your new Genevieve is far better than the old. So well done. But one question. Have you made sure you aren't writing someone else, so there will be another do-over?"

There is a silence. I decide that the truth is best. "Well, it's me. I mean obviously not entirely, because I'm not a woman but..."

"Obviously. Why didn't I see it? Anyway I like it a lot. It is feminist without being didactic. There is humour to carry a person in who doesn't get feminism. Have you always been a feminist?"

This floors me as I am not even sure that I know what feminism is. I admit that ignorance, and go on: "I don't know – I just react to the world as I find it. Some things are terribly unfair."

On the way down to his office, Bill says: "I don't know anyone else who has hit it off so well with her. Whatever you have, you should bottle it."

"I don't know if there is much of a market for social awkwardness that somehow doesn't break everything."

After discussing a schedule of future meetings and deadlines for finishing off episodes, I am still in good time to get to the shelter before lunch. I check my watch: Hazel should be at work. So the shelter it is.

As I arrive, Jill walks in laden with veg and spices. I greet her then: "That looks exciting. What's the plan?"

"I've been talking to Abdul about the sort of curry he makes, sweet, not very hot. It reminds me of how you spiced that breyani. So that is the plan for today. Are you pitching in?"

"For sure, if my help is wanted."

"Of course it is. Come on."

Martha greets me like a long-lost buddy, then we get into prep. The plan is to do a veg curry spiced Cape Malay style and yellow rice with raisins. "The yellow comes from turmeric because saffron was scarce and expensive in colonial South Africa," I explain.

Martha gives me a look. "You mean it is not scarce and

expensive here and now?"

Suitably chastened, I get my head down and chop.

By 12:30, the kitchen is smelling of sweet spice and we have a large pot of yellow raisined rice at the ready.

As the residents file in, one of them notices me serving. "Mate, you're back here. I thought you was too good for us now."

"No, never."

"Last time before you run off, married?"

I recognize him. He was the one who got help when Harry was dying. "No such thoughts. We will carry on honouring Harry and being part of the shelter is part of that. In fact, if the residents don't mind, I would like to have a party right here as part of getting married. Do you all mind?"

No one minds, signified by a raucous cheer.

While I have their attention, I mention the new project, including the cooking school and professional help for anyone who wants to get off the street.

This results in a buzz of conversation. Then the one I recognized pipes up. "How do you know we want to get off the streets? What if we don't like cooking?"

I hold up both hands. "Wait. This is not about forcing anyone. It's about options. When I was here, I always had options, so it isn't the same, I know, but if you don't have options, you're stuck. If you are stuck, the least we can do is make conditions better and make this a real home."

I see there is a babble of disagreement, "Look, no one is making any choices for you. The only thing I really forced on anyone is better food and I hope no one is complaining about that."

A rawboned woman with straggly ginger hair, who is new

to me, pipes up. "No, mate. You've done a bloody lot more than that. You treat us as humans. I used to go to another shelter and I up and moved here because of what everyone is saying about you. Even if I am stuck on the streets, that's me. But no apologies from you." She glares around the room and everyone subsides into silence. Then slow applause breaks out.

I decide I should open another prickly subject. "Actually, I did kind of force another thing on you. Letting outsiders eat here." There is a table in a corner with four people in expensive-looking suits, who are looking decidedly uncomfortable to be singled out. "Did I do the right thing? I know it brings in money, but it's your home."

A ragged-looking resident, one I recognize from way back, pushes his chair back and walks up to me and shakes my hand. "Mate, if I walked into the place where those suits over there normally eat, I would walk straight out again with eyes burning through the back of my head. Let them bloody wait for us to be served and feel out of place so they know what it's like."

I grin and give him a hug; clearly, from his surprised reaction, this is not part of his life experience. It takes me back to that first time at Chez Henrique, when I worried that I was an embarrassment. The suits look at each other uncomfortably. Then applaud.

That out of the way, I mosey over to the school, which is close to ready to go. As I walk in, Zibi greets me loudly. "Hey! Over here! I have a suprise for you!"

There's a cauldron simmering with an odour that takes me way back to my gran's farm kitchen. He lifts the lid and offers a spoon to sample. "Wow! Samp! Where did you get that?"

"Actually, hominy." I am puzzled. "American, popular in the South. Black food over there. Beans not exactly the same, but close enough."

I sample and test my memory, "Nice. But not exactly samp. I remember my gran always had a huge pot of this stuff going. She said she couldn't afford to pay a decent wage but at least no one would starve on her farm. I used to dig in and take a bowl of my own." I have a disturbing thought. "Would the farm people have resented me eating their food?"

"Oh, no. They would have been delighted. By eating the same food as them, you recognized their humanity."

Abdul has joined us while this conversation is going on. "See? I told you we have to improvise, make do, like my ancestors and our Indian friends' ancestors did. Come on, don't tell me it's bad because it's different."

"No, of course not, Zibi is a great cook. We know that already. But I am here to tell you about something else."

I tell them about the wedding party plan in the shelter. "Ah," says Abdul, "are you wanting us to cook there?"

"It had crossed my mind but that is between you and the shelter cooks. It's about time that you started working together. That is still the plan, not so?"

"Yes," says Zibi. "Clearly you are not keeping up. We actually had that as the next step once this place is ready."

"So, talk to them about that. But what I would like is if the two of you can join the main party earlier in the day, so if you do help with the cooking here, you will still be guests for part of the time."

"With family?" asks Zibi.

"Of course. None of my family will be here so I need

someone from home, otherwise it's all Hazel. I'll chat to Carol about invitations." I don't add that with my lack of social skills, I wouldn't have many friends to invite, even back in South Africa.

Chapter 47

Finale

It's Friday, the day before we're getting married, and I have a meeting with Bill. We have rewritten all my original episodes, and Gina wants to see us. I am at the office at 9:00 sharp, in time for seeing her at 9:30.

Bill ushers me in. "Sit, lad. This is your big day."

"Oh? I thought I was getting married tomorrow."

"That? Of course, but Gina was very upbeat when I last spoke to her."

"What are you expecting?"

"Hmm. I think we should let it be a surprise. Tell me about your plans for tomorrow. But first, where's Hazel?"

"She took the day off to work on plans for tomorrow. I'm useless at that stuff so she told me to leave it to her and delegated me to talk to you."

"A pity because she should be here, but anyway, tell me the plan for tomorrow."

I explain how Carol has had her way in certain areas, like using a church and a traditional party, but we have kept that smaller than she would like and we are following up with another small party at the shelter, ending up by regrouping with an even smaller party at home.

"Interesting. Five minutes to go. Let's go to Gina."

Gina for once is waiting for us at the door and ushers us in. Bill gives me a glance; this is clearly not usual.

"Sit! Sit! Where's Hazel?"

I explain.

"Well, I suppose I can't top that can I? Or can I? Your series is going into production. Your job is done. I will sign the paperwork for your payment today."

Just like that, all that hard work has come to a close. I sit back feeling numb. Then: "I think I know where Hazel is. May I use your phone?"

"Of course."

I have another thought. "Will Hazel's secondment to your department continue?"

"Definitely, if she wants it. In fact, I would like to transfer her over here from News. She added a lot to your writing. And we can use her science skills as a special advisor just as much as the News department. The Doctor, for a start. They owe you." Gina winks.

I am about to say, *yes, definitely*, then back off. "I know what Hazel's answer will be but she should be the one that accepts your kind offer to keep her on here."

Gina nods and gestures towards the phone.

I phone Hazel's parents' home and Carol answers. "Is Hazel there?"

"No, just popped out to the shops."

I am about to stop there then decide, no. Let Carol be the bearer of good news. "When she gets back, could you tell her we are going into production and the BBC is committing to paying for the screenplays? And Gina wants to transfer her to her department, if she wants that."

Carol lets out a whoop loud enough for everyone in the office to hear. It's such a good feeling to be so accepted by her but I suddenly feel down because I remember that Geoff is not with us.

As we are about to leave, Gina stops us. "Do you have any further plans? If your life circumstances change, one of you could need to spend more time at home."

"That would be me," I say without further thought.

"Ah, the man of the house puts his foot down. Patriarchy lives."

"Come on. You know me better than that. Of course we will talk it through, but it makes no sense to do anything else."

Gina stands up and walks up to me as we are about to leave. "On a personal note, I am so happy this worked out. You don't have any of the usual scary person markers. You aren't black, you aren't gay and you aren't a pushy woman. But you are different, and that scares people.

"Being 'other' is enough to make you a target. Embrace being 'other'. It is you. You can't be someone else."

I nod, thinking of the discomfort of the "suits" at being singled out at Chez Harry, and she goes on. "My big break-through came when I pitched my first major production to a room full of men who thought they knew everything. They absolutely eviscerated my proposal. I was about to tear them all another one when this decrepit old man tottered to his feet. I thought, *oh no, am I going to have to fight someone who's on his last legs?* But no. He ripped into them. I remember it as if it was today. 'Do you even listen to yourselves? Everything you have criticized would have been positive if it was a man pitching. Your attitude is utterly shameful. I will use every part of my considerable network to shame you if you don't see sense and take your collective heads out of your over-padded bums. This proposal should have a standing ovation, not this ridiculous attack. It's innovative, it will bring in new and younger audiences and it will change the way people see societal stereotypes.'

"There was a silence as he sat down. Then, one after another, the others got to their feet and started applauding. I like to believe that I would have made it without him, but support matters. I never felt stronger. My only regret is that I was so carried away with the moment that I did not find out who he was and never saw him again.

"Be yourself. Stand up for who you are. But value support. It matters. You didn't get here by luck. You recovered from major blunders. Embrace 'other'. Not just in yourself but wherever else you see it."

On the way out, as we walk towards his office, I ask Bill: "Is it really all over for me?"

"Yes – though of course you should be available if there are any issues with the screenplay as production unfolds. However, we will shortly – I hope – have a new staff writer with keen insight into what you are about. Well done. This has to be a great success. The original series had a following that was getting jaded. This more than refreshes it. It's very likely that you will be called on for a follow-up."

When I get home, I phone Geoff. He is upbeat and says, "I am not physically there but as always, I am with you. I have a surprise for you. Two people you appreciate are on their way over. They asked me to hold off until the last minute, but you need to expect them and have space for them at your party."

Who would that be? But I decide that a surprise is a surprise so I leave it and instead tell him about inviting Abdul and Zibi.

"Good, so you have someone from home, even without me. My best to them. Things are grim here. One of my clients was killed recently, and it can only be by apartheid agents. I feel safe because white South African opponents of the system are usually not that kind of target."

On that sombre note ('usually' isn't 'always'), I walk over to a picture of Geoff. I once again remind myself that whatever difficulties I've been through, others have been through far worse. And besides, big day tomorrow... Though I still don't know how I was persuaded to wear a suit. I distinctly recall promising myself I would only ever wear one to my own funeral. I decide to try it on. It is not a comfortable feeling – so not me. No matter how much I look at it in the mirror, it looks wrong. I am so engrossed in this hopeless endeavour that I don't notice Hazel walking in.

"My! You are turning into quite the narcissist! Admiring your suited self in the mirror."

"Well, no. I am wondering whoever got me into this."

"Judging from the otherwise empty state of the flat, it must be you."

That seems a good moment to remove the suit. I don't remember much after that, except that whatever it was, it was better than wearing a suit.

It's the big day. Carol is with her mum, to satisfy her desire to be in control. We're due in the church at 10:00. I still don't know who persuaded me that is the place to go; that memory is buried somewhere with the suit memory. I don't intend to bring those up with Richard at our next session. Being blissfully unaware so far is a great coping strategy. But wait! Of course I know how this all happened. I have a Best Person. Claudette took care of all this stuff. And made damn sure I did not have a stag party."Stag party?" I ask, showing my ignorance.

"Your male friends get you blind drunk and do everything possible for you to make a fool of yourself."

I roll my eyes. "What have I missed by having almost no male friends?" In fact, the only ones I can think of are Stan and Simon. And I should not forget Abdul and Zibi, now becoming friends. Surely not the type to do something like that.

But back to here and now, where Hazel's best friend is my Best Person and has steered me through all this without pressure to conform. Except for the suit. And the church. The big reminder of this is that she is due at the flat any minute to get my act together, for which I am profoundly grateful.

So no, definitely no problem for my shrink Richard to fix. Putting her in charge of all the details is the most sane thing I ever did. There is a knock at the door. It's Claudette. I almost suffocate her with a hug. Then let her go. "Whoa boy! You already have someone else."

I hold her at arms length. "Just for getting through today, I have you."

She wriggles free. "And what I need to do right now is get you into that stupid suit. I don't know how Carol persuaded me to force that on you. Do you know how to do a good tie knot?"

"I think so. I went to a school that did that." Not so fond

memories of teachers calling me out for a badly tied knot.

"Just as well. That's not a skill I ever needed. Come on. Put that thing on and I will check if anything needs straightening up. Then I will call us a cab in good time to get there. And don't forget your stage prop."

Once we are in the cab, Claudette says, "I hear you and Gina are hitting it off."

I share the story about the decrepit old man who stood up for her. "That would be my dad. I often wondered if his story was about Gina."

"I'm sorry..."

"Oh, he called himself decrepit. That isn't the point. He and I used to have huge fights about feminism. He believed that treating all men as enemies was a sure way of making that true. He died a few days after that incident and I only heard about it from one of his work colleagues at the funeral. It really changed me. And I am pleased now to know for sure that it was Gina."

"Hence your soft approach to me?"

Despite my lack of social skills, I have managed to convey irony. "The knife thing? You awakened the old me but, believe me, I am so sorry I said something like that particularly now I know you better."

"No apology needed. I want Hazel to have friends who stand up for her. So many times in the past, I had no one when I needed support. Kindness of strangers was sometimes all that I had."

"Kindness of strangers isn't nothing. Look where your kindness to Harry led." I nod. There is nothing left to say.

Once we get there, fortunately there is not much for me to remember. I think the order of events is something like 'aisle altar hymn' but that doesn't sound like us. I remember something involving rings and a kiss, then we are at a party. It's a crowd. I wonder what Carol considers to be a big party. Magnums of Dom Pérignon Rosé are navigating the room. I lean over to Hazel: "We know that can't be cheap. Did your parents…"

She whispers back: "No, if they were slightly wealthy before, they wouldn't be anymore. That's a gift from Arthur." I nod. *Obviously, it's his thing.*

We get through various formalities. Several times, I have to draw on my coping strategies, sometimes on professional psychiatric tricks from Richard. Finally it gets to my speech. The crunch. Time to check if Claudette has worked on me well enough. No. It is up to me. But I appreciate what she put into it. And I also appreciate that I have no old-school male friends to rag me. I stand up and say: "I am a man of few words," and sit down. There's an uproar so I stand up again, and reach for my stage prop. It's a pile of printer paper, the kind that's one long sheet with page perforations and sprocket holes down the side. "Just in case someone did want a longer speech, I prepared one." I lift the top page, showing that this is a *lot* of paper.

This scores a good laugh. I look around the room. I am out of punchlines so this is it. I drop the page. "I actually don't need a prepared speech. All I need is people who care about me and people I care about. I am sorry that I don't know most of you here. I am also socially awkward so if what I just said came out as an insult, I slipped my excuse in just in time." I get a mild laugh. "But seriously, I am not used to having lots of friends or even much of a caring family. Hazel, Carol and Robert are all the family I have here, which is far

more than I ever had before." Then I remember the predicted
surprise guests and spot two familiar faces; seeing who they
are is a real lift. "And I must add, my two good friends from
California, Stan and Simon are here as surprise guests. I
would also like to single out Abdul and Zibi from South Africa,
who have become friends. And Claudette, who is the best
friend a person could have and definitely my Best Person for
today.

"But to all the rest of you: Hazel is what connects us and
I can't think of a better way for a socially awkward person
to make friends. And I truly hope that did not come out
sounding weird."

I sit down, wondering if I have messed up again. There is
a slightly confused buzz in the room. But Carol drags me to
my feet, gives me a hug and raises her glass. "To weird!"

I don't remember too much after that aside from a dentist's drill adorned with serious knives but I make it through
the party somehow and we are off to the shelter for the next
one. Once in the cab, I turn to Hazel. "Did I mess up?"

"You confused some of my friends. But that in my book
makes them messed up. Come on, we are going to party now
with your people. I bet the odds are that I will make a social
blunder."

"It isn't a contest."

"Quite. Stop over-thinking and enjoy yourself."

"That reminds me." I share the conversation with Gina
about "changed life circumstances".

Oh. She looks at me with feigned joy. "Why do we need
to talk about this? Are you expecting?"

"No, idiot. What I mean is, we never talked about having
kids. If we do, you have to do the hard part for nine months.

I don't see why you need to make a career sacrifice after that. I actually like working from home. And cooking. And I actually don't know if I have a career, I mean I only sold one screenplay. You have an actual job."

"You're so sweet. I should marry you. Oh, wait..."

"You're not cross with me for making the decision without debate?"

"Yes. But you caught me in a forgiving mood. Come on, we don't have to decide now anyway. I mean, you aren't actually pregnant, right?"

"I'm different but not that different."

That takes us to the shelter, where Abdul, Zibi, Martha and Jill are hard at work when I walk into the kitchen, which is smelling fantastic. "Out!" Yells Martha. "You are the guest of honour tonight so stay out of the kitchen!"

I decide not to argue; I am only there to say hi, not to force my way into the cookery. I rejoin Hazel. "They chased me out of the kitchen. But not before I got to pick up a delicious odour."

She sniffs me. "All I'm getting is deodorant and sweat."

We go back outside and greet guests as they arrive; a short list of ours – mostly Hazel's closest friends – as well as the residents. To my surprise, Stan and Simon show up again – the only ones other than Claudette and Hazel's parents who are guests at both parties. I give them both big hugs. Carol explains. "They are the nearest to family that you have here. I thought you would like them at the smaller party too." I like the New Carol very much.

I spot George and we exchange cheerful waves. It's been a while since I did the greengrocer forage. I turn to Carol. "Henrique and Eleni...?"

"Henrique will be here as soon as he has service settled. We will send a delegation to Eleni to fetch her with dessert." Of course: they cannot abandon their businesses, even for this. I anticipate refusing apologies.

Some of the residents are new to me but all clearly know what is going on. Out of habit, I count the outside guests. Then remember that I am not running the kitchen; I'm sure Martha has this under control.

Once everyone is seated, including the outside guests, I go round the serving area to the kitchen. Martha fixes me with a gaze. "Scoot! Didn't we clear this up? You're the guest this time."

"Ah, but the place where I most feel at home is when I am serving. I don't do parties well."

Martha grudgingly allows me to take my place. There is a row of glasses of orange juice, a clear homage to Harry. There is toast, which mystifies me at first. "Aha, for the toast!" Martha looks at me as if I am slow. Then I see a large baking pan with a set custard topping and piles of yellow rice with raisins. Abdul nods in my direction. "Veg bobotie with yellow rice. Zibi has made samp and beans with a hot Durban curry sauce for those with the stomach for it."

Jill adds: "And Eleni will be in later with baklava and pistachio ice cream."

This is not a totally coherent menu, but it fits the occasion – memories of this place, a tribute to Harry, memories from home for the exiles. "That sounds wonderful," I say, and notice that the residents are starting to queue up for food – which takes us back to where I started my story, with the intrusion of the media scrum headed by Henrique, with Eleni in tow.

Having chased the media out, we get down to a meal with lots of nostalgia, including jokes about toast and toasts. The last, best one, is where one of the residents stands up and says, "To Harry!" No one complains that it is supposed to be our day; I certainly do not. It is Harry as much as anyone who has brought us to where we are.

Then, I go out to see what the fuss is. Henrique is holding back a gaggle of journalists with cameras flashing in my face; Abdul, Zibi and Jill push past to fetch Eleni, who has departed the scene, and the dessert. Thankfully, the TV crews have found another ambulance to chase. My inner anti-bully conquers my flight reflex. "Henrique, what is going on?"

"You have been awarded a Michelin star."

"A what?" The only Michelin I know of is a brand of tyre.

"One of the top culinary accolades. A selection of restaurants have one star, a smaller number have two and the very best have three."

A journalist thrusts a mic in my face. "That is quite an achievement for a homeless kitchen. What do you say?"

"I say, shove off, the homeless do not need to be part of a media circus. Where I come from, people are dying for their rights and no one is allowed to report it. This isn't news. It's voyeurism."

I hear voices saying things like "wedding party" and "exploiting the homeless". My weird head converts them all to a very large dentist's drill. Flanked by Nebuchadnezzar-sized knives – that resolve into Claudette and Hazel. I turn and walk back inside with them flanking me, followed closely by Henrique, with Martha's ladle guarding our backs.

Dramatis Personæ

Characters are approximately in order of first appearance; some are grouped together as they relate to a specific event or scenario.

Luke Fredericks – virtually disowned by his parents, brought up by his grandmother; interests in writing and cuisine; draft dodger from the apartheid military

Gran Timson – Luke's maternal grandmother who stood in for his parents until she was too old to look after him

Jamie – Luke's older brother; favoured by the parents

Geoff Fredericks – Luke's uncle; put him on the path to becoming a draft dodger

Ian Fredericks – Geoff's son, noteworthy only for not being around

De Villiers – rugby fan teacher who took Luke's side against a bully

Simpson – bully who was the first to experience Luke's anti-bully rage

Harriet – Honours-year girlfriend who cruelly dumps Luke

Stan – Geoff's gay friend in San Francisco; he and Simon sharpen Luke's culinary skills and interest

Simon – Stan's partner

Millie – Green Tortoise bus driver

Charlie – Millie's assistant

Hazel – girlfriend first met at Yosemite, invited Luke to visit her in London

Robert – Hazel's dad

Carol – Hazel's mother

Fred – on night duty at homeless shelter; unfriendly at first

Bill – on early morning duty at homeless shelter; friendly from the start

Harry Whitmore – homeless polylinguist, the inspiration for Chez Harry

Martha – head cook at the homeless shelter kitchen

Jill – Martha's deputy

Henrique – owner and head chef of Chez Henrique and chief early benefactor of the shelter gourmet project

George – greengrocer favoured by Henrique and also a benefactor

Eleni – coffee shop owner; a later benefactor

Claudette – long-time friend of Hazel

Jonathan Childs – COSAWR case worker, handling Luke's asylum application

Julian Holmes – Second Permanent Secretary, Home Office; passes the Harry story to his brother, as part of the Oxbridge network

Sir Charles – Permanent Secretary, Home Office; fails to be available for Luke's pre-ministerial meeting

Arthur Whitmore, QC – Harry's brother; in the UK, a barrister is in the top echelon of legal practice, and generally has the suffix Queen's Counsel (QC) or King's Counsel (KC), depending on whether the monarch is a queen or king

Hamish Leery – broker for a large investment firm; backer of Chez Harry

Andrew McGill – runs a software company; backer of Chez Harry

Judith Simons – runs an upmarket retail chain; backer of Chez Harry

Gina Gibbons – producer

Genevieve Mullins – fictional character in crime detective screenplay

Bill Locke – senior BBC screenwriter

Ian McLennan – head cook at *Dr Who* location

Abdul Hendricks – Cape Malay cuisine specialist; refugee from South Africa

Hlakaniphile Zibi – Durban Indian cuisine specialist; refugee from South Africa; Zulu rather than Indian (known as Zibi); his first name translates to Intelligent or, more idiomatically: Smart.

Richard Doyle – psychiatrist; helped Carol and Luke understand their issues

Al – in charge of supplies in the homeless shelter kitchen

Jen – general assistant in the homeless shelter kitchen

Bea – general dogsbody and dish washer in the homeless shelter kitchen

Notes on Mental Health and Autism

Autism spectrum disorder (ASD) is a neurodevelopmental disorder that affects interaction with others. It can take many forms.

Asperger, as it is sometimes called, rather than Asperger's Syndrome, its earlier name, is a form of ASD and some argue that it is not a separate condition, as it is part of the variability of ASD.

I don't like to see ASD and Asperger as illnesses but rather as personality types, as they are attributes of an individual, not something that can be "cured" though high-function individuals can learn compensations for behaviours that make them socially challenged. A person living with ASD should not be be shunned by society; nor should anyone who has any other attribute that is not their fault, like skin colour, gender identity or sexual orientation.

The exact form that Luke has is fictional, a composite of behaviours I have seen in others. His mental tricks are partially inspired by a book on obsessive-compulsive disorder, *Brain Lock* by Jeffrey Schwartz, in which he describes mind tricks that can be used to escape repetitive behaviours. I am not a psychiatrist and do not want to enter into the rights and wrongs of any particular approach. I do however want to point out that Luke ends up getting therapy, which is the best approach to dealing with behavioural problems, particularly where they may have an external trigger, like traumatic memories.

Luke's accommodations may come across as weird but that's me. I tried to put myself into the head of a person going through what Luke went through and ended up there. If anyone else has had similar experiences, I am sure their accommodations and approaches to processing such experiences will be completely different.

Acknowledgements

I would like to thank my wife Fiona Semple, who is the liberated kind of feminist and let me keep my own surname when we married, for her careful proofreading.

Nhlanhla Mabaso also did a proofread for which I am most thankful. Not only did he correct some of my misremembered childhood Zulu but also some of my English.

I would also like to thank aMan Bloom for some insightful comments.